IF I COULD TELL IT

Camden Martin

IF I COULD TELL IT

Camden Martin

DREAMING BIG PUBLICATIONS

If I Could Tell It

Copyright © 2019 Camden Martin

Content Editor: London Koffler

Copy Editor: Amanda Clarke

Cover Art: Camden Martin

Cover Design: Kristi King-Morgan

Editor-in-Chief: Kristi King-Morgan

Formatting: Kristi King-Morgan

Assistant Editor: Maddy Drake

ISBN- 978-1-947381-23-0

www.dreamingbigpublications.com

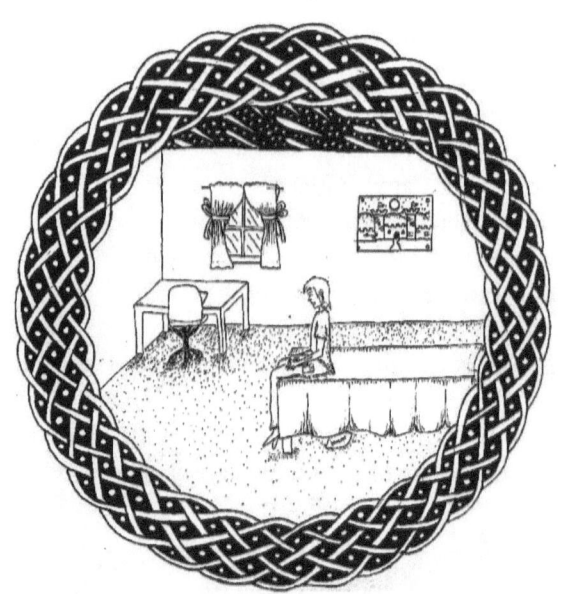

Hi.

My name is Camden Martin, and I wrote this piece when I was fifteen years old. I suppose you could technically say that I began writing it when I was twelve because I wrote the first draft when I was in the seventh grade—Arthur's age at the beginning of the story. I believe that my youth qualifies me to write Arthur's story as he is known by legend as the *boy king*. And even though I am not a teenage boy, or from medieval Britain, I have found many parallels between Arthur and myself. I am head over heels in love with the legend and everything to do with it, and for that reason, it is my ambition for everyone else to feel as I do.

This piece is a testament to me, my generation, and most of all, Arthur. I hope that you fall in love with this epic tale just as I have. Thank you, and happy reading.

Sincerely,

Camden Alyse Martin

P.S.
Fall asleep in my American dreams.

Arthur

Circles are my favorite shape. They make sense. Every circle is the same, aside from size. Every single one has the same ratios and the same look and the same never-ending edges. Every part of every circle is the same. The curvature never changes; it just goes around and around until you stop tracing your finger around the outside edge.

I think that people should be circles. Then everyone would be the same. There would be no short, or tall, or fat, or brown, or white, or male, or female. That would be better. Everyone equal. Then no wars would be fought, and there would be no disagreements, and all the circle people would live in their circular world, and everyone would work together to survive, and be happy.

I would be an architect in this circular world. I would sit in a little room, at the top of the tallest tower in the circular palace and look out over the circular land and make a circular structure that nobody would ever forget. Just like in Rome. In Rome, they had architects, and they designed bridges, and palaces, and houses, and bathhouses, all made to help people. And then, everyone in this circular world would look at the structure I built, and they would think, *Arthur made that.*

And then, the circular emperor would come up to me in that little room, and he would tell me that I did a great thing by making that circular structure out there in the circular land. I would tell him that it was my honor to do so and that I was only trying to do something good for the circular people of our circular city.

And the best part of all?

The emperor would not be me.
Christopher Columbus was wrong. The world is flat.

Chapter 1

Colorado Springs, America, 2008

Things that make sense:
- Circles
- Mathematics
- Swordplay
- Latin

Things that do not make sense:
- People
- Contractions
- Christians
- My Father
- Ranks
- Me

That was the list I was making during my seventh grade, fifth period, language arts class. Mrs. Hamilton had told us to make a list of four to six things that made sense to us and four to six things that did not.

She was gliding through the rows of wooden desks, scanning each person's paper, and maybe saying a thing or two about it to each student.

Then she got to me.

"Arthur, why do you have 'people' down for things that *don't* make sense to you?" she asked me. I looked up at her.

"Because they do not."

"And contractions?" she questioned. "I would think that your generation would have the easiest time of all with them."

If only she knew.

"Not me."

"Why didn't you write football down under things that make sense?" she asked. "I thought you loved playing."

I shrugged and blew my longish, golden blonde hair out of my face. She said to be honest, so that is what I had done.

"And what about playing the trumpet in band?" she tried, obviously not satisfied with my lists.

I shrugged again. I did not want to talk to her. Talking made me feel out of place; the accent was too foreign.

"Well, okay," she said, frowning. I noticed she did not say anything about the fact that I wrote 'me' and 'my father' down.

It was universal knowledge among my teachers that I was a foster child. I was the one who people looked at and said, "Oh I feel so sorry for that poor boy." That was me, the one whose parents left him on the doorstep of an orphanage when he was twelve years old, or so they thought. At least they did not question me too much. Questions were bad. Questions meant more lies I had to remember. More things I had to cover up.

"Now, get started on your paper about what the things that make sense to you all have in common and the same with the ones that don't," Mrs. Hamilton said; she looked at me for a second. She probably thought I had fleas and slept in a cardboard box at night. "Arthur, just remember if you ever need any help that you can come to me."

I nodded and looked down at my notebook—at my lists—the lists that apparently were not good enough for Mrs. Hamilton.

I sat there in the red metal chair at the brown wooden desk in the center of the green painted classroom on top of a short gray carpet. There was a girl with long, brown hair on my right who had black marks smeared across her eyelids. She was concentrating on her lists. I saw 'school' under her 'does not make sense' list; she must have been struggling. On my left, there was a boy with short, dark hair wearing a black sweatshirt advertising a beach city somewhere. I searched my mind for their names, but I could not remember. I suppose this was because I did not care enough about them when we met.

I looked up at the front of the classroom and saw Mrs. Hamilton gazing at me as if in deep thought. I think she did not understand me because when people did not understand something, they either decided not to think about it, or they had the desperate need to figure it out. Unfortunately, she had the desire to figure me out. If Mrs. Hamilton had a list of things that did not make sense to her, then I would have been at the top of it at that moment.

There were only five periods in the day at Carmel Middle School. First was mathematics: pre-algebra, second was band, third was physical science, fourth was history, and fifth was language arts. So Mrs. Hamilton was my dominant teacher and therefore, she believed that it was her personal mission to help me and figure me out.

The bell rang and I closed my notebook and tucked my pencil into the side of my jeans. I shoved the red notebook with 'Language Arts' written across it into the black backpack that my foster parents had given me. They really were nice people. They just could not figure me out either.

Mrs. Marion Ector met me at the front door of the school as she had done after football practice for the past month of September. Practice was canceled today, however, so she met me at two thirty-four. She was my foster mother, and she had told me it was alright for me to call her mom or mother, but I did not like that. I had a mother. Just not here. So, I stuck with Miss Marion.

You see Mrs., Miss, or Mr. were titles for people who did not have titles. It did not matter their profession: if they were older than eighteen, and you were not, then you called them Mrs., or Miss, or Mr. At least that was how I saw it. Maybe there were certain types of people that you did not use titles for, like the people who sat on the sides of the road with brown signs saying things like 'Help' or 'God Bless.' Miss Marion cursed them and said they would go straight to the drug dealers if you gave them any money.

Miss Marion was a medium-sized, forty-something, very stressed-out woman who was always doing something with her very busy social schedule. She had told me that she and Mr. Ector had had their children when they were young, twenty-four, so now they were off at somewhere called college. Twenty-four did not seem very young to me; my sister was only fifteen and my father was constantly trying to marry her off. Plus, my mother had had me when she was sixteen.

"Ready, Arthur?" she asked, holding her hand over her cell phone for a second.

I nodded, and she resumed her conversation with whoever was on the other end of the cell phone and put her hand on my shoulder as if to push me out the door.

We walked out to the parking lot where all of the other students were either being picked up by their parents or getting onto big, yellow school buses. Miss Marion ushered me into the front seat of her small, white car, and I set my backpack between my legs. She finally hung up with the person on the phone and flipped the device closed, setting it in the car cup holder between us.

"How was school?" she asked me, trying a little too hard to be friendly.

"Fine," I said simply. Keep talking short, that was how to make people not ask me about things.

"I just got off the phone with my friend, Carey," she said as she put the car in gear and backed out of the parking lot. "She really wants to meet you."

"Okay," I said. *Okay* was kind of like *yes*, except it could be used for more things, like simple acknowledgements or *alright*.

I noticed that the Ectors keeping me as their foster child was kind of like a social advance for them. People saw them taking care of me and they thought that they were such nice, generous people. They were helping that poor, orphan boy. It was alright though. They were helping me, so I did not mind helping them out in their social aspects of life.

"What's your favorite class?" she asked. I had to come up with a decent answer; she was getting annoyed with my lack of talking.

"Math," I said, shortening the word like everyone did. "It is the easiest."

"Oh?" she asked. She was really just prompting me to continue.

"Yes," I said. She was not going to get any more out of me.

She continued asking me questions, and I continued answering them without any description the entire ride to the Ectors' house.

Their house was rather large as houses go; I think. It was painted pale blue with white trim and was three stories high. A lawn of green grass and river stones stretched out in front of the house, and a blacktop driveway made a path from the road to the three-car garage. The garage was the only place in the entire house that was messy. It had all sorts of things shoved in all sorts of places. For example, there was a canoe paddle stuck in the rafters of the roof.

"Thank you," I said quietly, grabbing my backpack, and getting out of the car.

"Sure…?" I do not think she quite understood why I always said thank you whenever she did anything for me. It was just respectful in my mind.

I lay awake in bed that night.

The ceiling was a dull gray color and I stared at it as if it could tell me all the answers I wished. The answers to the reason that when, in a few moments, I would close my eyes and drift off to sleep only instead of dreaming, I would wake up where I was from. I would wake up in reality. I would wake up *there*.

*****

Cadbury Castle, Britain, 645

The stick was slammed down on my hands for the ninth time that hour. I was counting the number of times before my fingers broke. I looked up at Father Patricius in defiance.

"Arthur, focus!" he yelled at me as if I were some sort of dog.

I blew my hair out of my eyes and glared at him. I was done with these ridiculous Latin lessons. I knew what I needed to know, and that was that. I wanted to learn Greek anyway. Then, I could read the texts in the library about the studies that the Greeks had done on mathematics—especially circles.

"Now what is the *nos preterite* tense of *venire*?" he asked me. His face was red, and I knew he was very close to hitting me in the face with the ruler.

"*Nos venit*," I said, still glaring at him. I just wanted to be done with the lesson so I could leave. "We came."

He nodded. I glared at him some more.

So he hit me with the stick again. I cringed. No matter how many times he slammed that stick down it still felt like he was breaking all my fingers. "Be respectful!"

I looked down and away from his icy gaze. And people said the Old People were cruel. In my opinion, the Christians were much, much worse.

"To Britain to save the people," he said, asking me to translate the rest of the sentence. I did not like the sentence because we were *not* saving the people of Britain. We were killing them. We, being Christians, and people like my father.

"*Nos venit a Britannium salvabit populi*," I said, still glaring at him.

He slapped my hands again. I thought about how easy it would be to twist the stick out of his hands and shove it through his chest. I softened my look.

"*Vale*," he said, which meant *farewell*.

I stood and bowed to him. "*Vale*."

Father Patricius left my chambers, and I leaned back in my chair. I picked up the piece of papyrus I had been writing on, crumpled it into a ball, and threw it at the cobblestone wall. I hated Father Patricius, *hated him*. In his mind, only Christian men were people. Everyone else was an animal, not worthy of any attention or effort. Women, we needed, but they did not receive any rights. The rest of them deserved to be either slaves or killed.

Lancelot was sitting on a table in the armory, staring at the wall. I tackled him off the table to the ground and laughed with my hands planted on either side of him.

"What are you doing, Arthur?!" he yelled in my face.

"Greetings," I said sarcastically and got off of him. "You were not prepared, my friend."

"I was thinking," he said defensively, standing up and brushing himself off.

"Mm," I said. I picked a staff from the nearby rack. "And what were you thinking about?"

"Avalon," he said. I adjusted my grip on the staff, feeling the weight of it. "Do you think that is where I really came from?"

"That may be," I said. I swung the staff around and spun on my heel. Unfortunately, I did not gauge my surroundings as well as I should have, and I tumbled into the rack of staffs. They clattered to the ground.

"Arthur." He rolled his eyes. I cringed and bent to pick them up before someone came in and saw.

I set the rack back up and shrugged my shoulders.

"Maybe you could ask your mother," Lancelot said, sitting back on the table.

"About what?" I asked, slowly backing away from the wall.

"She grew up on the Isle of Avalon," Lancelot said, "maybe she knows if that's where I'm from." He picked a staff from the opposite wall and followed me out of the armory into the grassy training yard.

"Maybe…" I responded.

The training yard was a *very* large rectangular courtyard in the center of the palace. It had covered hallways along the outer edges in the Roman style with tall stone pillars and a few floral trees around the edges alternating with flower beds. On the side closest to the armory, there were training dummies, which were really just burlap bags of straw on a metal stick with armor and a helmet on, in neat little lines. On the side furthest away from the armory were archery targets: furthest away so no one would accidentally be shot. In the center, there was a fairly small, circular arena with grass instead of dust for padding. Throughout the entire yard, there were podiums, for masters to teach from, and other various training aids.

Currently, about fourteen archers were shooting crossbows at the timed command of someone I could not make out. A couple of the older boys, Kay and Bedivere, were fighting with maces in the corner across from the armory entrance. There were not many more men practicing or even just having fun with each other. They were all out at war. The war of my father.

You see, I hated my father. *Hated* him. Uther Pendragon was the bane of my existence. The absolute reason that I loathed the day I would become king.

All he did was sit in the palace in luxury, coming up with new ways to tax people so he could send more men to the ridiculous war he had started with the Saxons. A common misconception is that they started it. While it is true that they invaded us first, Ambrosius, my grandfather, was the real reason for the war. He pissed them off. Then they invaded, and my father, being the pompous idiot he was, pissed them off more. Instead of trying to make peace with them, he just sent more and more of his men to kill more and more of their men, and then be killed themselves.

That is why I do not want to be the High King of Britain: because all being king seems to be is sending more people to die while you encourage a problem that could easily be solved with peace.

Lancelot and I walked over near Kay and Bedivere, careful not to get too close so they would not harass us. They glanced our way but made no move to instigate communication.

We stood across from each other, slammed our staffs on the ground once, and then went at it. Lancelot struck first. I blocked on my left side and used the momentum from the blow to spin around on my feet and strike at him from the right. My staff collided with his and he flung it over his head. I tapped it once on the ground to get it to bounce back up, then spun it around my back and whipped my body around, nailing him hard in the side. It made a loud *crack* sound against his ribs and I cringed.

"Sorry?" I gave a forced smile while he glared at me, holding his hand over his side.

"You do know you are not supposed to hit the other person *hard* right?" he said, irritated, leaning on his wooden staff.

"I know," I said. I smiled inwardly. I may have hit a bit too hard, but I had definitely executed that strike perfectly. If I had had a sword in my hands, he would have been dead. I just needed to hope that nobody who was a snitch saw me do it so I did not get punished.

"Arthur!" Too late. I think if I had been a dog, at that moment my ears would have been all the way back against my head and I would have been leaning my chin on my paws looking pitifully up at my punisher.

"Yes, Mother?" I asked weakly. Maybe she did not see it.

"Why did you hit Lancelot like that?" she asked me angrily. Unfortunately for me, she had seen it.

"It was an accident." *Of course it was not an accident. Can we focus on the fact that it was a perfect blow?*

Lancelot snorted. I wanted to kick him in the shins, but I do not think my mother would have approved of that.

"Well," she said very sweetly, "I suppose you could not have meant harm to your best friend."

Sometimes, I think my mother is the only person who loves me. Sometimes, I *know* my mother is the only person who loves me. And she always believes in me, no matter what. She was the one who believed in me when I was just a baby and no one thought I would live to see summer. She was the one who did not doubt me when I said that I knew what the future was like. She is the one who stands up to my father for me. She is the only one brave enough.

"I came to ask if the both of you wanted to go riding with me," she said.

"Yes please," Lancelot said. Lancelot was a bit like my adopted brother. Not by my father though. The only reason he had not been killed when my father ransacked the Isle of Avalon ten years ago was because my mother had seen three-year-old Lancelot and took pity on him. She convinced my father that she could raise him in the New Ways and that he and I could be brothers. My father hates him even more than me because of this because he was born from someone who believed the Old Ways.

She looked at me with her fierce gray eyes. I nodded, and she smiled.

"Off we go then."

"Austin?" I asked my manservant as I sat in a chair in my chambers and sipped a cup of hot milk. He was currently preparing my bed for me to sleep.

"Yes, my lord?" he asked and brushed his ear length red hair out of his freckled face.

"Do you ever have strange dreams?" I questioned. He pulled back the covers and I climbed into bed.

Austin shook his head. "Not really."

"Oh." I pulled my covers up to my chest. I yawned in tiredness. "You are dismissed."

He bowed to me and blew out the remaining candle on my bedtable.

I settled into my featherbed and closed my eyes, drifting off to sleep—or whatever it was.

*****

Colorado Springs, America, 2008

The reason I like mathematics is simple: it makes sense. Everything builds off something else in a neat and orderly fashion. There are only right answers or wrong answers. Black and white, no gray. No questions asked.

In pre-algebra, we were learning about the simple rules of algebraic properties. Like whatever you did to one side of an equation, you must do to the other in order to get the correct answer. This seemed like it applied to my life in a way. Whenever something happened to me on one side of my life, it seemed to trickle over to the other side.

"Arthur, do you know how to do number five?" my friend Ty asked me from across our four desk group. He was a tall, dark-skinned and curly-haired boy, with full lips and dark brown eyes.

"Ah, yes," I said, tracing my finger down the list of equations to the bolded '5.' "Factor out the three first."

"Thanks," he said and went back to his work. I finished my paper and got up to put it in the metal basket on Mr. Jefferson's desk.

He smiled at me and I gave a forced smile back.

"Do you like math?" he asked me.

"Yes sir," I said. I just wanted to sit down and finish my drawing of the apartment complex I was designing for my friend Helix, who said that he was going to have to move because a fire had destroyed his home last week. I thought if he saw my drawing, then maybe he would feel more hopeful.

"That's good," he said, nodding, "I hope you continue to like it."

I nodded and went back to my seat.

I pulled out my ruler and the sheet of paper I had been drawing on from my binder, smoothing the paper out on my desk.

It was a big rectangular building with an angled roof so the rain and snow would slide off. The windows were circular and kind of nautical-like. Helix had said that when he was older, he wanted to join the navy and captain a ship. All the angles of my drawing were the exact same as they would be in real life, and I made sure that it was all to scale. Every line was perfectly straight, and I think, if you were to want to, you could have used my drawing as a blueprint for the real thing.

"You going to practice?" Ty asked me as we packed up our things for the next class. The bell was to ring in about a minute and a half.

"Yes," I said. The class started to line up at the door.

"You know," Ty said, standing next to me, "you're kinda weird Arthur, but you're pretty cool too."

Was that a compliment? I think so. It was hard to tell sometimes, especially since Ty spoke African-American Vernacular English.

"Thank you."

"Yeah," he said and patted me on the shoulder. I only came up to his ear. I was still waiting for my predicted growth spurt to happen so I could be taller and stronger. At least, I hoped it would happen. "Whatcha got next?"

What do you have next? I mentally translated. "Band."

"Oh, you're one of those," he said. One of what?

I did not answer because I did not know what he meant. I just looked at him, confused.

"Never mind," he said, shaking his head and half smiling. "Go unleash your inner geek."

Well alright then.

That night after football practice, I retreated to my room at the Ectors' household to finish my paper on the similarities between the things that made sense to me and the similarities between the things that did not.

So far, I basically had an introduction on what the things were and a couple of similarities. The biggest similarity I had between the things that made sense to me was that none of them had to do with other people. I had left a blank spot on the page for the similarities between the things that did not make sense to me.

I thought that my handwriting was rather bad compared to the other students. This was probably because I learned to write with a quill and ink instead of a pencil. I had only been using a pencil for about a month.

"Arthur," Miss Marion knocked on the doorframe because I had left the door open. "It's time for dinner."

"Okay," I said and set my pencil down on the paper. I looked around the room for a second.

The walls were a plain, eggshell white and the carpet was a light gray. The bedspread on the twin bed in the corner was a scarlet red and the desk in the corner opposite the door, which I was sitting at, was a plain oak wood with a black cushioned chair that spun around. Miss Marion said I could put things up on the walls if I wanted, but I did not have anything. Maybe, someday, I could put up one of my drawings.

I followed her into the upstairs hallway, down the stairs, and through the living room to the wooden-floored dining room. Mr. Ector was already seated at the end of the table. I sat at his right. Miss Marion brought a pan of some sort of pasta and cheese dish that she called "lasagna" and set it on the table between the three of our seats. There was also, a green salad and a loaf of fresh bread that she had bought at the grocery store.

The Ectors did not pray before their meals, which was strange to me because I always had. Miss Marion served both of us some of her concoction and sat down to eat herself. I thought it tasted fairly good, but, then again, I have been told that I will eat anything.

"How's school going, Arthur?" Mr. Ector asked. That seemed to be the staple question of adults nowadays. *How is school going?* Was what they asked when they did not know you very well, and they had no idea what else to say.

"Fine, sir," I said. I knew to be respectful to adult males. They were the ones with the power. They were the ones who made decisions, so, therefore, in order to get what you wanted, it was smart to be respectful.

"Please call me Anthony," he said, exasperated. He had said that to me many times. Anthony was his first name. I knew I could not call him by his first name, though. It was extremely disrespectful. I nodded anyway.

"I think we should do something about your hair," Miss Marion said, breaking the silence.

What was wrong with my hair? It was about shoulder-length, and I tended to just cut it with a knife, so it was a bit choppy in some places. I did not think anything needed to be done to it.

"Do what to my hair?" I asked nervously, forgetting to add a *ma'am* to the end so it did not sound so cavalier.

"Cut it," she said. "On Monday I can take you to my salon when I get mine styled." Today was Thursday, so that meant three days.

"Cut it how, ma'am?" I did *not* forget this time.

"Short," Anthony piped in. "I bet you can barely see with that mop in your face."

Miss Marion punched her husband in the arm to say that his comment was rather rude.

"I'll just take you in with me and you can cut your hair however you like," she said, giving Mr. Ector a curt look.

I finished my paper when the digital clock read '8:30' in bright red numerals. I slid it to the side and looked out the window over the desk.

The neighborhood streetlights were all on over the concrete road, illuminating the houses. It was beautiful, really. Each house was a little bit different, but all of them matched in a certain way. They complimented each other. A neighborhood would be an interesting project to design, it would help people, but it would also be a work of art in its own right. I gazed out the window for a bit, picturing all the scales and measures and angles that went into designing this complex housing development.

I did a quick sketch of the neighborhood with a pencil and a ruler on printer paper. As soon as I finished, I held it out in front of my face, then immediately crumpled it up and threw it in the wastebasket underneath my desk. It was imperfect, and imperfection bothered me.

I tucked myself into bed after that, listening to the outward sounds of the American city. The modern sounds: the cars in the street, the electronic hum of a radiator, the wind against the window shutters. It was funny how familiar those sounds had grown to me in the past month that I had been waking up in America. They no longer seemed so strange and foreign. They had simply become a part of my reality. My utterly confused and unidentified reality, the reality that flip-flopped back and forth between my two lives.

Fall asleep in America, wake up in Britain. Fall asleep in Britain, wake up in America. Dream in Britain, Daydream in America.

*****

Cadbury Castle, Britain, 645

I looked at the doors to the trial room. Should I have left them closed and walked away? Maybe. But that was not what I did. I walked right up to that door and I told the guards to open it for me. Am I stupid? Most likely.

"Arthur," my father said as I walked down the cobblestone aisle to his throne.

"My Lord." I bowed in front of him and stayed on my knee.

He waved his hand to release me and I stood up. "What is it that you want?"

Uther Pendragon was a tall, muscular, blonde man with a bit of a large stomach and a wicked scar across his face stretching from his left eyebrow to his right cheek. He had pale blue eyes and a square jaw. His skin was even whiter than mine, almost transparent. He hated everyone, except for my mother at times. People knew not to disrespect him though. I had seen him cut the throat of someone for forgetting to use the correct title.

I had come to ask him not to kill the young girl from Avalon that had wandered into our city by mistake. Lancelot had asked me.

"Um," I said. His hard stare was drilling holes into my soul. How could this man be my father?

"Spit it out, boy." I could not remember one time that he had called me son. And still, for some reason I desperately wanted his favor, his attention.

"I came to say that I want to represent the Pendragon crest in the winter solstice tournament," I said. *I am sorry Lancelot, but I was afraid that my father would have killed me if I had asked,* I rehearsed in my head.

"You have represented me for the last five years," he stated. His stare narrowed even more, if that was possible. "Are you some kind of idiot?"

"No, my lord," I said. I bowed my head.

"Get out," he said harshly. "I have work to do."

I did not lift my head up. I turned around and quickly began to walk toward the door.

"And Arthur," he said. I could not help but be a little excited. Maybe *this* time he would tell me that he loved me, or at least did not hate me as much as I thought. "You will be punished if you do not win this year."

A chill went through me and I continued speed walking out the door. The guards looked sympathetically at me. They had heard the whole thing.

I was supposed to be going to my chambers for my Latin lesson. However, I felt I needed to get out to the training yard to practice. I was afraid of what "you will be punished" meant. It could be anything between being lashed with a whip with glass stuck in it to having my sword hand cut off because my father thought it was useless.

"Why are you afraid of him?" A smooth voice drifted into my ears. A small hand grabbed my arm and drew me into a niche in the hallway. My sister's face looked up at me, her gray eyes shining in anger.

"I am not, Morgain," I said, brushing her hand off of me. "Leave me alone."

Morgain was one of those people who did not really understand the line between being normal and being a creepy stalker. She was three years older than me and had midnight black hair that flowed down her back in soft waves. She never put it up, even though it was considered rather promiscuous for women to always have the hair down. She had the same eyes as mine—the gray eyes of our mother—but she had the shorter, darker features of her father, Gorlois, our mother's first husband. You can add Morgain to the list of people who hated me, right under my father.

"Arthur, stop lying," she commanded me. I realized that was what I was doing, and I *hated* lying.

I just looked at her.

She shook her head at me. "You are a coward Arthur Pendragon. A coward!"

"I said leave me alone," I demanded and pushed her away by her shoulder.

She growled at me, "You could never stand up to evil. You are going to end up just like your father: sitting fat on that throne while sending people to die."

"Shut up," I growled back. I was nothing like my father and I never would be. "I am not like him."

She snickered, "Whatever you say, brother."

I glared at her and walked off. I stopped mid-stride when I realized I was going the wrong way, turned around, and walked back past Morgain who had her arms crossed over her chest and was smirking at me. I ignored her and kept walking.

"Did you talk to him?" Lancelot asked me enthusiastically as I pulled my sweaty, white training tunic over my head in the armory.

"No, sorry," I lied. "He was busy."

"Oh," Lancelot said, looking down. I felt guilty.

"Yes," I said quietly because I did not know what else to say. This was when the word *okay* would have come in handy.

There was an awkward silence.

"Kay says that he is going to slay the dragon that is supposedly terrorizing the people of the village Meredith," he said, breaking the veil of silence.

I smiled. Kay loved to talk a big game, but he never actually did the things he said he was going to do. "Of course he is."

Lancelot laughed, "You are more likely to do it."

That is when inspiration struck me. I would slay the dragon. Then my father would see me doing something great and Morgain would stop calling me a coward! I would go with Kay to Meredith, saying that I was to help him, and then I would slay the dragon instead of him! I would be a hero if I did that. "Well, why not?"

"What?" Lancelot asked. I forgot he could not read my mind.

"I could slay the dragon!" I said excitedly. "Then my father will finally see some worth in me!"

"Arthur, no offense, but you will die if you go against the dragon," Lancelot told me with a doubting look.

"Well, then I will work as hard as I can, training until I am good enough," I said proudly.

"Alright, Arthur." Lancelot rolled his eyes. He did not think I could do it. That only made me want to work harder.

We had supper in the dining hall that night. We, being me, Lancelot, Morgain, and my mother and father. My father sat at the end, my mother at his left, me at his right, Lancelot next to me, and Morgain next to my mother. It looked like we were having goose or swan, some sort of large bird.

"How was the day?" my mother asked, trying to be cheerful. One of the servants served me some of the meat, a ripped-off piece of barley bread, and what looked like glazed carrots. I looked up at her and stayed silent.

"Fine, Ygraine," my father answered, "other than the fact that we are losing the war, and my only son is going to lose our land to the Saxons because he lacks a spine and a brain!"

I did not look up. I felt Lancelot glance at me. Morgain was definitely smirking.

"I am sure Arthur will mature with time," my mother said, trying to sound hopeful.

"Oh yes, time," he said callously. "I almost forgot; he can see the future!"

I bit my tongue. I never should have told anyone about the strange, free land of America.

"What do you have to say for yourself, *son*?" The gaze of everyone at the table was on me.

I stood up. "I am not hungry."

And then I left.

Left to go where? I was not sure. *There* I supposed, America, an escape from this place into another. An escape that started with the closing of eyes in one place and the opening of the same eyes in another.

*****

Colorado Springs, America, 2008

"Hello Arthur," the school counselor, Mr. Franklin, smiled at me as I came in through the glass door to his office. He shut the blinds.

"Hello," I repeated.

"Please, sit down," he said, motioning for me to have a seat in the brown office chair. I complied.

Mr. Franklin was a tall, skinny man with short, dark hair and black, thick-framed glasses. He had an almost fake expression on his face that looked as if he were trying to be friendly but could not quite do it naturally. It looked like he was hiding some sort of pain beneath those thick glasses. I just could not quite figure out what it was.

"So how are *you*, Arthur?" he asked me. Believe it or not, this seemed like the first time that someone had asked me that and actually meant it. Maybe it was because it was his job to ask "troubled" students that question.

"Fine," I said. I needed to be undescriptive in order for him not to find out too much about me. I had a feeling this man had an aptitude for finding things out.

"Really?" he asked. He did not believe me. "Arthur, you can tell me anything. I promise. I am here to help you."

Somehow, I did not think that telling him I was born in the year 633 would help anyone. "Okay."

"Do you like it here at Carmel?" he asked me.

"Yes, it is fine," I said. I looked at a poster on the wall that had a cartoon boy with skin made of a rainbow that said 'Be You' on it.

"Do you know why you're here?" he asked me.

"No, sir," I said. I folded my hands in my lap.

"Your language arts teacher, Mrs. Hamilton, told me that you wrote yourself on a list of things that didn't make sense to you," he said. So it was Mrs. Hamilton's fault I was here. "Why did you write that Arthur?"

"I do not know," I lied. Maybe it was because I was in a strange land thirteen hundred and sixty-three years away from where I should have been.

"You seem to be a fairly intelligent individual, Arthur," he said, carefully gauging my expression, "and I don't think you would write something for no reason."

I shrugged and kept my face in monotone.

"You seem very respectful," he told me. Of course I was respectful. I did not want to be punished. "What do you want to be when you grow up?"

I had never been asked that question before. Never. It was always "Arthur you are going to be the High King of Britain and you will marry a beautiful young woman and have lots of children so that when you die there will be someone else to be the High King of Britain." I did not receive a choice. That was just the way things were.

"I do not know," I said.

"If you could do anything for the rest of your life, what would it be?" he prompted me.

I thought about this. If I could do anything for the rest of my life. Well, I did not want to do just one thing for the rest of my life, I wanted to do lots of things. I wanted to play football, and do mathematics, and talk to people, and do my drawings, and design structures.

"...Maybe an architect," I said. He regarded me. I regarded him.

"That is a great career choice," he said. He seemed thankful that I had finally given him a bit of information. "Why do you want to be an architect?"

"Because I want to help people," I said simply, "and I like mathematics."

He nodded, then looked down at his papers. He furrowed his eyebrows. "What's your last name, Arthur?"

I shrugged my shoulders. My last name was Pendragon, but I could not go around telling people that was my name.

"Well, you must have a last name," Mr. Franklin leaned back in his chair and crossed his arms over his chest.

"I suppose," I said. I looked down at my hands "I just do not know what it is."

He studied me for a moment. "I suppose you could take your foster parents' name if you wanted, and they agreed of course."

"Okay," I said. *Arthur Ector.* "That would be fine."

"Why did you go to the counselor?" Nathan whispered to me as Coach Hunter explained to us the importance of working hard at practice.

"Mrs. Hamilton said I had issues or something," I lied. I knew exactly why.

"I swear that woman's crazy," Nathan laughed quietly. He pushed his brown hair off his forehead.

"Maybe," I smiled halfheartedly. She was not crazy. She just knew there was something wrong with me.

Both Mr. and Mrs. Ector picked me up that afternoon after practice. This was a rare occurrence. Miss Marion always picked me up except for the few times that she had charity fundraisers to attend with the women from her church.

Mr. Ector made small talk all the way to the electronics store, where he parked in the parking lot, and ushered me and Miss Marion inside. I walked just a little behind them and dragged my sneakers on the asphalt. The dull hum of electronics made me nervous. They did not seem natural: images captured by foreign objects, human tasks done by machines.

"Why have we come here, sir?" I asked as Mr. Ector led me through the store. Miss Marion had wandered off to look at washing machines.

"To get you a present," he said enthusiastically. I blew my hair out of my face.

"You need not buy me anything," I said quietly. Also, I was not sure I wanted anything that came from this store.

"Yes, I need..." he paused for a second. I think my way of talking sometimes confused him. "I want to buy you this."

I stayed quiet as he stopped in front of a table of opened laptops with the illuminated Apple sign on the screen. Ty had said that he received one for his birthday a couple of weeks ago. Also, that they were *extremely* expensive.

"Pick one," he said. I looked up at him. He could not possibly be serious. What would I do with a computer anyways? "I mean it, Arthur. I want to get one for you."

I thought for a moment. It was generally considered polite to refuse such an expensive gift at first, but it began to irritate the other person if you refused too much.

"I do not know which one to choose," I said quietly. I really did not; they all looked about the same to me.

"Well, what's your favorite color?" he asked me. He bent down a little so he was more at my level.

"Red," I answered. I had always liked the color. It reminded me of power, and somehow it also felt hopeful, like something good was coming.

"Then get this one," he said and pointed to one that was painted a shiny scarlet.

Chapter II

Cadbury Castle, Britain, 645

I looked down at myself as I stood naked in the center of my room. I suppose I was fairly tall for my age, just not as tall as I wanted to be. I was athletic, but I did not have defined muscles in my stomach and arms like Lancelot did. My skin was too pale, and it looked off with the golden color of my hair. My eyes were a silvery gray, like my mother's. I think my eyes were my favorite feature of myself.

I had snuck into Kay's chambers last night and asked him if I could join him on his journey to defeat the dragon. He had squinted his eyes at me and shrugged his shoulders like *why not?* Kay was that kind of person, the *why not?* kind of person. Except on occasion when he was mean to Lancelot and me, then he was very mean.

Technically, I outranked him by a lot because I was the son of the king and heir to the high throne of Britain. I did not like ranks, so I really never used mine to push people around. After all, I had never done anything to receive my rank: I was just born.

He had told me to wear my most protective armor and bring the sharpest weapon I could find. It was before the sun had even risen, so Austin had not come to help me get ready yet. No one would know that I had left with Kay.

I picked some brown leather trousers from my wardrobe and pulled them over a pair of breeches. I found my sturdier plates at the bottom of my trunk by the door. I had never put on my armor by myself before, and it was a bit trickier than I expected. I had to use my teeth to grip one of the straps and pull with my hand on the other to fasten the plates properly. It took me about twenty minutes to get all of it on my body. I grabbed my hunting sword from the table; after all, it was the sharpest thing I had. I also tucked a little leather sack of silvers into the waistband of my trousers, underneath my tunic. It felt cold against my skin.

After I had fastened all of the things I was bringing onto my body, I tied a thick rope around the bedpost and threw it out the window. Then I carefully began to lower myself down the stone wall to the public window below. Thankfully, I made it to the glassless window opening and pulled myself into the hallway. This whole debacle of getting from one window to another was, of course, to avoid being seen by the guards outside my room and to avoid being heard by my parents whose chambers were down the hallway.

Kay was waiting for me at the end of the hallway with his arms crossed over his chest.

"What took you so long?" he asked me, irritated.

I shook my head as if to say *I know not*. I thought I had gotten ready quite quickly. After all, I had met Kay before sunrise as he had requested.

"Come on," he said, dropping the subject, turning and beginning a brisk pace down the hallway. I followed him down six flights of stairs on the servants' stairwell, and out to the lesser-used stables on the north side.

He had already gotten someone to prepare two horses for us with leather saddles and reins. He untied them from the posts they were attached to and handed me the reins to the brown one with white patches.

"Are you going to take a spear or a lance?" I asked him as we began to walk the horses out behind the north wall of the palace to the dusty road that led to Meredith.

"Arthur, we are not going to actually kill the dragon," he said condescendingly.

We mounted and set off on the trail at an easy trot. "We are not?"

"Of course not," he said shaking his head. "I doubt there even is an actual dragon. Some idiots probably made it up to get their village more attention."

"Then why are we going?" I asked, looking at him carefully.

Kay was three years older than me, fifteen. He had chestnut brown hair that reached just below his ears and a burn scar on his left cheek. He was tall and lean, and sometimes this made his movements seem a little awkward. He had sort of an arrogant aura about him, as if he owned the world. It was false though, I could tell. Underneath it lay a layer of insecurity, uncertainty, and fear of the unknown.

That was probably why he always went on these "adventures" where nothing ever actually happened. He *wanted* to prove himself; he wanted to show that he had some worth besides the fact that his father, Sir Halpin, was of noble blood. I suppose he and I had that in common. Both of us wanted to prove our worth. Both of us had highly respected fathers. The difference was that people respected Kay's father because he was a war hero and an honorable man. They respected my father purely out of fear.

"Because sometimes we do things so people can feel safe," Kay answered me. "If we tell the people of Meredith that we have slayed the dragon then they will no longer be afraid to go out into the forest."

"How do we make them believe that we actually did it if there really is no dragon?" I asked him. We passed by a very peculiar looking charred tree, and I stopped the conversation for a second to gaze at it. "We will have no evidence."

"The people are uncivilized faerie folk," Kay said. "They will believe anything we tell them. Especially their future king."

Oh yes. That.

The faerie folk were one of the tribes that roamed Britain before the Romans and the Christians came. They had dark features, and all of them were relatively small and short. The people of the New Ways thought they were above them. It was not that they were stupid or uncivilized, they just did not believe the same way as *us* so they were thought of as lower. The faerie folk were not a problem, however. They were very compliant. They lived in the villages they were told to live in and did the things they were told to do, and in return, they received protection and also were allowed to, you know, *live*.

"I guess."

We did not talk much after that. It was only small exchanges like Kay telling me to watch out for a branch that I was about to run into. About a half hour later, we passed another charred tree like the one we had seen before. We slowed our horses a little to look at it this time. It was strange because it did not look like a lightning strike, but rather more like someone had held up several torches to the tree and let it catch fire.

The ride to Meredith at a mild trot was generally about an hour long. The village was fairly close to Camelot and Cadbury Castle, so it was a popular place for knights to travel. Or used to travel, I suppose. Now they were all away fighting in that ridiculous war.

About fifty minutes into the journey, we began to see more of the charred trees, oftentimes grouped together in clusters as if someone had taken a gigantic torch and set fire to them all at once. We also began to see strange marks on the trees; marks that looked like someone had carved lines into the trees with a dull knife, ragged and uneven. The marks bothered me; they were so imperfect, yet still in organized lines.

Kay held his hand up, and we both stopped and dismounted, holding the reins in our hands. The horses stamped nervously as if they knew something but did not know how to tell us.

"What is going on?" I asked, looking around. The forest looked completely normal, aside from the marked and charred trees.

"I know not..." Kay trailed off, gauging his surroundings the same way I was.

He drew his sword, and I swallowed, then copied him.

I had never been in a situation where I had had to use my sword in a real way. It was always during training or Lancelot and me just being stupid. I was not quite sure if the skills I so frequently practiced would be up to par if I really needed them.

It was so silent, my ears felt like they had stopped working. The forest was not supposed to be silent. The forest was supposed to be filled with birds and animals that all made *noise*. The silence made it seem afraid. But afraid of what?

Afraid of *that*.

A huge reptilian creature had risen up behind us. Kay and I turned around slowly. My heart was beating so fast and loud I thought that Kay would be able to hear it.

"I thought you said that there was no dragon," I whispered to him.

Kay was frozen in fear, so he did not answer.

"Kay, what do we do?"

Kay shook his head because he did not know and was probably too afraid to move.

I had never seen a dragon before that day, so I had not been sure what to expect. I suppose I expected a large, green lizard with wings, sort of like an alligator. The dragon that stood before me now was much more terrifying.

The scales were a metallic black that had an almost silvery tint to them. It had sharp, white claws that dug into the forest floor and had remnants of blood on them. It had a drooping chest and belly that dragged on the ground, but it still looked like a sheer mass of pure muscle. A long swooping neck came off of the thick body up to a large, horrific head. The eyes of the dragon were pure white like pearls, and it had an extended snout with smoke rising out of the nostrils.

The mouth was the most terrifying by far. The white teeth were long, sharp, and jagged. They were also smeared with blood, and out of the side of the mouth was a bloody, human leg. That was the worst part. It was not only the most terrible creature I had ever seen, but there was now proof that there was no chance it was friendly. It was a demon.

The moment Kay and I and the dragon all regarded one another seemed to be the longest moment of my life. Which I suppose was probably good because it was likely to be my last moment before the dragon killed us. My blood rushing in my ears and my heart pounding in my chest were the only sounds I could hear. It was not a matter of *if* the dragon was going to kill me, it was a matter of how long.

I looked at Kay, but Kay was no longer next to me. He was gone. I spun in a circle, searching for him. I saw a smear in the dirt where Kay had been. He must have run off to hide. Leaving me alone. With the focus of the dragon completely on me. That was when my body stopped responding to my own thoughts, the thoughts that I was thinking to run, *to flee*, to get to safety.

Instead, I ran straight at the dragon with my sword drawn, having no clue about what I was doing. It was like my movements were being instructed by a greater force, something that had always been there, but had never been used.

The huge claw of the dragon rose up to smack me to my death, but I blocked it. *Perfectly.* I had never done that before. I did not even think about what I was doing, it just happened. My sword left a reasonable, bloody gash in the foot of the dragon. I continued on my rampage and the dragon spewed fire at me. I rolled to avoid it and used my forward momentum to get to my feet, jumping to not be hit by the spiny, black tail that lashed out.

I noticed a pattern in the strikes of the dragon: claw, fire, tail, tail, fire, claw. Block, roll, jump, jump, roll, block. It clawed at me twice, and it did two tail spins in a row, but it never blew fire twice in a row. I figured this was probably because it took more effort to generate fire, so it was able to do it less often. I figured my best shot at killing the thing, or at least injuring it, was to stab it in the mouth, as the rest of the body of the dragon was covered in hard scales that worked as armor. This was actually good because fire was the least used attack; the teeth, however, could be an issue.

I blocked a swipe from the claw and jumped, grabbing a scale that had begun to come loose from the body. I slid my sword into my belt and held on to it, tucking myself against the scales of the dragon to avoid the fire. It worked, and I began to climb sideways across the scales of the dragon toward the neck like a leech. It stamped around and tried to shake me off, but my grip was iron strong. It roared in frustration. I continued climbing until I was hanging on to the neck, just below the head. Somehow, I was not afraid anymore. It was almost natural, as if I were born to kill dragons and the instructions on how to do it were written on the backs of my eyelids.

I drew my sword with my right hand while holding onto a loose scale with my left and desperately trying to find footholds with my feet. I steadied myself for a second and then tried to plunge my sword into the pink mouth of the creature while still avoiding the teeth. Blood gushed out onto my arm, and I pulled my sword back out. I noticed that the scale I was using as a handhold was beginning to separate from the skin beneath the armor. I stabbed my hunting sword there next, into the soft pink flesh; it felt like cutting into warm butter. The blood from the neck drenched me, and I jumped the seven feet back down to the ground, cringing at the impact, and ran to what I considered a safe distance away from the now lumbering and blood gushing creature.

My surroundings were drenched in the warm scarlet liquid. Blood wet the ground, and my clothes, and seemingly everything around me. The dragon fell to the ground. Its head fell with a thunk, and I slit the throat quickly to end the creature's suffering.

I stared at the dead dragon silently. My racing heart slowly began to calm itself. I let out my breath that I had not even realized I had been holding. I stumbled back and fell to the ground. Tiredness overtook me, and also guilt. The adrenaline of battle trickled out of my system. My nose burned with the scent of blood and my own sweat. The coolness of the fresh October air flooded my system and I breathed deeply.

Yes, I felt bad about killing the dragon. However, not as bad as you might think. The dragon had been killing innocent people for no apparent reason other than the fact that it had developed the taste for human flesh instead of wild deer or other forest animals that I assumed dragons might eat. I was saving lives by killing that dragon. It was one life compared to possibly hundreds. The people in Meredith did not know how to defend themselves; the entire village could have been destroyed. Burned to ashes and bones by this mighty creature that I had slain.

"Arthur…" Kay came out from behind a tree that he must have been hiding behind.

I glared at him. My first feeling toward him was anger. He left me to die. He ran off in the hopes that the dragon would kill me instead of him. He did not even try to help me or even make an effort to slay the dragon and save the people that he had supposedly set off to save. He was a coward.

"Look I…" He started and then trailed off, having a sudden interest in the ground.

I shook my head at him and clicked my tongue against the roof of my mouth loudly to call for the horses. Surprisingly enough, they came. Even they were more loyal than Kay.

Before I mounted mine, I ripped one of the black scales off of the dragon. It fit in the palm of my hand and looked almost like a piece of obsidian. Then I mounted and kicked the flank of the horse, setting off at a gallop in the direction of Meredith.

*****

Colorado Springs, America, 2008

"Are you *sure* this is a good idea?" I asked Ty as we stood by the chicken wire fence at the far end of the graveyard near his neighborhood.

"Yeah, duh, Arthur," he said, rolling his eyes. "I've done it thousands of times."

It was highly unlikely that he had done it thousands of times, considering that he was only thirteen years old, and there were only about three hundred and sixty-five days in a year. He probably could not have done it until he was six years old, which only left seven years. That left only about twenty-five hundred days that he could have possibly done it, and he was implying that he had done it at least two thousand times. That meant that he was doing it at least four out of every five days, and that was highly unlikely considering that he had things like school and football practice almost every day. However, I did not feel that Ty would properly appreciate my logic against why he could not have done it thousands of times, so I just went along with the inference that it was okay to do because Ty had done it *thousands* of times.

We scaled the fence and jumped down onto the perfectly trimmed green grass of the graveyard. The soil sunk softly underneath our sneakers and I cringed: we were going to leave footprints.

"Relax," Ty commanded me. "Nobody will be here on a Saturday."

I looked around the cemetery nervously. It was dead silent—excuse the pun. Various tombstones marked the ground where different people lay. Toward the center of the place was a modest concrete building with bright flower beds around it. That was our destination. We were going to sneak inside the office of the Gravedigger and take his keys. Why? I was not really sure. Bragging rights, I suppose.

It was easy enough to get to the building. We just walked across the grass to the nearest sidewalk and then traveled down the sidewalk; we sidled up against the wall behind the flowerbeds and listened for what was going on inside. We did not hear anything at first, and then we heard off-tune whistling.

"That's the guy," Ty said. He nodded, and we began to creep around the side of the building until we reached a window with the blinds pulled down halfway.

We crouched beneath the windowsill and peeked through the bottom of the window, being careful not to be seen.

The Gravedigger was a short, skinny man in ripped overalls and a dirt-stained, long-sleeved white shirt. He had a long, scraggly brown beard, and the same scraggly brown hair on his head. The keys that we were after jangled on his belt. He was seated in a wooden chair at a computer desk and was scrolling through something. He continued to whistle badly.

"Ready?" Ty stood up and patted my shoulder. I shrugged and stood up with him.

I followed Ty around to the back of the building where he unlocked the back door with a key he had stolen a couple of weeks ago.

We crept into the building through a black and white tiled laundry room. There was a washing machine turning loudly. If you asked me, the Gravedigger needed to wash his own clothes. Ty shut the door softly behind us, and we stood on either side of the doorframe leading into the main office where the Gravedigger was.

Ty smiled manically at me and raised his eyebrows. I closed my eyes for a second and hoped we did not get caught. Mr. and Mrs. Ector would *not* be pleased if they found their foster son arrested for breaking into a graveyard. Ty held up one finger, then two, then three, and then he ran out into the room yelling, "I'M A ZOMBIE!!!"

I let my head fall into my hands. *Really Ty?* I stayed behind the laundry room door, listening carefully through the wall.

"AAAHHHH!!!" I heard the Gravedigger yell. "You son of a gun. Little pest!!!"

Obviously, Ty had been here before because the Gravedigger recognized him.

"I will take these!" Ty said. I guessed he was reaching for the keys.

"No, you will not, you little punk!" Gravedigger yelled at him. I heard the sound of metal on metal and a harsh *click*.

I burst through the door into the main office of the room to see the Gravedigger aiming a hunting rifle at Ty who was running around the room like mad trying to avoid being shot.

I did not think. I acted.

I tackled the Gravedigger to the ground and ripped the rifle out of his hands, straddling his chest. He punched me in the eye, and I grabbed his hands and pressed them to his chest like I remembered from training *there*.

"Who the heck are you?" the Gravedigger yelled at me. He spit in my face, and I cringed.

I did not respond to him. I just left him there, wrestled to the ground. "What do we do Ty?"

"Uhhhhh…" Ty seemed utterly confused.

"Ty!" I said loudly. I needed him to focus, so we could come up with a plan, so I did not spend the rest of my life sitting on this man.

"How did you do that…?" He asked me, staring wide-eyed. Gravedigger tried to yell at me again, and I covered his mouth with my hand.

"I do not know," I said, which was the truth. It had felt the same as fighting the dragon, everything flowed from somewhere inside me. "But I really need you to tell me what to do right now, Ty!"

"We can't call the cops cuz ya know…we broke in…" Ty reasoned. "However, he did almost shoot me."

"So, we are not calling the cops," I said. The Gravedigger began to struggle again. "What else?"

"Ah…" He set his face in a thoughtful look.

"Think!" I yelled at him.

"Jeez, Arthur, you're usually so chill," he said shrugging.

Maybe it is a good thing I am not "chill" right now because then we would be in serious trouble! I am literally sitting on some man who just tried to shoot you in the middle of a cemetery! Maybe you should be a little less "chill"!!!

"Look, we need to do something quick," I said, taking a deep breath.

"We probably need to just get out of here," he said. "The Gravedigger can't prove it's us, so we're home free if we can get out without being seen."

"Okay," I nodded. I motioned to the person I was sitting on. "So what do we do with him?"

Ty smiled mischievously. "The closet."

"What about the closet?" I asked irritated.

"Let's put him in the closet," Ty said. "Then we can get out without being seen."

The Gravedigger struggled beneath me. Apparently he did not want to be put into a closet.

I nodded. "How do we get him in?"

"Uh…" He trailed off.

I thought for a moment, then I got up off of him, gripping his arms together with my hands and dragged him to his feet. "Open the closet door."

The closet was on the left side of the room, about ten feet away from where I was currently holding the Gravedigger who was still struggling like mad.

Ty opened it, and I dragged the Gravedigger to the closet and shoved him inside. I held the door shut while Ty took a wooden chair and propped it under the door handle.

The Gravedigger was screaming an awful lot of curse words, and I felt like he might cause enough commotion that someone would come and find us.

"Okay, let's get outta here," Ty said, slapping me on the shoulder. "Oh wait!"

He reopened the closet and quickly grabbed the keys from the Gravedigger's belt. The Gravedigger tried to punch him, but Ty dodged and slammed the door shut, repositioning the chair. I rolled my eyes at him.

We ran back through the office, through the laundry room, and out the back door to the cemetery. We trekked across the perfect grass at a full sprint, climbed the fence, and jumped to the other side. We ran to the nearest tree and collapsed behind it, breathing hard.

And then Ty started laughing.

Laughing. Like it was the funniest thing ever that he was almost shot and that we shoved someone into a closet. And I do not know why, but I started laughing too.

I went over to Ty's house that night for dinner.

His parents, Theresa and John Douglas, were very nice people. His younger brother, Landon, who was in the sixth grade at Carmel, was a bit of a tattletale, but he seemed to like me well enough.

"How was your guys's day?" Mrs. Douglas asked us as we sat at the dining room table.

"Fine," Ty said, cleverly undescriptive. I nodded to say that I agreed with him.

Mrs. Douglas rolled her brown eyes and her puffy black afro bounced as she did.

"What did you do today?" she prompted us. Mr. Douglas passed a basket of golden brown biscuits to me, and I took one. That was one of the reasons I liked going over to Ty's house. His mother made the best southern-style food.

I glanced at Ty, watching how he was going to answer this question. "We went to the park and hung with some of the guys from school."

I nodded again. Best to just go along.

"Sure," Landon mocked us.

"Shut up," Ty glared at him.

The phone rang, "Sorry, I gotta take this," said Mr. Douglas as he got up to answer it.

Mr. Douglas was a police officer, so he always received phone calls about things happening at his work or problems that his co-workers needed help with. The funny part was that Ty's father's job was to keep people out of trouble and enforce the law, and Ty was…well, a troublemaker.

"Arthur and me are gonna go up to my room 'kay mom?" Ty said, already getting up.

I would have liked to have a second helping, but whatever Ty needed to do in his room sounded important so I followed him.

"Thank you, Mrs. Douglas," I said. I almost bowed to her and then I remembered that that would be strange.

I followed Ty down the picture strewn hallway to his room that was painted a vibrant, electric blue and had pictures of pro football and basketball players pasted all over the walls. That was what Ty wanted to do when he became an adult after all, be some sort of pro sportsman. I hoped he made it. Miss Marion had told me it was stupid of Ty to dream that way because it would only result in hopeless failure. Apparently, pro sportsmen who did well in the world were quite rare.

Ty turned on his boxy, gray computer and drummed his fingers on the keyboard. When it finally loaded, he opened the internet 'e' icon.

He typed 'Evergreen Cemetery, Colorado Springs, Caretakers' into the search box. He clicked on the first link to find information on burials at the cemetery. He went back and clicked on the second link. Then we heard a knock at the door and we both turned our heads. Ty minimized the search engine so the intruder would not see what we were doing.

"What're you guys doing?" It was Landon.

"Nothin'," said Ty, glaring at him. "Go away."

"Mom said Marion called and said she wants Arthur home," Landon said, crossing his arms.

I stood up. "I will see you at school Ty."

"Yeah, I'll finish the project," he said, smirking at Landon.

Chapter III

Meredith, Britain, 645

The night before I had walked through Meredith to the inn on the northside of the village. I had paid for one night with five silver even though the innkeeper had recognized me as the prince and insisted that I not pay. Part of the reason I had paid was because then the innkeeper would not tell my father where I was. I did not need to be punished for running off just yet. After all, I had slain the dragon and quite possibly saved a lot of innocent people. The servants at the inn had brought me supper and now breakfast free of charge, and they had insisted they wash my clothes and shine my armor. So now I was sitting in my breeches and my undertunic on the grass mattress on the floor of the inn room.

There was black mold crawling up the walls from the floorboard and I swore I had seen a rat the night before, crawling through a crack by the door. Nevertheless, I had a safe place to stay away from my father in a village that might worship me after I told them about how I had slayed the dragon that had been terrorizing them.

My hunting sword was hanging from my belt and scabbard on a peg next to the door. Yesterday, before I went to bed, I had cleaned the blade of the dragon's blood with a rag that one of the servants had given me. Somehow the sword seemed polluted now. I did not know why. I had killed deer and rabbits with it before when Lancelot and I went on hunting escapades in the forest. It just seemed that killing a creature as magnificent as a dragon was different. Something so big, so mighty, and I had killed it. It fell to the ground with its blood on my hands. It would never taste the air of the world again; it would never taste the blood of another again.

Part of me wondered what had happened to Kay, but part of me did not. He had been planning to lie to the people of Meredith without actually taking care of the problem at hand. And then when the problem arose, he fled in fear. He left me to die without even trying to help me. He was too much of a coward to stand up to it, to try to save the people he said he came to save. I was not though. I stood up to my fear and conquered it. I knew what had to be done and I did it.

In Rome, there used to be men called gladiators. Gladiators were men who feared nothing. They defeated lions and all sorts of beasts in front of giant crowds to prove their worth and their bravery. In Britain we had men called knights. Knights were like gladiators; they were supposed to be the bravest men in the land and defeat beasts and protect the people so that everything was right and well. The knights that I knew were not like this however. They were mean and heartless. All they cared for was glory and money and women. Not to love. To rape.

And becoming a knight was no task of honor either. All you needed was to be of noble blood and have the favor of someone who was higher in rank than you. And the worst part was that you could not become a knight, no matter how great a man you were, if you were born of common blood. A man could have slayed a thousand dragons and saved a thousand villages and he still would not be good enough to enjoy knighthood. All because he happened to not be in the right family.

The *right* family. What decided which family was noble or not? Obviously not the actions of people. The definition of noble is "possessing very high or excellent qualities or properties." My father was supposedly the most *noble* man in Britain and yet he did not have any fine or excellent qualities. He was just mean, greedy, and lustful, without integrity.

Someday, when I am king, I will have the opportunity to knight men. I will not knight anyone that is not honorable. Even if they tie me down and make me. I think that the honor of knighthood should only be received by those that are worthy, and I will not judge their worth by the blood that flows in their veins. They would be deemed worthy because of their actions, and the great things they would have done in their life. They will live by a code of honor and integrity and they will be the most respected men in the land. Not because of their family. Because they earned it.

"Your clothes my lord." A servant bowed to me and set a stack of folded clothes on the floor in front of me.

"Thank you." I gave a half-hearted smile, and he bowed again and left.

I hastily put on my clothes and fastened my armor to my body. I was going to tell the people about my victory against the dragon. Starting with the Lord of Meredith, Sir Lewys.

The night before, I had left my horse in the tiny inn stables where it had been fed and groomed, once again, free of charge. I untied it from the post and walked it out of the stables to the central village road where I mounted and trotted north through the village to the large manor in the distance. A few people looked twice at me as I rode through the village, but I think most of them just assumed that I was a messenger or a knight going to stay with Sir Lewys, so they paid little attention.

The manor of Meredith was fairly small as manors go, I believe. I am not one to say, however, considering that I lived in Cadbury Castle which was thought to be the largest structure in Britain. The manor had a small, ivy-covered stone gateway that led into the front steps and the main doors. The main doors were about ten feet tall and made of a plain oakwood without any crests or designs on them. There was a small courtyard area in front of the main entryway that had a statue of a dog at its center. I rode into this area and dismounted in front of the steps.

I waited for about ten minutes before coming to the conclusion that no one was going to welcome me in which, although I was unannounced, seemed odd. Generally, there were at least a couple of guards watching to see if anyone wished to enter. That seemed like a good safety measure. I tied my horse to the drooping branch of an old willow tree in hopes that it would be compliant and meandered up to the front doors. I considered knocking, it seemed polite, but then, whoever was supposed to be at the door had already neglected to invite me in so I went right ahead and opened the doors myself.

I entered into a torch-lit hallway seemingly devoid of other people. I followed the long straight hallway to a cross path where I turned right and began to hear voices. Voices accompanied by Kay.

I sidled up against the wall to listen, careful not to be seen. I heard the dull hum of subtle breathing. There were obviously several people in the room.

"And the dragon just fell over after it had been stabbed?" a voice asked.

"Yes," Kay said, "as if an unknown force had been pulling it down."

I realized what was happening. Kay had finally come to his senses and was now telling Sir Lewys about my defeat of the dragon for me. He had decided to make up for his cowardly behavior yesterday. Maybe Kay was cut out to be a knight after all.

A hand gripped my arm and spun me away from the wall. "Who are you?"

I ripped my arm away from my captor and drew my sword, holding the point to his throat. "You tell me first."

"I did not mean any harm!" He backed away, surprised at my threat.

I looked him up and down without moving my sword. He had shoulder-length, wavy dark hair and black eyes and looked about my age. He came just up to my eye level, and so was about two inches shorter than me. His build was thin and wiry. He did not look very strong.

"What are you called?" I asked him fiercely. I was surprised at how menacing I could sound when the need arose.

"Gawain," he said. His eyes were crossed from looking at my sword point. "Now can you please not run me through?"

I slid my sword back into my belt. "Sorry," I muttered.

"What are you called?" he asked me, sizing me up.

"I have a cousin called Gawain," I said, purposely not answering his question. He did not need to find out who I was just yet. "He lives north in Orkney."

Gawain looked to the side. "Just tell me your name."

I had a feeling I knew who this was. I had not seen him since I was six, but I was fairly certain that this was the son of my aunt, Morgause, and King Lot. According to a letter my aunt had sent my mother, her son Gawain had recently gone missing and there was a countrywide search for him. Well as "countrywide" as there could be when the country was at war.

"Arthur," I gave him a sideways look. His face dropped; he knew that I knew. Somehow, when he had told me his name I just knew that this boy and I were related and that we were meant to meet. "It has been quite a while."

"Yes, yes it has," he said in monotone.

"Why are you here Gawain?" I asked him. I suppose I could not blame him too much for running away, considering that I had done the same thing, just not for three weeks.

"Here?" he asked. "I heard someone had slayed a dragon and I came to see if it was true."

"That was me," I said proudly.

"What!?" Gawain wrinkled his brow. He pointed to the room I had been listening in on and had momentarily forgotten about. "That boy in there did. His name is Kay or something."

"What!" My anger from yesterday came flooding back, turning my stomach into a roiling pit of rage. "He said that he did it?"

"Yes," Gawain nodded. Then he whisper-yelled, "keep your voice down, I do not want to be caught eavesdropping!"

"That lying little—" seething, I started to walk into the room that Kay was lying to everyone in, but Gawain stopped me.

"Are you crazy?" he asked. "You might be the prince of Britain and want to be sent home, but I for one do not!"

"He is lying to everyone about something I did!" I whisper-yelled at him. He started to drag me down the hall.

"I would too!" Gawain said. "You have no proof that you killed the dragon instead of him!"

I clenched my fists and sighed angrily. "I have to set it right somehow."

Gawain just rolled his eyes and continued dragging me away from the room where Kay was lying to everyone about *my* accomplishments.

We walked out to the front courtyard and sat down under the willow tree where my horse was and I sighed, leaning against the massive, rough tree trunk.

"Why did you run away?" I asked him.

"I decided that I was tired of my parents," he said, playing with a willow leaf. "So I left."

"I wish," I muttered.

"Why?" Gawain asked me. "You are the richest child in the country. Why would you run away?"

"Because I hate my father," I said. We made eye contact for a moment, and then he looked away. "You are fairly wealthy too if I remember correctly, why did you leave?"

He shrugged. "I just wanted to I guess."

I smiled. I wished that I could do things just because I wanted to.

"Are you going to go home?" he asked me.

"Yes," I answered. "I only came to slay the dragon."

Gawain smiled, "Of course you are."

"And what is that supposed to mean?" I asked sharply.

"Nothing." Gawain shook his head and looked down. "Are you still angry about your friend taking the credit for what you believe you did?"

"I *did* do it," I said firmly. "And I am."

"Good luck with that."

I glared at him and stood up. "Just you wait."

I marched right back into the manor, through those large oak doors, and down the dimly lit corridor all the way to the room where I had heard the voice of Kay. I did not bother to pause and listen around the corner this time. I dove right into the chaos that was an open cobblestone room filled with people listening to the stories that Kay was telling. False stories.

"Arthur!" Kay said, surprised as I barged into the room and marched up to him. He smiled nervously, "What are you doing here?"

"I came to tell the people about the dragon *I* slayed!" I said loudly in his face. It was slightly awkward because he was at least three inches taller than me.

He frantically shook his head at me to tell me to stop talking. I did no such thing.

"Do you not remember?" I asked. I turned and swept my eyes over the crowd. I felt the rage in my core roiling like a volcano again. "When you hid behind that tree, I turned and fought?"

"Young man," a deep voice said from behind me. I felt a large hand on my shoulder.

I turned. It was Sir Lewys. He immediately recognized me and knelt on the stone floor. The rest of the men in the room did the same, bowing their heads as if I were some sort of god.

I clenched my fists. I *hated* when this happened. I had done nothing to deserve their groveling. *I was born*; that was all. And I was not even born to a great man. I was born to a greedy, unrelenting, selfish man who happened to be a king who had people killed for fun and encouraged war in his free time. And for that, these people were kneeling at my feet.

"Get up!" I yelled, irritated. Never before in my life had I been this angry. Not even when my father made fun of me for saying I was able to see the future, or when Morgain manipulated things so they looked like my fault, or when Lancelot bested me in training. I was not even sure why; the current events just stirred my emotions like nothing else.

The people in the room quickly got to their feet. There were about fifteen men and women in fairly bland clothing all staring at me, wide-eyed. I wanted them to disappear so I could talk to Kay and ask him why he had betrayed me as he just had. However, I was not a magician and therefore could not make all the people around me disappear, so I just had to deal with the issue at hand the best I could.

I wanted to yell at everyone the truth and then yell at Kay for lying and then just yell some more. I could have done that, but that would only perpetuate the belief that I was a stuck-up child of noble birth that just wanted my own way. That was not the goal.

I breathed in deeply. Out of the corner of my eye, I saw the edge of Gawain's too big, black tunic flutter around the entrance to the stone chamber from the hall. He was listening.

"I am not worthy for you to kneel before me," I said softly, it was what I had been thinking after all. I found myself more nervous than I had felt when I had rage bubbling up inside me, and I wanted to yell my thoughts to the people in the room. I was only twelve years old after all. It was highly unlikely that I would be able to talk to all these adults without a speck of fear in my mind.

The people in the room looked around awkwardly, not sure of exactly what to do.

"I-I am the one who slayed the dragon," my voice shook a little and I cringed. I did not sound confident in the fact that I was the one who had saved the village. I sounded like a small child that would run back to his mother's embrace at even the mere story of a dragon. I repeated myself, trying to make my voice sound deeper, older, "I *am* the one that slayed the dragon."

I looked at Kay, he was slowly slinking toward the entrance of the chamber where Gawain was listening.

I wanted to say that Kay had lied to them, but that did not seem honorable either. It seemed downright petty. *I* knew that I had slayed the dragon, and that was what mattered really. That the dragon had been slayed and the people had been saved. It really did not matter *who* had done it, just that it had been done. It was for my own selfishness that I wanted everyone to know that it was I who had done the task. Now the people had heard both opinions, mine and Kay's. It was up to them to decide which of us was telling the truth.

It did not seem right for Kay to get the glory for something I had done, however, and it was definitely not right for him to lie so blatantly. I suppose I could have told someone, like a training master or a senior knight, what he had done so he could be punished, but I did not want to tattle like a child.

I slowly backed away from the people who were all looking at me as if I were going to say something interesting that would better their lives. I thought that they were expecting a bit too much from me. Maybe when I was older, I could enlighten people with a mere speech that I conjured up in the heat of the moment. Maybe then I would be worthy of the respect that people gave me, the respect that I had not earned.

"Yes…" I said meekly, not knowing what else to say. I willed words to form in my mouth, but they did not. I wanted to run all the way back home and fall asleep in my mother's warm embrace. Forget that any of this ever happened. Gawain was right. I should have just let Kay be the liar that he was.

I turned, lifted my chin ever so slightly, and walked out of the room, trying to portray an air of confidence to my audience who was watching my every move.

Gawain was waiting outside the entrance to the room as predicted. I looked at him for a moment, then continued walking down the hall. He followed a good ten feet behind me. I walked down the stone steps to the willow tree where my horse was, only to find Kay frantically undoing the knots I had tied to keep the horse there.

"What are you doing?" I exclaimed, running up to him and forcing his hands off the reins of my horse.

Kay backed away, his pale face bright red with embarrassment. He opened his mouth to say something, and then shut it. That was probably a good thing. Anything he said would have probably made me even more angry than I already was.

We just looked at each other for a moment. I felt as if I were looking down upon him even though he stood taller than me. His eyes were turned toward the ground in shame. I wanted to do something to set things right. I was too young to punish him, and I was also not his direct authority.

I untied my horse from the willow branch and mounted. I looked down at Kay who was trying not to meet my eyes. I looked up toward the path I was planning to take out of the courtyard. I needed to forget about Kay and just leave. If he could convince people that he had done something he had not, then he could convince someone to give him a method of transportation home.

I trotted out of the manor grounds and about two hundred yards down the dirt village road before I remembered Gawain. I suppose I did not have to help him. Something about his laid-back disposition bothered me, I am not sure why, but it did. He was my cousin, however, and he had at least tried to help me, so I went back for him. I could at least try to convince him to return home to Orkney.

"I had a feeling you were coming back," Gawain said as I dismounted just inside the manor courtyard.

I smiled and walked my horse back over to the willow tree. I noticed that Kay was nowhere to be seen.

I sat down in the shade of the drooping willow tree on the soft grass of the courtyard. *There,* in America, it seemed that all the grass on peoples' property was trimmed short so that not one piece was out of place. Although I considered myself a perfectionist in the things I did, I did not like the American way of trying to make everything perfect. From bathrooms to the trees on the sides of streets, it seemed that there were constantly people in place to trim and critique everything. Some things were not meant to be perfect, like grass. Grass was wild. It had been here since before people roamed the earth, tromping over beautiful things like dirt. Grass was meant to be long and yellow and form a bed for whoever wished to lie on it.

"I suppose I should tell you to go home," I said, sitting with my legs crossed, facing Gawain.

"So why do you not?" Gawain asked with a tilting smile tugging at his mouth.

That was what bothered me about Gawain. He was arrogant. He had the same way about him as the young knights who walked about the palace as if they owned the world.

"Because I do not want to tell you what to do with your life," I said, I picked a piece of grass and rubbed it between my fingers. "I have had enough of that in my own experience."

He flipped his long, thick, dark hair out of his face. Gawain had beautiful hair, in fact, Gawain was a very beautiful person. Almost beautiful like a girl. That bothered me too. I knew that girls would look at him instead of me if we were together.

"Alright," he said. I had made this deep confession of my life's experience to him and his reply was *alright*. Add that to the list of things that bothered me about him: he was too stupid to give meaningful replies.

I looked at him for a moment. He made no move to extend his reply. "So, are you going to go back to Orkney or not?"

He did not pay any attention to my question. "Do you think your parents would recognize me?"

I shook my head. I squinted at him, trying to decipher what he might be thinking. "I did not recognize you."

"Let me come with you to Camelot," he said. It was more of a command than a request. I did not like that.

"Why?" I asked. I noticed my friendly tone gradually trickling out of my voice.

"I have a plan."

And that was how Gawain came to Camelot.

Chapter IV

Colorado Springs, America, 2008

History was the best class of the day. This was mainly because of our teacher, Miss Adams. Miss Adams was only twenty-five years old, which was young for a teacher here. She was short, shorter than me (which was one of the reasons I liked her), and she had a bright reddish orange pixie cut that did not even come to the tips of her ears. For that reason, almost everyone called her Miss Carrot. She was very skinny and she looked like she might just fall over if someone were to blow on her hard enough. Her personality, however, was the exact opposite of her delicate looks. Every time a student interrupted, she slammed a worn metal yardstick against the whiteboard, followed by a tally on the punishment sheet.

The punishment sheet was a piece of paper that all the teachers used to record how many times we did something wrong. Every time you spoke out of turn, or slept in class, or were leaning back in your chair, or writing curse words on your desk, it was a tally mark. No one knew what happened with the tally marks. I thought it was more the idea of the *tally* that was meant to scare the students into doing the right things. Ty said that at the end of the year, Miss Adams whacked you with her metal yardstick once for every tally you had. I knew what it was like to be whacked with sticks by teachers, and I did not enjoy it. So I did everything I could to avoid getting little purple tallies next to my name.

Miss Adams took a blue marker and wrote the word 'Aqueduct' on the whiteboard. Then she wrote the word

'Coliseum' under that, and then 'Gladiator', and then 'Jupiter', and then 'Empire'.

I was in the third row back from the board, so I had to lift my head to see above the girl in front of me.

"What do these things have in common?" Miss Adams asked the class.

Rome, I thought. Jupiter was the King of the Gods in Rome, or used to be anyways, now most of the people in Rome were Christians.

A girl in the front, who seemed to know about everything Miss Adams taught, raised her hand.

"Hailey," Miss Adams pointed to her.

"They're all things from ancient Rome," she said proudly. "Just so everyone knows, an aqueduct was how they moved water from one place to another." she continued in usual Hailey fashion.

"Right," Miss Adams agreed. "We're going to spend the next month learning about the ancient Roman civilization."

That sounded interesting. I already knew quite a bit about Rome since it was where some of my family had come from, and during my Latin lessons, Father Patricius always told me about what it was like to grow up there.

My grandfather, whom I never met, came from Rome. His name was Ambrosius Aurelianus and he was the one who started the war against the Saxons. He was also the first one to defeat them and invoke a period of peace that lasted about fifteen years. He went to battle with them again and died in battle, leaving the problem to my father, whom I assumed would leave the problem to me.

Miss Adams pulled the large world map down over the whiteboard. She took her metal yardstick and snapped it over Italy.

"This is where the great city of Rome is," she said. She ran her hand in all directions over the area around Italy. "And this is where the Roman Empire was."

The Romans were a conquering people. That was how they got to Britain. I suppose if it was not for the fact that they were greedy and wanted more land, I would not be alive. Or maybe I would be alive, but live on Avalon and be a wizard. Or maybe I would be painting myself blue and practicing cannibalism as a Pict. It was probably a good thing that the Romans came, at least for my sake.

"We are going to do an activity. I want you to get into groups of four," she said.

I turned around and looked for boys from football to form a group. Helix was diagonally from me to the right, and he motioned for me to come to him, so I got up and sat on his desk.

"We still need two more people," I said, looking around. A couple girls were sitting nearby. I was pretty sure one of them liked Helix because she giggled and started whispering to her friends whenever he looked in her general direction.

"Trinity and Sequoia are staring at me again," Helix complained. It felt more like he was bragging.

"They are the only ones left without a group," I commented.

"Fine, whatever," Helix said and stood up. Underneath, I could tell that he was happy for their flattery.

Helix walked over to Trinity and Sequoia and started talking to them. Who knew making groups could be such a political hardship?

"Arthur!" I heard Miss Adams harshly yell my name. I turned my gaze to her. "Get off that desk!"

I practically sprung off the desk to the floor in fear of a tally mark or a whack from that stick.

"Graceful," Helix laughed at me, coming back with the two girls that would complete our group of four.

63

"Shut up," I said and glared at him.

We moved four desks together and all sat down to face Miss Adams who was quite outwardly irritated with us.

"Thank you," Miss Adams said sarcastically, and most likely directed toward our group.

"Carrot needs to calm the heck down," Helix commented to me from across our group of desks.

"Mr. O'Krier." Miss Adams slammed her stick onto the whiteboard and I cringed. I could almost feel the stick slamming into the tops of hands. "That's a tally for you."

Helix leaned back and rolled his eyes. Everyone was looking at him.

"Don't roll your eyes at me young man!" she commanded harshly.

"I didn't!" he defended himself. Everyone knew he had.

She made another mark on the punishment sheet and recomposed herself.

"We're going to do an activity that demonstrates the groups of people that the Roman Empire conquered," she began. Well, I knew all about that. "First, I am going to assign each group a different civilization."

She held up a blue velvet cinch bag. "I need one representative from each group to come up and choose a civilization out of this bag."

"Arthur," Helix decided for our group. Maybe he thought that I would have the best statistical luck.

Trinity and Sequoia shrugged.

At least our group did not get into a fight about who got to draw the slip of paper out of the bag. Really it seemed silly that some of the groups were.

Miss Adams slammed her stick. "Please form a line up here."

Most of the students rushed up to the front so they could be at the front of the line. It really did not make a lot of sense. It was statistics. No matter where they went in line, they could not control which civilization they received. People could be so stupid sometimes.

Hailey was in front of me, and she read her civilization out loud to the class, "The Celts." She looked at Miss Adams. "The Romans didn't conquer the Celtic Empire. I thought they were the barbarians that brought it down."

I cringed at the use of the word *barbarian*. It was a choice word of my father's to describe the Old People.

"Haven't you ever heard of the Druids?" Miss Adams asked her.

"Like wizards and stuff? Of course!"

"The Druids were a part of the Celtic Empire, and the Romans did conquer them," Miss Adams said. "You'll find out about that. Now go sit down."

I already had found out about that, and it was terrible.

"Your turn, Arthur," Miss Adams smiled at me and opened the bag. I reached my hand in and grabbed a slip of paper.

"The Ancient Greeks," I read.

"Sparta!!!" Helix yelled as if the only thing the Greeks had achieved was that one group of violent people.

Miss Adams chose not to pay any attention to Helix's comment. "That will be an interesting one."

I nodded and took my seat at our desk-table.

"Each group will be researching their civilization and how the Romans affected their culture. Then, you'll present that civilization to the class as if you're a part of it," she explained, walking around the room passing out a rubric. "I expect all of you to dress up and say a few words in that culture's language."

Everyone in the class groaned. Dressing up was *not* something middle school students generally preferred.

"Then the group that has the Roman Empire, raise your hands—" A group near the front raised their hands. Miss Adams smiled mischievously, "will 'conquer' you."

The bell rang and everyone hurried to gather up their things without bothering to put the desks back in order or waiting to hear a dismissal from Miss Adams. That was one thing about American people, they had very little respect for authority and people's property.

"I'll finish explaining the project tomorrow!" Miss Adams called as the students rushed out the door.

I stopped before exiting into the hall. I smiled weakly at her, "Thank you, Miss Adams."

She smiled back, in my opinion, thankful that at least one person appreciated her project. "You're very welcome, Arthur."

I smiled awkwardly one last time and then left her classroom.

I think that one of the reasons I was decent at football is because I was not afraid of pain.

I was not afraid of pain because of *there*. Because every single time I did the slightest thing wrong in Britain, I was hit or whipped or slapped. So when another boy hit me or tackled me it did not hurt so bad.

American boys had an apparent aversion to pain. I think this was because their discipline often consisted of taking a technological device away rather than an infliction of physical pain. I suppose this made sense. I did not really have anything *there* that my father could take away from me. Well, maybe he could take away my food and starve me. I must not give my father the idea of starving me, although he had probably already thought of that.

I also did not have an aversion to hitting anybody else. This was because I thought that most people, especially American people, could have done with a bit more hitting. It was a way for me to take out my bottled anger, which I suppose I had a lot of because things seemed to frustrate me more than they did other people. I am not sure why this was; maybe it was because other people did not seem to see the inherent stupidity which most people carried with them.

We had just finished the chant that we did after each practice, and before and after each game we played when Coach Hunter came up to me.

"I think you have real potential Arthur," he told me, placing his hand on my shoulder. This made me edgy, I did not like it when people I did not know very well touched me. Actually, I did not really like anyone to touch me.

"Uh, thanks," I said. I shifted from foot to foot.

"Well it's good you're on the team," he told me. This was beginning to get more awkward than I thought it was intended to be.

"Yes." I must keep my words short and concise.

"See you tomorrow then," he said.

I nodded, and without looking back hurried to the parking lot where Miss Marion was waiting for me.

*****

Arthur

I think that most people who know me think that I am insane.

I really do not mind; it is only thoughts after all. I suppose it is my fault that they think I am insane. I never should have told anyone about America. I should have kept it in my head and never told a single soul. But really, that is much more difficult than it might be perceived to be.

I do not think it is perceived to be difficult to others because they see it as something that began in my head, so it should stay there. Or they think that I made it all up like a bard telling a tale of how someday, the world will be presumed to be round. Because if people do not understand something, then it is nonsense to them. It makes very little sense for the world to be round because the ground that we walk on is flat and no matter how far we walk or ride on horseback the ground remains flat. So if I were to tell someone that every time I fell asleep at night I woke up in a land across the sea more than a thousand years in the future that would be sort of like telling them that the world is round.

I think that may be another reason why I like circles. Because I can relate the circular shape of the world and people not understanding it to *there*. To America. To my supposed insanity.

Lancelot told me that he believes me.

I do not think he was telling the truth. I think he only said it for my sake so that I would not be alone. But I am alone. I will always be alone.

*****

Cadbury Castle, Britain, 645

Tournaments happened four times a year. Spring equinox, summer solstice, autumn equinox (Beltane, which was sort of a harvest festival), and winter solstice. They generally lasted around four days and after finals, on the last day, there was a feast where the champions were recognized. The competitions generally consisted of six different events: jousting, quarterstaff, mace, archery, swordplay, melee, and the free event which was where all sorts of people with all sorts of weapons competed.

If I Could Tell It

I had competed at each of the four tournaments in swordplay and melee since I was ten years old, forced by my father. I was never very good at any of the other events, and my mother always pleaded with my father to not have me compete in the free duels because that was where the most men were killed or seriously injured.

That was another thing about tournaments. It was fine for someone to kill another person for the entertainment of the crowd. I suppose that each person who entered the tournament knew that they could be killed though, so in a sense, it was their own fault for entering. Unless they were like me. I did not get to choose to enter or not. I was forced to put my life on the line.

The first day of the tournament was always the worst. That was the day that the most people died. The more barbaric of the competitors lost on the first or second day because of a lack of skill so they did the most damage they could on the days that they competed. After the first two days, the violence seemed to die off a bit because it was mostly noblemen left.

Technically, you could kill someone of high rank in a tournament if you wanted, but that would most likely result in making quite a few enemies, so generally, it was not done. For example, if someone were to kill me (although I doubt my father would mind) they would definitely invoke the wrath of my mother and of the whole of Britain, as there would be no more heir to the high king.

Today was December 18, 645. The first day of the winter solstice tournament. It had been over two months since I had slain the dragon and Gawain had come to Camelot with me.

I had told my mother that Gawain had come back with me from my "trip" to Meredith in hopes of becoming a servant at Cadbury Castle. Thankfully she did not recognize him as her nephew although I was sure she had her suspicions. We decided that he could keep his name as Gawain as long as he never mentioned Orkney, or his parents, to *anyone*. Well, except for Lancelot. I told Lancelot. In my defense, I told Lancelot *everything*, even about things that happened *there*. He was a very good listener and he was very good at keeping secrets. I knew that Lancelot would never betray me.

Gawain kept his head down well for the most part, aside from his occasional arrogant speech about things he had supposedly done. I did not think he had done most of them. After all, how could he have taken down a Saxon warrior when I could have easily beaten him with a wooden broomstick?

I let him sleep in the firewood closet next to the cobblestone fireplace at the far end of my room. I had made Austin drag a cot in there and I had taken a couple furs from under my bed for him. Austin was one of the many who thought I was positively crazy, so he did not question me. He just did as I asked.

I was not sure what Gawain did during the day. He left in the morning after I sneaked him food from my breakfast, and then he came back for me to sneak him food from my supper. I thought that he might have been getting drunk in the village below Cadbury Castle. He certainly acted that way. I was not sure where he would have gotten the money to buy ale though. Maybe he stole it.

Austin was my squire for tournaments as well as my manservant. I considered him my friend. I was not sure if he thought of me the same way. In my mind, I was not better than him and he was not lesser than me. I needed him to help me, and he was one of the people "grooming" me for my imposing kingship. Someday I would have a job to do, even if it was not a job I preferred, and he was helping me to prepare.

I think that my tourney armor weighed about sixty pounds. I do not think that I could have fought in much more than that. Maybe when I was older. My tournament sword only weighed about twenty-five pounds and even that was a bit heavy to swing.

Gawain came out of my firewood closet while I was in the midst of having Austin strap on my armor.

"Leaving so soon?" I asked as he ran his hands through his hair in front of a wall mirror.

"Going to compete," he said simply.

"At what? Bragging?" I asked sarcastically.

"Funny," he said back sardonically. "At free."

"Have fun publicly dying." I rolled my eyes at him.

"Turn," Austin commanded me and I complied. He strapped a shoulder plate on.

"When I win, I am going to buy my own village with the prize money. Then you will not have to see me anymore," Gawain glared at me.

I glared back, "Oh, but I would miss you so much."

Austin paid no attention to Gawain and greased my hair back with olive oil. Ick. I suppose it kept it out of my face though.

"Goodbye, Arthur," Gawain said to me. And with a flip of his silky, black hair, he left.

There was no exciting beginning to tournaments as one might think. I suppose that people did not want to compete in fake fighting so much when there was a real war going on. Maybe after the war was over there would be. Until then, we just went to our tents in the field behind the arena next to the palace and waited until it was our time to compete.

The order of the events each day was always the same. Joust, mace, staff, sword, free, melee. That meant that my two events were toward the end of the day. It would be at least five hours, around one o'clock, before it was my turn to duel sword.

"Arthur." My mother lifted the red tent flap and appeared inside the makeshift room. I was sitting on a chair analyzing the marks on my hands from Father Patricius hitting my hands with his stick. There were little purple bruises and red marks all over them, combined with callouses from my sword training on my palms.

"Yes, Mother?" I looked up at her. Her soft, auburn red hair was pulled out of her face in one thick braid down her back.

"I wanted to come and wish you luck before you compete," she said. She wandered over next to where I was sitting.

"Thank you," I said. I looked at the ground.

"Are you nervous?" she asked me. She absentmindedly put her hands on my shoulders.

"A little…" I trailed off. "I suppose I am more afraid of what Father will do to me if I lose."

"He is only bluffing," she said, her hands moved from my shoulders to my hair where she smoothed my grease-covered mane back against my head. "You know how he is…"

I did not look up at her. I did know how he was and I was tired of being whipped and yelled at for speaking out of turn or tripping in the hall. He probably would not kill me for losing the tournament, but he would find some way to inflict pain upon me and make my life miserable.

I sighed.

"I love you, Arthur," she told me.

"I love you too," I replied because that is what you say when someone tells you that they love you.

Lancelot was best at jousting. I suppose that this was ironic because of his name, *lance*-lot. A lance was the very thing used in jousting. It was interesting to watch him joust because he was small, smaller than me. He was dwarfed by the size of his lance and the horse that he was riding.

He still managed to knock the other man off more often than one might think, despite his small stature. He used physics, I think, as I learned in science class *there*, to push the other man off. Only Lancelot did not know what physics was because he had never been to America and he had never heard any of the theories, and as many times as I had tried to explain advanced mathematics or the process of a valid experiment, he still did not seem to understand.

Lancelot won his first joust against someone I did not know. The person did seem to be a short man however, not a boy, at least five years older than Lancelot. At least he was off to a good start.

Kay was competing at the tournament as well, but only in staff. I saw him as I was walking to the well in the center of the field of tents to fill up my leather wineskin with water. I looked at him and he pretended as if he did not see me, just as he had done since that day in Meredith when I confronted him. I never told anyone in Camelot about the dragon. I figured that they would simply think I was making it up, as they had thought when I told them about my vivid "dreams" of America. I did not need to further validate the suspicions of my insanity.

I did not see Gawain in the tent field or in the arena stands. It was as if he had disappeared. Maybe he was camped out in the woods behind the field, waiting for the time to come when he would compete in his free event. I did not even know what weapon he was going to use. He had none that I had seen. Maybe he would use a metal pole like some barbaric warrior. I doubted he could win with that, just get himself injured.

Gawain did seem to have some supply of money, of which I knew not, from where he was drawing his funds. He had to be eating somewhere during the day. I doubted the table scraps I took to him would be enough to sustain him. I thought he may have taken on a job or an apprenticeship, at least that would explain where he hurried off to each day.

I was walking back to my tent from the well when I met a strange woman.

"Do you have any money?" a feminine voice asked me. I looked to my right.

"No," I said truthfully, "not with me at least." I looked the woman up and down. She was plump and seemed to be bursting out of her too-tight scarlet dress. Large breasts hung out of a half laced corset and her lips were ruby red with carmine. Her white blonde hair was long and hung freely beneath her waist.

"Oh, well that is such a shame," she said. The woman came very, very close to me and pressed her large, overflowing breasts against my arm.

I did not like this. I did not like it when people touched me and I especially did not like it when strangers touched me. I also did not understand why this woman was touching me with her breasts as if I were her baby and she was trying to feed me. I just stared down at her in shock.

"I could give you such a lovely time," she told me smoothly, her voice silky and warm. She continued to press her breasts against my arm. I inched away slowly.

"How?" I asked suspiciously. Maybe she was a witch and she wanted to sell me a magic potion that would make me lucky or excessively happy.

"Oh, you know." She walked her fingers up my shoulders. I did not know, and I was not sure that I wanted to know. I wanted her to stop touching me.

I moved her hand off my shoulder, "I-I think I will be going now."

"You must be bent," she frowned. Bent? What did that have to do with her creepily touching me?

"For your information, I *am not* bent," I informed her. Then I lifted my chin and walked away. I started to run once I was sure I was out of her sight. That woman scared me.

My father and my mother sat side by side in the covered section of the stands. Morgain sat next to my mother who was on the left of my father. She looked absolutely miserable.

I was waiting at the gateway to the dirt arena where I had a perfect view of my father's hard stare toward me. I felt as if he were taunting me, telling me that there was no way that I could win even one duel. I had been training at least four hours a day since my father told me that I would be punished if I did not win the tournament.

I had definitely gained muscle over the time I had been training so intensely. It also helped that I had grown over an inch in those couple of months. Now I was five feet and seven inches tall. I had gotten much better at fighting. I had begun to incorporate my mathematics into it as well. I found that if I could knock my opponent slightly off-balance and I delivered one last blow, then gravity would do the rest. That was the goal in tournaments after all, to knock the other person to the ground where you could kill them if you so wished.

Last year I had made it to the semi-semi-finals. But I was shorter then and less muscular. I also had not had my father's punishment floating over my head.

The two men from the previous duel exited the arena. Neither of them had been hurt. The person announcing things announced my opponent first and he walked out into the arena. I did not hear his name, a wave of nerves had drowned me. My heart was beating in my ears. It felt a bit like when I fought the dragon, that same adrenaline rush overwhelmed my body and made me feel like I needed to do everything ten times faster.

The person announced me, "Prince Arthur Ambrosius Pendragon, heir to the High King of Britain."

That made me even more nervous and on edge. Partially because of the mention of my middle name and my Roman Grandfather, and partially because of the announcement of my someday becoming the High King of Britain.

I was practically shaking as I walked slowly into the arena. I tried to keep myself composed. I heard cheers from the stands for me. I reminded myself that it was not as if I would be killed in this fight. Nobody would kill a twelve-year-old boy who was the entire future of the country. At least I did not think they would.

I set the point of my sword in the dirt and put my hands on the bronze hilt to keep it from tipping over. I watched my opponent do the same.

He was an average-sized man with a slender figure and shoulder-length curly brown hair. His eyebrows were thick. They looked like two caterpillars lost on his face. His eyes were a deep chocolate, almost the same color as his hair, and I could feel him sizing me up as I was doing with him.

We both looked at my father who, through his unwavering glare at me, gave us the signal to put our helmets on and bow to one another.

I slipped my helmet on over my greased hair and stared at my opponent's feet through the slit for my eyes. He had on dark brown, knee-high boots with a bronze buckle near his ankle. I had a moment of wondering if he liked that buckle. I wanted a buckle on my boots like that.

I heard the sound of a deep drum. The fight was beginning. I bowed my head and leapt back. I had found that it was best if I went on the defensive in my fights. I was more strategic than aggressive. It was harder for me to strike first because I was not strong; however, I could use my opponent's strike against them.

My opponent jabbed at the left side of my chest with his sword. I caught his blade with my own and with both hands flipped his sword over, knocking him off-balance, just as I had planned. My actions were no longer functions of my mind. They were purely muscle reactions that seemed to be going without my command. I spun on my heel and planted my foot into my opponent's breastplate while he was still off-balance. He fell to the ground and I stood over him with my foot on his chest and my sword pointed at his neck.

I looked up at my father. He looked down at me critically. I knew he would find *something* wrong with my performance even though I had won in no time at all.

It was the first time I had ever taken anyone down that easily. At first, I thought that it was because my opponent was very bad at fighting. I doubted my skill. But then I saw the crest on his dirtied tunic and I saw that he was from a southern kingdom that was famous for their agile swordsmanship. Maybe I really had become better due to my frequent and intense practice.

My father pointed to me to acknowledge that I had won, and I slowly walked out of the arena, my heart still beating in my ears, the flow of adrenaline unwavering.

*****

Arthur

I have not told anyone in America about *there*. This is because I do not wish to become known as insane in both places. Maybe, someday, I will meet someone that I know I can trust, who will never betray me, and then I will tell them.

I hope that when I marry, I will have a wife that I can tell about *there*. And I hope that she does not see me as crazy as everyone else does. I have dismissed the idea that there is anyone else like me, who also has the experience of *there*. I think that if I hope, then I will only disappoint myself.

Chapter V

Cadbury Castle, Britain, 645

I had won my two other duels from the first day, so I advanced to the second day. The melee was not until the fourth day of the tournament, winter solstice day, so I had not competed in anything else.

My father said nothing to me during dinner the night of the first day of the tournament. He just watched me carefully, as if we were playing an elaborate game of chess with our eyes, and his life depended on the outcome.

Gawain, surprisingly, had also won his duels from the first day. Somehow, he had come up with a sword with which to compete. My guess was that he had been working for the village smithy in order to receive the sword.

My favorite thing to eat in the morning was apple pastry with honey. It had been since I was six years old and my mother let me try some during a breakfast that my father had hosted for some of his knights. Because of this, I was very happy when I found a soft, sugary dough filled with crushed, golden apples, wrapped in a cloth on the table inside of my tent in the arena field. The kitchen maid Halaina, who seemed to always be watching me, must have brought it.

I sat down at the table and scarfed down the pastry as if I were starving. It tasted sweet and fresh, as if the apples had only been picked that morning.

Lancelot glided into the tent through the flap.

"Oh good! You are here already," he said a little too excitedly.

"Why so good?" I asked suspiciously.

"Well, not good I suppose," he thought for a moment. "Never mind that! Your sister has run away again!"

"Again?" I stood up to face him. "Seriously?"

You see, Morgain had this interesting habit of running away for a few days at a time. Then search parties were formed and there was a state of panic and then she came back. I knew where she went. She went to Avalon to talk to the Lady of the Lake. I had promised her that I would not tell anyone though.

"Yes!" Lancelot said. His dark brown eyes were wide and nervous. I was not exactly sure why. She did this all the time. "We have to find her!"

"Why?" I asked, crossing my arms over my chest. "She will come back."

"Are you not the slightest bit concerned about the welfare of *your sister*?!" Lancelot accused me.

"Not really," I shrugged and sat back down in my chair. "She is always mean to me."

Lancelot followed me to my chair, "Have you ever thought that maybe *you* are mean to her, Arthur?"

"I am not," I said simply.

"Sure," he said sarcastically, "just like you are nice to everyone else."

"What are you trying to say?!" I asked angrily.

"That you are mean, Arthur!" he yelled at me. "I do not know why, but you are!"

Lancelot thought that I was mean. How interesting.

I did not see how I was mean. I thought that I treated people only as they should be treated. I suppose that I saw people as stupid quite a lot, but I had a reason for that: they were. People were so utterly stupid that it bothered me to the point of anger. I may react sharply, but it was their fault for having been stupid. Morgain was oftentimes one of those people.

It made no sense to run away. Her life was fine. She lived in luxury as if she were a princess. Maybe my father did not particularly like her, but it was not as if he liked me either. I did not run away. That was probably because I recognized that I had responsibilities and I was not so selfish that I ran away from them. Morgain was, and therefore, I did not believe she deserved me to be actively nice to her.

As for average people, while they were still sometimes irritating, I tried to be fairly pleasant toward them. I had been told in America that I was blunt, inconsiderate. But they only thought that because I was honest. I would rather be honest and have people a little irritated with me than lie. I did not understand how people could live with so many lies on their backs. I lied enough to cover up my strangeness due to *there*. I did not want to lie any more than that.

"I do not think that I am," I stood up again and lifted my chin although I was already a few inches taller than him. "I am honest, and I treat people as they should be treated."

Lancelot shook his head. "You have no empathy whatsoever."

I thought Lancelot maybe had a little too much empathy. Anyone who thought that much about feelings probably had his head so full that he could not learn anything more.

"Whatever. I cannot talk to you right now." Lancelot sucked air in through his nose. I did not see what I had done to make him so upset.

My mother came into my tent in a state of panic about a half hour after Lancelot.

"I told Uther to cancel the tournament," she said to me. I was sitting on the ground examining a blade of grass. I found that it was made up of lots of little, green strings.

"Why?" I asked. For some reason, the grass was greatly interesting to me.

"Did Lancelot not tell you?" my mother asked. She looked very concerned.

"Oh…" I trailed off for a moment, "about Morgain running away again?"

"Yes!" She pushed my ungreased hair out of my face. I looked up at her from my grass. "Are you not concerned?"

"She will come back," I told her. "She always does."

"Arthur!" she scolded me. "How dare you act so cavalierly!"

Cavalier. That was an interesting word. I must remember to look it up in a dictionary *there*.

I just looked at her.

She glared at me, "You know where she is."

I did not say anything. As much as I disliked my sister, I could not betray her. She had told me where she had been going in complete confidentiality.

"Arthur tell me," my mother commanded me harshly.

This was one of those moments that I hated. I had to lie, lying was the only way to not betray my sister's trust. "I do not know where she is."

"Arthur," she looked into my eyes and we had a moment of challenging each other to see who could hold the other's stare longer. It was also my goal to hide my thoughts from her. I kept my glare hard and steely, I would not betray my sister. She sighed, "I wish you would show a little more emotion."

I kept my mouth shut. I thought I showed plenty of emotion. In my opinion, most people showed way too much emotion. It was drippy.

My mother sighed, "Goodbye my son."

And then she left, having given up that I was ever going to tell her about the destination of my sister.

It turned out that my mother had convinced my father to cancel the tournament, or at least put it off until

Morgain was found. In other words, I had no choice but to join the search for her because I could not continue until she was found.

It was noon before I decided to leave my tent. Everyone that I was even sort of friends with had gone to look for Morgain. Well, except for Gawain. He was sitting next to the well drinking wassail, spiced apple cider, from a wineskin. But really, I doubted I would consider myself friends with him.

I went back to my chambers in the tower where all my family's quarters were. Mostly because I was done sitting in my tent staring at my grass.

I stared out the window for a while, looking at the palace square. It was made of a pale, worn cobblestone, and was surrounded by buildings on all sides. An iron portcullis made a guarded entrance and exit. There was a wooden block that was moved to the right side, for now, that was used for executions. It was bloodstained and molding. In the area just before the grand palace steps there was a stone statue of a lion. The lion was from when Ambrosius was king. In Rome, lions were considered quite mighty I suppose. When we had presented our projects in history class *there*, the group that had been doing ancient Rome had said that oftentimes gladiators would fight lions to prove their strength.

Tiny white flakes began to fall from the sky like clouds or angel feathers. They fell on the lion's head and back and began to form a soft white coat to cover his chiseled, stone fur.

I wondered if Morgain really had gone to Avalon this time. What if she had gotten lost? As I said before, she was not very intelligent in my opinion. She had never been pleasant to me, but Lancelot was right, she was still my sister, I would feel bad if she froze to death in the forest.

I continued to stare out at the palace square, thinking, until the lion's snow coat had thickened to a good inch and a half. That was when I got up from sitting on my windowsill, pulled on a too big fur coat, and headed out with the cold bronze of my tourney sword pressing through my thin undertunic to my side.

Avalon was northwest of Camelot. It was a short distance away, probably around three miles, only taking about forty-five minutes to walk there. Lancelot and I found a trail last summer that led from the arena field, around the back wall of the palace, and entered onto a worn path through the Darkling Woods, and went all the way to Avalon. My theory was that it was how Morgain had been getting there undetected by the guards.

I did my best to avoid all of the people that were in the arena field and glued myself tight to the stone castle wall so I would not be seen. Once I was out of sight, I resumed a casual walking pace down the trail through the forest.

It took me about thirty-five minutes to reach the tree line at the shore of the lake. I emerged onto thick, smooth, pure white pebbles that clicked together under my leather boots. A permanent layer of mist shrouded the lake and the island that I knew was beyond.

Avalon was a rather dreamlike place. It was as cold as the snow that fell onto my hair, and yet I felt a blunt warmth that started in my core and spread to my arms, but never quite reached my hands. It never quite felt real. Lancelot and I had been here dozens of times, and I still could not completely remember what we had done. By the time we reached home after a day of searching for treasure and splashing each other with water, I could barely remember what had happened. It was like my mind became as foggy as the mist that covered the lake.

I stood, looking out to the mist, not knowing what to do. I did not know how to reach the island for I had no boat and I was a terrible swimmer. Also, even if I were half decent at swimming, it was currently snowing and the water would be as cold as ice. I figured that you had to use magic to reach the island where the Lady of the Lake lived.

I crouched down to the water's edge. It gently lapped at the pure white pebbles. I put my fingertips in the water and felt something like liquid ice gently caress my calloused hand.

That was when the boat came.

It glided across the glassy, mist-covered lake with swanlike gracefulness and stopped just before it would have bumped my hand. I stood up and looked at the weathered wooden boat for a few moments before presumptuously deciding to step into the small vessel and see where it would take me.

I never much cared for boats, or anything to do with water for that matter. They made me nervous, as if one wrong shift would send me sinking into the icy depths below. Drowning seemed like a terrible way to die, the world gradually disappearing above as you sank into the abyss that was ripping the air from your lungs and taking the life from your heart.

If I had to die, I think I would like to be burned to death.

I had seen it before at witch burnings. The flesh of the victim turning brown and then charcoal black as their skin withered and blistered and they looked out at the crowd that was full of eyes avidly watching for pain. Because that was what the audience cared about. Pain. It was sad really, what the people of Camelot desired for entertainment. If I burned to death, then I could see the world one last time as I felt my lungs no longer able to process air from the smoke, and I could feel one last burst of feeling as my heart exploded in my chest with a final hot beat of anguish.

I suppose that having a sharp sword shoved through your chest or neck would not be so bad either.

If I Could Tell It

It would be fast if anything. The pain would not last long, just a single sharp jab to destroy every feeling that you had ever had in your mind so that nobody else could read its contents.

Humans are such fragile things. One poke with a sharp, metal stick could snuff out the light of a person forever. A mere abundance of heat could cause the body to cease to function. A lack of oxygen stops the production of energy. The tiniest sip from a poisoned cup stops the heart. And I dare think, one's own mind could destroy them; the relentless hounding of insanity.

I sat on the moist floor of the boat while it slowly took me through the mist. It was moving by some force that I could not figure out, for it had no oars, motor, or sail. The moving of the boat was completely flawless, no sounds, or bumps, or tilts. Not even the feeling of rushing water plagued the moss-laden hull of the boat.

It was only about ten yards before we hit the white, pebbled shore that I saw the island and the tall gray tower rising out of the mist on the top of a tall green hill and meager forest. That was how thick the mist was.

The boat hit the shore with the smallest possible thud, and I exited the boat quickly. As I said before, I am not a fan of water. I walked about ten feet up the shore before I looked back to see that my vehicle from the mainland had completely disappeared, almost as if I had imagined it.

I had no choice but to begin walking up the dull, grassy green hill to the single tower that I hoped had someone who could help me, or at least remind me what I had come to Avalon for. Something about my sister, I think. My mind had started to become fuzzy.

I looked at the ground under my feet. It looked as if it were moving swiftly under my boots as I walked. It was strange looking, as if the ground were the thing moving and I was the one standing still.

"Who are you?" a melodic voice interrupted my train of thought, and I looked up from my discovery about the moving ground.

"Uh…" I was a bit shocked that someone had come to talk to me even though I knew that people lived here.

"Speak clearly." The voice belonged to a girl who was as tall as me in a long, white, flowing dress. She had dark black hair that was flowing all around her as if it had a mind of its own. Pale blue tattoos covered her naked arms that looked as thin as bone. I wondered if she was cold as I shivered in my heavy fur coat.

"My name is Arthur," I said, trying to sound as confident as I could.

"Why have you come?" she asked. Despite her melodic voice and serene appearance, she looked extremely irritated with me for some reason unknown to me. "And how did you get here?"

"Well…" I trailed off for a moment, searching my mind, desperately trying to remember. "I am not sure why I have come…but I am pretty sure that some sort of boat brought me here."

"How could a boat have brought you here?" the girl asked me. "You are not one of us. You are dirty, and you have violence in your blood."

I should have argued with her, or at least asked her what she meant, but that was the last thing I remember her saying to me. The girl with the serene beautiful features and the soft, white, flowing dress, telling me that I was dirty and that I had violence in my blood. Then I was waking up *there*.

*****

Colorado Springs, America, 2008

In America people did not celebrate winter solstice. They celebrated Christmas.

Christmas was a very fun time of the year in America. In fact, it was the most joyful thing I had experienced in America so far. Some traditions of Christmas were very strange, like putting strands of LED lights on the roofs of houses, or sending cards advertising one's family out to several people in order to brag about things that they had accomplished over the year. Most of the traditions of Christmas were based on winter solstice traditions though, like poinsettia flowers, decorating trees, or having a large feast with many distant family members.

The one tradition I could not seem to quite understand, however, was Santa Claus.

It made no sense that a fat man dressed in red with a big white beard went from house to house on the night of December 24 delivering presents to children. And he got in through a chimney. And he traveled by flying reindeer. And the scariest part of all? Apparently, he was constantly watching children to see if they were good enough to receive presents or not.

Frankly, the whole idea freaked me out.

The rest of Christmas seemed nice though. It snowed a couple of feet almost every day the week before the winter break from school, so we had gotten our break a week early. I went sledding with Ty almost every day on the big hill just outside our neighborhood. Sledding was very fun, other than the chill you got when a clump of snow makes its way down your jacket or snow pants when you fell off. We did not do anything like sledding *there*. Snow was more of a nuisance, not anything to rejoice over. I suppose I could have found something to sit on and sled down on a hill *there*, but that sounded a bit dangerous. Also, there were no hot showers to revive me after a freezing day of snow.

Today was December 20, four days until the great, fabled Christmas Eve, where we were supposed to hang stockings from the fireplace and then on Christmas morning they would be filled with presents. That was another especially strange tradition of American Christmas. Stockings hanging on the fireplace mantel.

I stepped out of the shower and wrapped a fluffy, navy blue towel around my waist. Miss Marion had a different color for each bathroom, and the one that was "mine" happened to be navy blue.

In America, people had all sorts of things that they used to enhance their bodies, and they kept these things in their bathrooms. Some things, like shampoo, conditioner, or body soap went inside the curtained, warm rain box of the shower, while other things, like hair gel, shaving cream, hand soap, cologne, and baby powder went on top of counters and in the cupboards of the bathroom. Some of these things made me nauseous with their overly sweet, chemical smells, like cologne, while other things, like shampoo, got rid of the grease in my hair, so I could at least appreciate them.

I pushed my sopping, shoulder-length hair out of my face with my hand and wiped some of the condensation off of the mirror. My gray eyes peered back at me through the blurry mirror along with my pale complexion. I was very pale. I had golden blonde hair, sheet white skin, and light, silver eyes. I did not like how I looked sometimes because I resembled my father instead of my mother. My father was very tall, probably over six and a half feet, with bleach blonde hair and pale blue eyes. My mother was about the same height as me, around five feet seven and had dark red hair and tanned skin. We had the same eyes, but other than that, I think we looked very different.

I hoped that when I was older, I would grow more. I hoped that I would have broad shoulders and I would rise above six feet. I thought that it was important for men to be big. If they were not, then they were either little boys or females. I knew that it was more complicated than that, but oftentimes I could see complicated things through more simplistic ones.

I secured the towel around my waist and made my way across the hall to my room.

I had put up a few of my drawings on the walls. They were in black frames, that matched the gray pencil marks that made up the intricate buildings and scaled plans. Some of the drawings were also pictures of circles. Circles that I had drawn with compasses and then divided into smaller sectors and then drawn designs over. Every sector of the circles was all the same, not one greater than the others.

The laptop that Mr. Ector had bought me that one day back in October was sitting half opened on my desk charging, an electronic blue light emanated from the screen. Water dripped from my feet and my legs to the floor and I shivered, the heat must have been turned down low. My small bed stood like a warm and welcoming beacon of comfort in the corner.

I wiped the remaining droplets of water from my chest and my legs and forcefully shook my hair out like a dog. I felt it sticking up in all sorts of unruly places and I smiled because that was the most comfortable way for it to sit. Then I climbed under the fluffy down comforter and closed my eyes.

When I woke, it was dark outside.

I climbed out of bed and pulled on a pair of discarded gray sweatpants that were crumpled on the floor. I flipped on the light that illuminated the place just outside the window to reveal that it was in fact, still snowing. I found a black T-shirt on the chair next to my desk and put it on before walking downstairs to the now very decorated living room.

The tree in the corner of the room was bright with yellow/white strands of light and red and gold ornaments hung delicately from fragile branches. On top, there was a golden star that shone from all the lights further down the tree.

Beneath the tree, amongst the brightly colored, papered boxes, there was a creepy little ceramic doll.

The doll had a shiny white face and unblinking circular blue eyes. A single lock of yellow hair stuck straight up off the top of the doll's head. It was dressed like Santa Claus in a red and white fur coat.

Now, I was not afraid of many things, especially *here*, but that elf doll, sitting there, under the tree, staring up at me as if it were watching my every move *freaked* me out. I did not like people to watch me and I definitely did not like *things* to watch me. So people, like things, were definitely something I wished to avoid.

I glared at the elf and sat down on the couch, just looking around at all of the different festive decorations. I was thinking about my experience *there*, going to Avalon, seeing that girl, then forgetting that I was there to search for my sister. All I could hear in my mind was her final words to me, *"You are not one of us. You are dirty, and you have violence in your blood."*

I did not know what that could mean. Well, I suppose I did a little. My father was violent, especially to the people of Avalon, and I had his blood in my veins. I knew I was not one of them; I was born noble in my father's palace. The one thing that completely baffled me, however, was her calling me dirty. Oftentimes Christians called witches and people of the Old Ways dirty. It was never the other way around.

"Arthur!" Miss Marion snapped her fingers in front of my face.

I snapped back into the present and looked at her.

"We are having company over remember?" she said, highly irritated that I had totally forgotten about the big Christmas party that she was throwing for the neighborhood. I guess I had forgotten that it was today, what with me being out all day sledding with Ty, and my mind still processing the events from *there*.

Miss Marion was wearing an elaborately knit red sweater with white snowflake patterns gracing the neckline. Beneath that, she had on jeans and a pair of socks with poinsettias on them.

"Oh, and your hair!" she said, running her hand through my messy mane. "It's atrocious!"

"Sorry," I muttered quietly. I hated the way combed hair felt. This felt much more natural.

"Now go up and get dressed!" she said frantically. "And brush your hair! Everyone's going to be here in ten minutes!"

I sprinted up the stairs to my room where I stripped off my clothes and searched my closet for something that Miss Marion would deem appropriate for her Christmas party. I found a blue and gray patterned sweater in my closet and a pair of jeans that I had only worn twice last week that did not smell too bad. I sprayed them with a bit of cologne to make sure.

I looked in the mirror at my mess of golden hair. I had a black metal brush with a cushioned grip that Miss Marion had bought me after we went to the beauty salon to get my hair trimmed. After that day, I decided never to go into a salon again. It smelled bad and all of the people in the place looked extremely weird with all sorts of piercings and brightly colored, half-shaved heads of thick hair. She had also bought me a comb and some sort of male shampoo and conditioner that smelled like chemically sweet apples.

I forcefully dragged the brush through my hair and cringed as it pulled on a knot of tangles. It felt like with every brush, my hair was being pulled out of my scalp. Eventually, I got it done. It really looked fine. It was smooth and the part was somewhat straight so it was probably good enough for Miss Marion.

When I went back down the stairs, a middle-aged couple was already inside the house and engaged in a flurry of greetings with Miss Marion. The woman was sort of fat and had curly brown hair. I noticed that she had long, perfectly manicured nails. That made me nervous. They looked like cat claws. Like she could draw blood from me with a poke. The man was also a bit round and had short, gray hair and a short, patchy gray beard. Neither of them was very aesthetically pleasing.

"Art*hur*," Miss Marion said my name sort of singsongy. I came down next to her and stared monotonously at the couple.

"Oh, he looks so sweet!" The woman's voice was a couple of tones too high. It added to the discomfort I was feeling in my stomach.

Then the woman wrapped me in a bear hug.

I hated people touching me. I hated strangers touching me even more. So this woman that I already felt very uncomfortable with was hugging me tight into her squishy body fat and lavender blouse. I wanted to run away.

I retreated to Miss Marion's side as fast as I could.

"This is Jennifer," Miss Marion told me. Jennifer smiled at me to reveal teeth that were way too white. "She works with me at the animal shelter."

"Nice to meet you," I mumbled. I wished that I had stayed in the bathroom to fight with my hair some more. Even that would have been better than Jennifer.

"A little shy aren't you?" Jennifer asked almost sarcastically.

I am not shy, I just do not like you. I stayed silent.

Miss Marion's eyes kept switching between me and Jennifer. I noticed Jennifer's husband was keeping to himself.

"Well, I better go greet more of our guests!" Miss Marion said, forcing cheerfulness into her voice.

"Anthony's in the kitchen. Feel free to help yourself to anything."

I stood still next to Miss Marion. Jennifer leaned over and whispered something in her ear. I knew that she did not want me to hear it, but I did anyway.

"You'd better teach that boy some respect, Mari. I don't think he understands what you and Anthony are doing for him."

Miss Marion squared her shoulders and lifted her chin. "As a matter of fact, Arthur is the most respectful boy I have ever seen Jen. Maybe it's just you."

I did not smile, but I wanted to. I could not believe that I meant so much to Miss Marion. Jennifer walked away to the kitchen in a huff as if she could not believe that her friend had just defended me.

"I didn't like the way she was acting toward you," Miss Marion said quickly. "Why don't you stay and greet people with me?"

"Sure," I agreed. I smiled to myself. Maybe Miss Marion cared about me more than I thought.

Chapter VI

Cadbury Castle, Britain, 645

Morgain was still missing when Austin woke me up the next morning. That also meant that the tournament was still canceled. And tomorrow was supposed to be the finals. Maybe the winter solstice tournament would not happen this year, all because of my sister's stupid choices. Sometimes people just did not make sense.

"Can I sleep for a bit longer?" I asked Austin. I was sitting up in my fur laden bed looking at the sunlight that was seeping in through the stained glass windows. "Everything I would have done today is canceled."

Austin looked at me a moment as if thinking. "I suppose so, my lord."

I thought it was strange that he still used my title even though he had been dressing and feeding me for a year and a half.

Austin was fourteen and he had started his service to me when he was thirteen and I was eleven. I did not know where his parents were from, only that they had died somehow and then, in one way or another, he became my manservant. He was very skinny, with thin shoulders, and devoid of any muscle or fat on his body. He had a gaunt, pale face and a swipe of foxtail red hair that rested against his forehead. Freckles covered his entire body like a plague.

I liked Austin. He was one of those people who tended to be very quiet and reserved and just went along and did their business without being noticed. He never talked back to me and I cannot remember him saying a single bad thing about anyone. He was a nice person to see first thing in the morning.

"I think you should just call me Arthur from here on," I told him, as I lay on my back and adjusted my hair on my pillow. "I do not want it to always be like I am better than you."

I noticed Austin stiffen. "If you wish," he replied. Maybe saying that it was always like I was better than him was not the right wording.

I smiled. Maybe I could begin to eliminate the silly rank system in place, very slowly, but eventually something might come of it. I closed my eyes, feeling accomplished, and turned over onto my stomach to try to sleep.

I think that living both *here* and *there* might have made me more tired than if I only lived in one place. I suppose, in a way, I was awake for twenty-four straight hours. I never seemed to be so tired that I could not function though, I just felt like I had developed a love of sleep, and I could fall asleep at almost any time I wanted. *There* may have been taking more of a toll on my body than I had once suspected.

*****

Arthur

It is funny how one moment can change a person's life forever. One event can send someone spiraling down into a never-ending pit of despair and depression. It can alter a person's values, how they see the world. Each and every time they think about something their perception will have skewed. Ten seconds can make or break the fragile reality that is the human soul. The next ten seconds may very well be the most important ten seconds of your entire life. What if you had to choose if your worst enemy lived or died in the next ten seconds? What if you had ten seconds to save the person dearest to you? What if you failed?

*****

Cadbury Castle, Britain, 646

Morgain never came back after she disappeared that winter solstice. No one ever heard from her. We had no idea if she was dead or living in Avalon or was a slave to the Saxons. She could have tripped on an arena stair, fallen beneath the stands, and died of starvation for all we knew.

My mother blamed my father. She said it was his fault that Morgain had run away because of the way that he mocked her and treated her poorly. My father denied this and escaped to his chambers, away from my mother and the rest of the world, every chance he got.

I was pretty sure that Lancelot blamed me for Morgain running away. He thought that if I had gone with him that morning then we might have found her and stopped her from leaving for good. I thought that Lancelot might have loved Morgain, the deep kind of love between a man and a woman. He never confessed that he did, but after how upset he had gotten after she left, I had my suspicions.

All the while, through the drama in Camelot of the queen's daughter running away and not returning, the war with the Saxons raged in both the south and the north. More and more men died on both sides and yet neither of the two groups would surrender or suggest peace.

I had turned thirteen on March 25, the Tuesday of last week. My mother had come into my chambers after the feast that my father, through no idea of his own, had thrown for me. I had been in the middle of undressing when she came in, and I had quickly pulled back on the dressy over tunic that I had worn for the feast. She sat on my bed next to me and held my hand.

"Arthur, I know that quite a lot of things have been going on lately, but I still want to do this for you," she said to me as she pushed the hair out of my face.

"Do what?" I asked. I looked everywhere but her face. Sometimes making eye contact with people made me uncomfortable.

"Give you this." She pulled out a dark steel ring from the folds of her dress and set it in the palm of my hand.

"Thank you," I said as I examined the ring. It was a very long, thin piece of metal that was wrapped around itself over and over again until it formed a perfect ring without any loose ends.

"It is made of meteor iron," she told me. "The Lady of the Lake gave it to me when I turned twelve, just before I left to marry Morgain's father, Gorlois. She told me that I was going to pass it on to someone very important when I felt it was right."

I nodded. Something in the back of my mind told me that receiving this was some sort of huge honor.

"When you look at this, I want you to remember me and my people and that they are a part of you," she told me. She picked up my right hand and slid the ring onto my ring finger. It was so big that it slipped off. She laughed, "I think that you will grow into it. For now, wear it on this cord."

She had handed me a deer hide strip of leather and tied the ring onto the cord. Then she had hung it on my neck where it had fallen in between the two sides of my chest.

"I know you will be a great king, Arthur."

*****

Somewhere near the Lake of Avalon, Britain, 646

I woke up in the forest.

I knew it was a forest because when I looked up, all I could see was a canopy of green spring leaves. It was quite serene, the grass beneath me was cool and dewy beneath my back and I could hear the faint rustling of leaves from a cool wind. In the distance, there was the faint trickle of a running stream. I could have lay there for hours being perfectly content.

I did not remember the night before, *there* or *here*, nor how I had come to be lying on the forest floor. I did not mind though. Somehow it felt as if I had been lying here forever.

"Thank goodness you are awake!" Lancelot's dark face and hair appeared in my vision, blocking my view of the forest canopy. "For a moment I thought that you would sleep forever!"

"Where are we?" I asked, ignoring his enthusiasm.

"In the forest."

Yes, Lancelot, I can see that. "But why are we in the forest?"

"The Saxons…" he trailed off for a moment, "they attacked Cadbury Castle."

I shook my head. That could not be true. Cadbury Castle was the ultimate stronghold. Ambrosius Aurelianus had made it himself. It was impossible for it to be taken by invaders.

"Where is everyone else?" I asked. If Lancelot and I, two teenaged boys, had escaped the Saxons, then my mother and father and a few other people must have.

"There is no one else," Lancelot told me softly. His eyes looked like pools of melted dark chocolate. He helped me to my feet. "I am sorry Arthur."

I looked at the ground. It was covered in tiny white flowers. They looked so pure and innocent. I stomped on them with my boot. "Why do I not remember any of this?"

"The physician made me give you a poppy seed potion," Lancelot looked down at his boots. "And then you passed out. Gawain helped me carry you out here."

Gawain? I thought Gawain hated me. Maybe underneath his arrogant exterior and devil-may-care disposition there really was a bit of compassion and appreciation for me allowing him to stay in my closet for several months.

"Oh…" My mind was still a bit hazy. My thoughts felt sluggish and my emotions lethargic. "Where are we again?"

"I am not exactly sure." Lancelot looked around at his surroundings as if he had not gotten a decent chance to look around before, being so preoccupied with making sure I was alright. "Somewhere on the other side of Avalon. We have never been here before."

Gawain and Lancelot had carried me farther than I imagined.

"So now what?" I asked. I probably should have been a little more upset about the fact that my home had just been taken over by invaders, but in my mind, I figured that being upset would not help anything, so I might as well assess the situation and find a way to solve the problem.

"I…I do not know." Lancelot sat with his legs crossed on the ground, crushing an array of wildflowers as he did.

I looked around. There were deciduous trees all around us and the forest floor was a carpet of soft, green grass and white flowers. There was no sign of any human civilization anywhere around us and all we could hear was rustling leaves and the faint ripple of water in the distance that must have been the Lake of Avalon.

"I do not think we should try to go back home now," Lancelot reasoned. *Duh*. "We should probably look around and try to find food and shelter before nightfall. We could be out here for a while."

I nodded in agreement. If Saxons really had taken over Cadbury Castle, that meant that the main headquarters of the British government and military were neutralized; therefore, we had almost no one left to come to our rescue. Unless the highlanders in the north decided to become our new best friends, as would be said in America: We were screwed.

Lancelot stood back up, leaving an imprint in the flowers that he had sat on. Without discussing it we began to walk toward the sound of the water in silence, each of us listening intently as not to go off track.

"Something just glimmered," Lancelot said, putting his arm out in front of my chest so I would not continue walking. I could almost see the clearing for the lake up ahead.

"What?" I asked. I noticed that Lancelot had no sword at his side, and I sighed. We had no food, shelter, *or* weapons. And Gawain had apparently abandoned us.

"Over there." He pointed to the left toward the water.

I looked in that direction. He was right. The sunlight from above *was* reflecting off of something. "Should we see what it is?"

"Why not?" he asked. "It is not like we are in a hurry."

We changed our trajectory toward the shiny spot to the left and walked at a slightly faster pace in that direction. As we got closer, the "thing" shone brighter and brighter and I noticed a faint gold sheen coming from it. Then it became apparent that the faint gold sheen was coming from the golden hilt of a sword.

I frowned, what was a sword doing sticking straight up in the middle of nowhere? And a gold hilted sword at that. Those were expensive.

If I Could Tell It

When we were about ten feet away Lancelot and I noticed something else. The sword was encased inside of a rock. And not just any rock, it was a giant mass of almost pure white stone, a boulder as opposed to the fine white pebbles that graced the shores of Avalon. The golden green sunlight dripped from the canopy of trees to coat the rock and the sword in a layer of bright light. It was beautiful.

I looked at Lancelot. He looked just as awestruck as I was. As if we were communicating without using words, we walked forward toward the sword in unison. We stopped when we were less than two feet away.

"What do you think it means?" I asked.

"I am not sure," Lancelot said. "But we had better not mess with it. It could be a Druid altar."

"The last thing we need now is Druids after us," I agreed. The Druids were ruthless people, and often times considered insane for their strange practices.

I went a little closer to the boulder. It was almost taller than I was and the rough surface would make perfect handholds. I grabbed hold of two niches in the stone, planted my foot near the base of the rock, and hoisted myself off of the ground. Then, feeling confident, I climbed up a step further.

"Arthur, stop!" Lancelot said frantically. "You do *not* want to break it!"

"I am not going to break it!" I yelled back at him, frustrated at his lack of confidence in me.

"Arthur you just tend to break stuff…a lot."

"I just want to get a better look at that sword!" I said and climbed a step further. I could now reach out and touch the shiny steel blade if I wanted.

Lancelot sighed and I heard him take a step back. I pulled myself up to the slightly flatter top surface of the boulder and sat down. I was about five feet off the ground, looking at Lancelot. The vibrant sword glimmered behind me.

"Nothing happened. See?" I taunted him. "Everything is fine."

The concerned look still did not fade out of Lancelot's face. "Arthur I just have a feeling that this is a bigger thing than you just being an idiot."

I frowned. One, I was offended that he had called me an idiot. Two, I was offended that he had told me that I broke things a lot. Three, I needed to prove to him that I was capable of not breaking the sword or the boulder that was its rocky sheath. So I stood up.

I felt so tall and powerful standing on top of that boulder with the sword encased inside of it, as if I really were destined to be king. Nothing could stand in my way. I was bigger, taller, and more successful than all of my enemies.

I grabbed the hilt of the sword as a handle so I would not fall. It was cold on my palms and the complicated welded designs pressed into my hands comfortably.

"Arthur, be careful!" Lancelot shouted at me.

That was when I fell.

I did not blame him for my fall, but he definitely did contribute to it with his startling shout.

I stumbled a bit and with my hands still quite attached to the sword, my feet slipped out from under me and I hit the rock on my back hard. It hurt bad and I felt like my spine was cracking under the pressure of my body and the hardness of the rough boulder. Then I felt the boulder's surface scrape across my back and the next thing I knew, my tailbone hit the hard, grassy ground.

I groaned and I looked to the left. My hand was clenched tightly around something, a gold and steel something. It was the sword that had been inside the boulder.

But that was impossible. The sword had likely been inside its rocky sheath for thousands of years. Sure, I was strong for my age, but it would have taken a demigod to pull the sword out from something that had been made around it.

"Arthur, you broke it," Lancelot said, half kidding.

I looked up at him through a lock of hair and glared. He was right. I had to find out some way to get the sword back inside of the boulder before I had Druid people coming after me.

I sat up and brought the sword in front of me to examine it. I set it on my thighs.

The golden hilt was beautifully crafted with tiny raised lines making swirls and knotwork in an elaborate pattern that seemed to fit in my hands perfectly. Slightly thicker black knotwork laced over the silvery steel blade growing up toward the point from the hilt like a vine. The edges on either side of the blade looked razor sharp, as if one touch could slice deep into flesh. I was lucky that the blade had landed off to the side of my body when I fell.

"Are you alright?" Lancelot asked me as he stuck out his hand.

I took it and he pulled me up.

"I think so. My head just hurts a little." I looked at the sword in my hands. "What am I supposed to do with this now?"

Lancelot shook his head as if to say he did not know.

"Maybe if we take it to Avalon," I thought aloud. "If we leave it on the shore the Druids might find it and understand."

"Maybe..." Lancelot was strangely nondescript.

I just looked at him a moment, confused, then decided not to push it with and left him in his quietness.

It only took us about five minutes to reach the tree line at the bright white shore of Avalon. Our boots made crunching sounds on the pebbles as we approached the water. The water lapped lightly at them and made soft splashing sounds.

"Who are you?" a voice rang out from across the shore. Lancelot and I both turned our heads to the left, where it seemed to be coming.

A short figure in a huge green cloak was running down the shore towards us. I looked at my friend. "Should we run?"

Lancelot shook his head, "We better just talk to him."

The green cloaked figure reached us and turned out, as expected, to be much shorter than me and even Lancelot. He only came up to my chest.

The boy looked around our age, other than his apparent shortness, and he had very short black hair and dark, caramel skin. His features were lean and sharp, and his dark eyes were intelligent, although devoid of warmth. The green cloak that was softly flowing around his body was much too big for him and was made out of a burlap-like material that I had never seen before.

"Who are you?" he repeated himself.

"My name is Arthur, and this is—" I started but the boy immediately cut me off and grabbed the hilt of the sword from my hand.

"Where did you get this?" he snapped at me. I held on to the sword and pulled it back.

"I found it," I said defiantly and lifted my chin. Lancelot elbowed me in the side.

"You *found* it?" The boy was practically seething. "That sword has been encased in stone for centuries and you just happen to *find* it?!"

"Now would be the time to tell him the truth, Arthur," Lancelot leaned over and whispered to me. "Before he curses us or something."

"Well, actually I was sort of…ah…I sort of fell and…" I thought for a moment. I did *not* want to tell him the real reason that I had gotten the sword. "I pulled it out of the rock."

"Oh, I am sure you did. Some *dirty blooded* Christian boy just happened to pull Caliburnus from the stone. I suppose you want to kill me with it now, too." Sarcasm dripped from his voice like drool. I noticed he used the words *dirty blooded* to describe me, just as that girl I had met on Avalon had done.

I looked at him sideways, "I did pull it out."

Well, sort of, I thought. *Technically my hands were holding the hilt when I fell over and it just slid out.*

The boy stared into my eyes as if he were looking for something. I took a step back. Then he did the same with Lancelot and Lancelot also took a step back.

"Are you sure you were not the one to do it?" the boy asked him without obstructing his intense eye contact. Their dark eyes were almost the exact same color, to the point where it was hypnotizing me.

Lancelot shook his head quickly. "Arthur definitely did it. I am not so stupid as to break your…altar."

"Altar?" the boy asked. He shook his head as if disregarding Lancelot's comment. "You just look so much purer. More faerie."

He was right about that. If he was talking about the dark coloring of the faerie folk, Lancelot was *much* purer than me. My skin was as white as a sheet and my hair was a bronze gold color that could never have been considered dark.

"Hold out your hand," he commanded me. I complied and the boy succeeded in taking the sword from me. I noticed that we still did not know his name.

He felt along my palms and my fingers and rubbed my callouses and looked closely at the little arches on my fingertips that were my fingerprints. He set the sword in my hands and stared in disbelief at the perfect fit of the puzzle piece. I saw him grit his teeth in frustration.

"It is you," he glared up at me. "In all my years of training, I never thought it would be a dirty blooded Roman and yet here you are. Some protector you will be."

105

"What am I?" I asked, utterly confused by the situation.

He ignored my question and continued to glare up at me. I glanced at Lancelot and he shrugged. The boy shoved the sword back at me and I slid it carefully into my belt. "Who did you say you were again?"

"Ah…Arthur," I scanned his face for anything that might give me the slightest clue about his identity.

"Not your name you idiot!"

I was not exactly sure what I had done to make him so mad. That I had fair features? He did not seem so upset with Lancelot.

"Where you are from! Your title! Your parents!"

I looked at Lancelot again as if to ask if I should tell him who I was. He shrugged again. Not helpful. I decided that I probably could not make him madder than he already was.

"I am from Camelot," I said slowly, still looking at Lancelot as I spoke, "and my father is…" I thought for a moment. I knew that the Druid people hated my father. I did not blame them. I hated him and he had not killed my family and friends in order to promote himself. "…Uther Pendragon…High King of Britain."

"*You!*" And then he shoved me. *Hard.* "You are the reason that sword even exists!"

I felt my stomach rage. I stepped back and took a deep breath. I *had* to keep my temper under control. I had a feeling that this boy could do very, very bad things if I made him mad enough.

"I hate him too," I said softly, swallowing down my rage.

The boy and I locked eyes for a moment. I did not let my stare waver. His dark eyes softened first and I saw some of his anger leave him. He sighed, "I suppose you cannot choose to whom you are born."

I nodded.

"Can you please explain to me what all of this means?"

"In time," he said, looking down at his light brown moccasins.

"Can you tell me your name at least?" I asked him. I needed *something* to call him besides *the boy*.

"Merlin."

Chapter VII

Somewhere in the forest near the Lake of Avalon, Britain,
646

I had heard the name Merlin before. Not *here* by anyone in Camelot, but *there*. It was in books, a few movies that I had watched, Miss Adams had mentioned the name once in one of her lessons where I had not been paying attention.

I nodded. It was probably just coincidence that he had the name of someone that was mentioned in America. I had heard of other people *there* with the name Arthur after all.

He took my hands in his own and I noticed that tiny blue tattoos stretched from the tips of his fingers up his arms. They almost blended in with the light brown of his skin. I felt as if his dark, intelligent eyes were burning holes into my pale hands and for a moment, I felt out of place as I never had before, being the fairest skinned of our trio. I supposed that was how Ty felt *there* quite often. Out of place. Different.

Lancelot broke the veil of silence that had come over us, "Are you mad at Arthur for breaking the sword in the stone?"

I cringed at him continuously reminding Merlin that I had broken his Druid ritual thing. Merlin shuddered, "What is your name?"

"Lancelot," he answered. I could tell he felt a little put out by Merlin being harsh to him.

Merlin nodded and kept fingering my hands which was beginning to scare me a bit.

"Do you live in the forest?" I asked him.

"No," Merlin answered quickly, "I have lived on the Isle of Avalon my whole life."

"Oh…" I decided not to tell him about my short trip and my brief conversation with the skinny girl in the white dress.

"I have not had many conversations with other people," he confessed. "So if I come across strange, please forgive me."

I nodded. He was strange indeed. "So are you some kind of warlock or something?"

"I suppose you could say that," Merlin said thoughtfully. "I have been told that I am going to be a guide though, to…to…" he trailed off.

"To what?" I asked. Merlin started to walk toward the green forest line and Lancelot and I followed.

"In time," he composed himself, "I will explain everything."

Merlin and Lancelot and I talked about several things, including why Lancelot had called the sword in the stone an altar, and how mean my father was to me. I asked Merlin if he knew anything about my sister going missing and he said that he had seen her once or twice on the Isle of Avalon but had never formally conversed with her. As of late, she had gone missing even from Avalon.

I never told either of them about my short trip to Avalon and my strange meeting with the skinny girl in the white dress. Merlin spoke of many girls though, especially one named Viviane, of whom he seemed very fond. He said that one day Viviane would be the Lady of Avalon, after the current one (a woman named Nimue) died. He also said that it seemed like Morgain had wanted to become the Lady of Avalon, but Viviane had gained the position of successor. That was about the time Morgain had disappeared from Avalon.

Merlin was also the only boy on the entire island and had been for as long as he could remember. He said that when he was very young, all of the other boys were taken by my father to be slaughtered. I noticed that Lancelot said nothing as he explained this.

"Where are we going?" I asked finally when I realized that we were walking through the forest with no regimented direction.

"I know not," Merlin answered. "I just feel that we must travel this way."

I was not sure how I felt about going a certain direction based on the feelings of someone who had practically been seething at me less than twenty minutes ago. All I knew was that we were walking away from the lake. In fact, we could have been heading toward my home for all I knew. My war-torn home.

Lancelot and I kept sneaking looks at each other as we blindly followed Merlin through the forest, through many shades of green and brown. I kept the sword from the boulder tucked safely in my belt. Merlin did not say anything to us, so we all walked in a forced silence for what felt like hours.

A shrill scream broke unceremoniously into our thoughts and the gentle hum of birds singing in the canopy of trees above our heads. We all stopped and stood completely still. Everything seemed even quieter than it had been before. Another scream tore through the air and I crept in front of Merlin to try and listen harder. For some reason, I recognized the feminine scream as if it were pouring out of the mouth of someone I knew.

I turned in a full circle and surveyed our surroundings. I had been here before. Not recently, but I had. I surged forward in a sprint. If I went just a little further, I knew where I would be.

Sadly, I was right. I broke through the rough tree line to face the western entrance to the palace square. The scream that we had heard was coming from there, almost as if there was an execution happening. A witch burning or a hanging. But that was impossible. The Saxons had taken over the palace. They would definitely not use the traditions of the Britons to kill anyone. It was more likely that they would cannibalize their victims like the Pictish tribes of the Old People.

I am not sure if entering the palace square where the high-pitched screams had faded into the dull sound of execution drums thumping out an ominous rhythm was the best or worst decision I had ever made. Those moments will haunt me forevermore. Those were my ten seconds. My decisions. My failure. My destruction. My utter depression and untold despair.

It was like a dream, those moments. Yet I remember them as vividly as if they had happened again and again and again. And I suppose they did as I played them over and over and over again in my mind, searching for what I could have done differently to change the terrible outcome. To make the right person die, instead of the innocent.

I walk proudly through the open gates. My head is held high even though I know that in this sequence of events, I am the defeated. The one that is sure to die an unwilling death, the boy who will come to be known as the one who was killed.

Rage roils in my stomach when I see what is happening on the execution block. My sister sits proudly on a dark wooden throne that is engraved with black obsidian knotwork. Her face is set in an unemotional stare as she watches the scene play out in front of her. Next to her sits a man with thick, dark black hair that falls beneath his waist. He is dressed all in dark brown deer hide that is tight against his dark skin and hugs his chest and thighs. My father sits with his hands and feet tied with rope, staring straight ahead as if the portcullis at the entrance of the palace square has sparked his interest immensely.

And then there is my mother.

My mother stands on top of a wooden plank on two flat rocks. Her hands are tied behind her back. Before her is a harsh, firm rope that forms a menacing noose knot. She looks through the loop with a fierce, unwavering determination that emanates from her, even to where I stand in the center of the western gateway, behind the group of people that has gathered to watch. Her flaming red hair is unbridled and flows behind her like a flag of rebellion to my sister and the leather-clad man that seems to be causing her this unceremonious departure from the world.

I stand frozen for a brief moment as I take in the situation before me. Fear flows from every part of my body, beginning in my plighted heart. My hands are covered in sweat and they clutch the sword Caliburnus from the stone. I feel the fear in my body melt into the white lightning of adrenaline. My breath becomes shallow and I sprint into the mass of the crowd that stands before me. Now is my chance to rise up against these people who have taken my parents captive, who have taken my home, my city, my kingdom, my country.

I sprint forward with a new passion that I have not felt before, not even when I had fought the dragon that day with Kay. The only thing I can hear is the sound of my beating heart and my shallow breathing. My vision seems to be covered with a faint silver tinge as I rush forward with the sword raised above my head, threatening death upon anyone who would dare to come into my path of destruction.

The sea of humanity splits like the red sea in front of me and I reach the block in what feels like slow motion. I leap up from the cobblestone ground and my boots thud loudly on the weathered wood. I feel the eyes of all the people in the square focus on me. I do not care. Their silent stares only urge my anger to rage further, my fire to burn hotter, brighter.

I jump into the air toward my sister. My arms collide with her chest and I feel the fabric of her black velvet dress brush against my cheek. Her arms flail for a moment before one hand grabs a fistful of my hair and the other attaches to the fabric on the back of my tunic. Her chair tips over with my weight and momentum, pushing her over onto her back. I shove us to the side of her chair and pin her down, sitting on top of her. I press my hands against her neck and wrap my fingers around soft flesh and feel her heartbeat and her veins struggle to pump oxygen and blood to her mind. Her face turns a light shade of purple and the color becomes deeper with every second I hold her there. I feel her life force draining out of her.

Rough hands that must belong to the leather laden man grab my arms and my waist and try to rip me off of Morgain. I do not budge. His prying hands dig deep into my stomach as he shoves and prods me, trying to weaken my grip on my sister. This only makes me hold on tighter. I know that with every second I am draining the life from her body. Thirty more seconds and she will be dead. This person who I used to think was my ally, my family, one with me in the disappointment and dissatisfaction of my father, was about to kill my mother. I need her to die. I have to hold on past the pain of the hands that are stabbing into my flesh and forcing me away from my goal. The only thing I can feel is her heartbeat in my hands. No longer can I hear my own heart. It is drowned out by the dying rhythm of my sister's.

I let up for less than one second. I felt sorry for her.

A sharp pain explodes in my left arm. A claw that hits the bone of my forearm and drags upward through my muscle and flesh. Warm blood pours down my wrist and onto Morgain's neck. The claw that has buried itself in my arm yanks me back and a yell hurdles itself from my throat as I am thrown backward solely by the flesh of my forearm.

The pain is almost unbearable. My head thuds against the rough wood of the execution block and I look up. All I can see is my mother's face, the utter terror that is erupting behind her eyes as she sees me, her only son, curled on the ground with blood spattered over him.

I try to get up to help her, but then my sister is above me, her face still in hues of purple and red from my attempt at justice. She holds me down, pinning my arms behind me, shoving her nails in the gash that the claw had made in my forearm. I want to scream, but I am incapable of making sound. She holds my head in the direction of my mother. Forcing me to watch.

A man dressed all in black with a mask covering his undoubtedly ugly face shoves the noose over my mother's head. I struggle with all of my strength, all of my will, all of my pain. My sister's grip is too strong with her nails forcing their way into my flesh. I can do nothing but watch.

The man kicks the board that my mother is standing on out from under her feet. She falls for a brief moment before the entirety of her weight is caught by the rope around her neck.

My voice works. I scream. My voice is high-pitched and feminine, but I do not care. I scream like the world is ending. Because my world is ending. She was the only one that loved me.

All I can look at is her face. Her terrible, horrifying face. Her once determined, loving, fierce gray eyes are empty. Nothing more will they see. Her mouth is set in a permanent scream that no one will ever hear.

My mother is gone.

*****

Colorado Springs, America, 2009

I sat straight up in my bed. My breathing was fast and shallow. All I could see was my mother's face. My mother's *dead* face. My mother as she descended into an unknown reality that none shall tell.

I heard an electronic beeping noise.

I was *here*. In America. That was my alarm clock. I needed to get up. Go to school. Be expressionless.

There was not real. Camelot did not exist, nor did my sister, or my father, or my mother, or dare I say it—me. I did not exist. I was nothing but a legend. A story to be told by bards and in books. Only America was real. Only this time. Only the year 2009.

I looked at my hands. They were red and white and had designs of tiny lines dancing across them. I scraped the nail of my right pointer finger across my left palm. I felt it. This was real.

I traced my nail further up my arm. Across my wrists. Along the bottom of my pale forearm.

"Arthur?" Miss Marion's voice rang in my ears from out in the hall. "Are you awake?"

"Ah…" I needed to reply, "yes!"

"You'd better hurry!" she said loudly. "Breakfast in twenty minutes, and *please* wash your hair!"

"I will!" I yelled back.

I turned my forearm over.

There was a long, ugly scar running from my wrist to my elbow.

*****

Cadbury Castle, Britain, 646

I slept for an entire day.

Well, I suppose that is not entirely true. I woke up around noon, looked at my surroundings to see that I was in fact, *here*, at Cadbury Castle, in my chambers. Then I went back to sleep and did not wake up until I had verified that I was in America again. Today was the day after that.

I could not sleep for another day though. I needed to see what had happened.

I think it was around ten when I finally forced myself out of bed.

I noticed that my arm was bandaged with a white cloth and it smelled like some kind of herb poultice that the physician had probably put on my wound. I could still feel all of my fingers and I could move my hand in all the ways that I should be able. At least no permanent damage had been done.

The sword that I had "pulled" out of the stone was lying on the table near the door to my chambers. I sat down at the table and lifted the sword onto my lap. I still could not make out what the strange symbols on the blade meant. I thought about what the boy Lancelot and I had met, Merlin, had said about the sword.

It was confusing, the way he had said it. But he did make one thing very clear. This sword in my hands was very, very important.

The door in front of me creaked open and Austin wearily crept in; he must have thought that I was still asleep. He caught sight of me and hurried to my side.

"I am glad you are no longer asleep," he said. He softly massaged my shoulders, but I pulled away from him. He must have forgotten my dislike of people touching me.

I nodded, hoisted the sword off of my lap and set it back on the table with a faint clanking sound.

"Where did you get that?" he asked me. He proceeded to change out my cloth bandages.

"Found it," I told him nondescriptly.

He understood that I did not wish to talk at the moment and he continued to unwrap the cloth on my arm silently. I cringed as the last coil of it came off and a stinging sensation pulsed throughout my arm. The wound really was quite disgusting. Ripped up red and white flesh and dried blood, all covered in a putrid smelling, green sludge. Somehow, I could not bring myself to look away. Austin wiped the wet green stuff off of my arm and applied more from a small plate that the physician likely had given him. Then he wrapped a fresh piece of cloth tightly around my arm and tied it all together with a piece of string.

"I hope you feel better Arthur," Austin said. Then he left, leaving me to stare at the shining sword in silence.

It must have been midday before I got up the nerve to go and see my father.

I hung the sword Caliburnus on my belt in a scabbard that I had found in a trunk in the corner of my room. The white tunic that I was wearing seemed relatively clean. My boots were polished. My hair was sticking up in a strange cowlick on one side, but it always did that. I needed to talk to him. Or at the least find out the entirety of what had happened. It seemed at least that we had taken the palace back from my sister who was now apparently a Saxon leader.

I am not sure if it was just my imagination, but people seemed to smile at me in the palace corridors as I journeyed to the throne room where I guessed that my father would be. They seemed to have a new respect for me that I could not quite place. It was probably just my imagination.

The guards bowed to me and opened the doors to the trial room. My father was sitting on his throne with his leg crossed over the other. A silver chalice was in his hand and a bit of dark red wine dripped down his chin as he took a long draft. A plump female servant that wore a dress and corset that was much too small for her body stood next to him with a pitcher in her hand

"Father," I said. I made sure to tilt my head down ever so slightly to admit his authority over me.

"Y-you!" he shouted/slurred at me. I looked at the floor. "Y-you god forbid T-terrible excuse for a boy! You killed her!"

"N-no father," I stammered. "I tried but something ripped me off of her."

"Not that insufferable bitch!" he yelled. "My *wife*!"

What? I was confused. Morgain's men had hung her I thought.

"You let her die!" He stood up and almost fell over from his drunkenness. He handed his chalice to the female servant and started to stumble toward me. I nervously retracted into myself. "This is all your fault!"

He slapped me across the face. *Hard.* And it hurt, as if he had slashed me across the face with a knife. Because he was right. I had let her die. It was my fault that my mother had been killed. If I had only been a little stronger. A little sooner to arrive at the palace square. The loss would have been avoided.

He was so close to my face that I could clearly smell the pungent scent of wine on his breath and see his rotting teeth. "If it were not for the fact that you are the only son I have I would run you through and run the blade of my sword from your beating heart to your defiant eyes."

I said nothing. I was frozen in fear of what he might do to me.

"Get out of my sight."

I complied and sprinted out of the trial room as fast as I could, forcing back tears with all of my might.

I ran and ran through the palace corridors, never slowing my pace. Eventually, I reached a door to the training yard at the outer edge of the castle and I ran across the cobblestone pathway and through the tree and grass landscape until I reached what I was looking for. I walked into an arch in the wall. It was decently concealed because of the flowering spring trees that covered the entrance. I climbed up into the stone niche, leaned against the wall, and cried.

Men were not supposed to cry. I knew this well enough. Even when the people they loved died, and when they were mad at themselves because they were the reason that that person had died. I was not a man. I was not even a boy. I was pathetic. I had killed my mother somehow. I probably could even be blamed for the successful invasion of the Saxons in the first place. I should not become king. I would be a terrible king. Much worse than my father. My ideas were ridiculous. I was insane. What kind of person said that they secretly traveled to a land in the distant future across the seas and believed it? Why was I even here? Why was I even alive?

I was alive because some higher power than I needed to have a good laugh. They put an insane boy in the position to someday become king so they could taunt him. That was all I was. A joke.

"Can I talk to you?" a smooth male voice entered into my thoughts. I lifted my head from my knees that were pressed against my chest and stared at the wall ahead of me without looking at the man.

"Why would you want to?" I asked, sniffing and wiping my nose.

"Why would I *not* want to?" he asked me. I finally turned towards him. He was cocking his head at me.

The man had a serene, smooth face and light curly blonde hair that flowed around his face like a mane. In fact, the man rather reminded me of a lion. His skin was just a shade darker than his hair and his eyes were slightly farther apart than they should have been which added to the lion effect that he had. I recognized him. He was the one my father had set in place to be the master of patrols; however, I had never formally talked to him and I did not even know of his name.

"I am a failure," I said, wiping my face and calming my tears the best I could.

"Surely that is not true," he told me. His light brown eyes were soft and gave me the impression that I could talk to him. "What have you done?"

"I killed my own mother," I muttered, shoving my head back into my knees, "and I think I caused the Saxon attack to be successful."

"What?" the man asked. He seemed very confused. "Please come down here and tell me why you think that."

I shook my head. I wanted to stay here until I died of starvation or dehydration. That way I could not hurt anyone else.

"Come on," he said and quite literally picked me up and set me on the ground.

I stood across from him and looked at him weakly. He was dressed in light training armor and had a wooden staff in his hand. He was about eight inches taller than me and I came just up to his upper chest.

"My name is Lionel," he told me and stuck his hand out. I found this slightly comedic considering that I had compared him to a lion only moments before. I still just looked at him. "This is when you introduce yourself and shake my hand."

"You already know my name," I said sullenly. "Everyone knows my name."

"At least shake my hand then," he tried. I sighed, and we grabbed hold of each other's wrists in the way that was the custom *here*.

My hands retreated to my sides where I felt my bandaged left arm bounce against Caliburnus for a second. My face was set in a permanent glare at the world.

"I organize all of the patrols from Camelot," Lionel told me. I already knew that. "I would like you to lead one sometime."

"Why?" I asked. There was no reason why he would want *me* to be in charge of something that important to the safety of the kingdom.

"Because I think you would be good at it, Arthur." He proved my theory that he did in fact know my name.

"Why?" I asked again. "I have already let everyone down once."

"What on earth are you talking about?" he asked as if in disbelief. "You made it possible to take back the palace when the Saxons attacked!"

"I did?" I asked, cocking my head at him.

"Yes!" he said enthusiastically. "When you attacked Morgain, the sorcerer that was making sure nobody was out of line became preoccupied with you and gave way to let the knights that were being forced to watch fight back against our guards! It was your surprise attack that allowed us to take back our home."

"Oh…" I really did not believe him. I thought he was only trying to cheer me up. And even if I had helped them take back the palace, I had still killed my mother. Nothing could change that fact.

"And what was that nonsense about you being the cause of Ygraine's death?" he asked me.

"My father told me," I said. "I *let* them kill her. It is my fault that she is dead."

"You *let them* kill her?!" he said angrily. "Uther told you that?"

I nodded.

"What a little liar," he said angrily. "If anyone *let* anyone do anything it was him! He tried to pay that sorcerer to let him go free and take the rest of us instead! And he told his own son that he killed his mother. What a bloody canker!"

Apparently, Lionel had a strong dislike for my father.

"But it is true," I said.

"No," he said firmly. "Sometimes bad things just happen."

We just looked at each other in awkward silence for a few moments.

"Do you like fighting staff?" he asked me.

"Yes," I told him. "I fight staff with my friend Lancelot quite a lot."

"Come on then." He jerked his head in the direction of the training yard.

I followed him blindly to where he handed me a big wooden staff and squared himself up with me. I sighed and took a defensive position.

And then we fought.

Lionel was the best fighter I had ever sparred. He seemed to be even better than some of the men that had fought staff in the tournament. In fact, I thought I had a faint memory of Lionel's name being called for winning the staff event once.

The most interesting thing about his fighting style was the way he swung the stick around his wrists and his hands. He did not hold the staff solely like a sword, and it flowed and spun in harmony with the movements of his body. It really was a magnificent technique, almost as if the stick were an extension of his body. He had me pinned in just a few moments and helped me back up to my feet.

"You are really good," I complimented him.

"Thank you," he said and smiled. "I saw you fighting sword at winter solstice, you looked pretty good then too. Too bad it was canceled. You definitely would have made finals."

"Maybe." I bit my lip and handed back the staff he had given me. "Did you make this?"

"Yes," he said. "I make all of my wooden staffs. The ones from the smithy just do not fit in my hands as well."

I never knew fighting staff could be such an exact science. I nodded.

"Where did you get that sword?" he asked, gesturing to Caliburnus at my side.

"I...found it," I said. I had a feeling that Merlin would not want me divulging the origins of the sword.

"You should consider yourself lucky," he told me. "That looks like a beautiful piece of craftsmanship."

I just nodded. Lionel began twirling his staff around his right wrist absentmindedly. It looked like he had practiced that one move for hours. "If you do not mind my asking, sir, how old are you?"

I realized that I had been quite rude before, not calling him by a title when he was very much in more authority than me. The master of patrols was a big position, which meant that people held him in high respect.

"Twenty-one years," he said, still focusing much of his attention on his staff. "How old are you?"

"Thirteen, sir," I answered. It was beginning to bother me that he was putting more attention on his staff than me considering that he was the one that had forced me to come out of my very secluded niche and talk to him. I stared at the ground.

Lionel's attention all of a sudden became extremely focused on two figures that I could not really make out across the training yard. It bothered me that I could not really make them out; my vision had always been like that though, I could not see far away objects as clearly as most people could. As they came closer, I could begin to make out their faces, Lancelot and Merlin. I could also see the tips of blue tattoos along Merlin's hands. Lionel's stare stayed hard focused on Merlin and his blue-stained hands.

"Who is that?" he asked me solidly and harshly. I suppose he assumed that I would know because Merlin was walking with Lancelot, who, everyone knew, was my best friend.

"Ah…" I trailed off for a moment, surprised at Lionel's sudden shift in mood. "A boy Lancelot and I met by Avalon before we came back to the palace that day. He helped me find the sword."

"He is a Druid, yes?" Lionel said without taking his eyes off him as they came closer to us. Lancelot was probably wondering why he had not seen me yesterday, or maybe he just wanted to talk to me about why I had slept for a day and a half. Or he wanted to talk to me about other recent events to make sure that I was alright.

"Yes," I answered. They were only a hundred yards away now.

"Then he does not belong here," Lionel said firmly. "You know that Arthur. It is best that you tell him to leave before I have to turn him in to your father's guard."

They arrived at our feet. Lionel's glare looked almost as menacing as mine was.

Lancelot looked very confused. He spoke to Lionel, "Sir, what is wrong?"

Lionel stepped back as if prompting me to speak. I complied. "Merlin needs to go home. Druids are to be executed if they enter Camelot remember?"

"But you hid Gawain in your chambers and nobody found out," Lancelot said as if he had carefully thought this through, "so I figured that I could hide Merlin in mine."

"Hold on," Lionel interjected. All three of us, including Merlin who currently looked as if he were trying to retract into himself, looked up at him in a respectful manner. "Who is Gawain? And why were you hiding him in your chambers?"

I glared at Lancelot. He should have thought about the fact that Lionel was standing right there when he spoke of my stowaway, who was my cousin and in Camelot illegally. And, on the topic of Gawain, I had no idea where he had gone. After Lancelot told me that he had run off after helping to carry me to Avalon, I had heard nothing of him or seen him in the past two days. In my defense, I had been slightly preoccupied.

I felt all eyes on me. "Gawain is…" I had to make up something fast in order not to get my "friend" into trouble. "….a really long story."

Lionel shook his head as if slightly confused. "Do you have a name?" he asked Merlin.

"Do *you* have a name?" Merlin fired back sarcastically. Lancelot and I looked at each other and then back at Merlin in shock. Addressing a knight like that was *not* something you did and lived to tell the tale. Especially not a high-ranking knight such as Lionel.

I do not think Lionel quite knew how to respond. He just stared at Merlin for a few moments and then looked at me for a few moments, I shrugged. He looked back at Merlin. Merlin stared defiantly back.

"Lionel," he said finally and stuck out his hand for Merlin to shake. He was still looking at him much too carefully, as if deciding which way to cook him.

Merlin took the hand and they locked wrists for a moment that seemed to last a lifetime. "Merlin."

"Welcome to Cadbury Castle, Merlin."

And to this day, I still do not know what happened in those awkward moments.

Chapter VIII

Colorado Springs, America, 2009

Sometimes I felt as if mischief followed me like a plague. A plague of destruction, clumsiness, and plain bad luck. This realization occurred to me as I was walking through the neighborhood with Ty at eight o'clock on the Saturday night of spring break. The rest of the week had actually gone quite well. I had gone with my foster parents to visit their son, Kyler, at college in Arizona and we had mostly gone on hikes and explored landmarks such as the Meteor Crater and Montezuma's Castle Museum. The climate was very, very hot and very, very dry which I appreciated because I am not one for humidity and cold weather. Their son had been very nice to me; he even gave me a shirt with 'University of Arizona' spelled out on it.

Now, as we were walking, I told Ty that I was thirsty and we stopped at the little general store to buy a soda pop. I had some of my allowance money with me, I did not often spend the ten dollars a week that Miss Marion gave me, and instead kept all of the oblong, green sheets of parchment in a jar on my desk next to my laptop. Ty and I were examining all of the different colorful, bottled flavors and choosing which ones to pick when a group of boys came up behind us. Well really, there were two boys and one girl who was dressed much too skimpily.

I recognized one of the boys. He was the son of one of Ty's parents' friends. He was very tall and African-American, with dark biceps that bulged out of his white, sleeveless T-shirt and braids descending down his neck to end in little golden beads at his shoulders. I knew that his name was Jaymore and that he was a sophomore at the high school. The other boy was slightly shorter and almost as pale as I was, but with a curly red afro and freckles covering his face and the legs that were visible out of the bottom of his neon green basketball shorts. The girl was brunette, very, very skinny, and had ripped washed out jean shorts that seemed to pull up her buttocks. They looked very uncomfortable. She had a beer bottle in her hand and her eyes did not seem to line up quite right.

"What do you want, Jaymore?" Ty asked defensively.

"Wanted to see if this kid is really as weird as people are sayin'," he motioned toward me. "What's your name again?"

"Um, Arthur," I said. I was slightly offended that he had not remembered my name, especially when one, I remembered his, and I did not usually bother to remember people's names, and two, they had come looking for me. They had just told us that.

"What do you think Hannah?" Jaymore asked the girl.

The girl kind of shrugged and said a few American swears that I will not recite. She seemed drunk, but in a different way than people got drunk *there*, a sickly sweet type of drunk. She pulled out a rolled paper tube from the side of her shorts and lit it with a lighter. That must have been from where the sickly sweet smell was coming. She inhaled on the tube and handed it to the red haired kid, who in turn inhaled from it as well. I just looked nervously at Ty. I was not sure what they were doing.

"Don't be rude," the redheaded boy said as he handed the paper tube back to Hannah. "Give them some."

"Sorry, Josh," Hannah said and rolled her eyes. She pulled another rolled paper tube from her jean shorts. I noticed that it was filled with green stuff. I, for one, was amazed that she kept all of these things in those tiny shorts. She lit the tube with the lighter and offered it to me. "Here ya go."

I did not take it. Mostly because it was on fire and smelled really strange. Ty looked nervously at me.

"What is it?" I asked suspiciously.

All of them joined in a chorus of laughter. I was utterly confused. I did not think it was a normal thing to accept a paper tube of green stuff that was on fire from a bunch of people you hardly knew or from anyone for that matter. I just looked at them strangely.

"God!" Jaymore laughed. "You're weirder than I thought!"

"*What is it?*" Josh mocked me.

They all laughed again. I felt very embarrassed and utterly stupid. I had no idea what it was and everyone else seemed to know.

Then the three of them walked out of the store still laughing hysterically and passing around the paper tubes. I just looked at Ty.

"What was that?" I asked quietly.

He looked at the ground. "Pot."

I decided to stop asking questions in order to not further embarrass myself. "Oh," I said as if I totally knew what pot was.

"Can we just go home?" I asked.

"Yeah, sure," he said.

And home we went.

*****

Cadbury Castle, Britain, 646

Merlin ended up staying in Lancelot's chambers and Lionel promised not to say anything to my father or any of the knights as long as he did not cause any trouble or perform any acts of sorcery. Lionel had also asked me to ride on a patrol with him the next day to see if I would be good at leading one or not. I liked Lionel. He was very nice to me, and he did not treat me like a little kid even though I was much younger than him.

I had not spoken to my father again since the day he had accused me of killing my mother. Instead, Lancelot and I ate supper in the palace kitchens with Merlin. I saw Halaina staring at me. I was starting to feel like I was being stalked.

I told Austin to wake me up early for dawn patrol with Lionel and he did. When I looked out the window while I was still in bed, I saw the night sky as the sun still had not risen. I pulled my bed furs off of my body and lowered myself onto the cold, cobblestone floor, cringing as my bare feet touched the chilled surface. I dressed in a plain brown tunic and trousers and I attached Caliburnus to my belt.

I sat down at my rectangular table close to the door that used to lead into my mother's chambers. I thought about how she used to come into my room at night when she heard me tossing and turning with nightmares, or when occasionally she would come to have breakfast with me, or help me pick out something to wear. Never again would that happen. Never again would I hear the smooth and rhythmic melody of her voice. Never again would I feel the warmth of her embrace and the softness of her fiery red hair.

Austin brought me a platter of biscuits and some crushed raspberry jam. I had asked for raspberry jam in particular; it was always my mother's favorite. I found I was not very hungry and stopped eating after two biscuits and a glass of milk. I just stared at the door to the empty queen's chambers. I pulled the leather rope out from under my chainmail and tunics and stared at the steel ring that hung on it. Maybe when I was older, I could wear it correctly. This was the last thing I had from my mother. This ring that was too big for my fingers.

I met Lionel at the stables where there were a few other men and boys just a bit older than me. One of them was Kay. I had been avoiding Kay since the incident in Meredith. He was not one of my favorite people. I glared at him as I went to stand next to Lionel and he pretended as if I did not exist. That was fine with me. Bedivere, to whom I had only spoken to a few times, was also there, standing next to Kay. I knew they were pretty good friends, so I figured that Bedivere was probably going to act as if I did not exist as well.

"Is everyone here?" Lionel asked loudly. He looked around and counted us. Then, feeling satisfied, "Let us leave then."

He mounted his horse and slid a metal staff into a scabbard by his horse's white mane. All of the others on patrol, including me, did the same. We fell into line behind Lionel as we headed down the trail through the western gates from the stables.

We were to be scouting along the western side of Britain to make sure that the Saxons had not invaded Cornwall and some of the western villages. Lionel said it was only about a two-and-a-half-hour ride there and that we would probably be back in time for supper at Camelot. I was thankful that Lionel had opted for me to ride at the front with him, considering that I did not really know any of the other men—aside from Kay and Bedivere of course.

"So are these the people that usually come on patrols with you?" I asked Lionel as I looked back at the seven other men that were with us.

"Sometimes," Lionel said. "The groups shift depending on the length and area of the patrol. There are also five others going in different directions. Those two boys," he pointed to Kay and Bedivere, "have not been on one this long yet. They usually just go on patrols to Avalon or Meredith. Sometimes we do run into trouble on the longer ones."

"What kind of trouble?" I asked nervously.

"Mostly just people of the Old Ways that are upset because we are on their native land," Lionel said and frowned, catching the hint of my nervousness. "I doubt we will come across any dangers today though."

I nodded and kicked my horse's flank in order to keep up with Lionel's fast paced trot.

The group decided to take a break a half hour into our journey, when we were just north of Avalon, to water the horses and map out our plan in more depth. We sat in a circle and looked at a crudely drawn papyrus map while Lionel explained to us what each of the lines and markings met. I could read the map well because of the geography study we did in history *there* so I did not feel the need to sit through a lecture on map reading. I asked Lionel if I could go and relieve myself. He gave me permission and instead of doing what I had asked, I decided to go on a walk to explore the forest. After all, this area was fairly close to where Lancelot and I had met Merlin.

It was funny when I thought about how quickly we had been able to get back to Cadbury Castle with Merlin's "senses" leading us. It had taken us a half hour at quick paced horseback to get to this location. Granted, the patrol had taken the long way because they did not know about Lancelot's and my trail, but it still seemed much too short of a time for us to be able to walk back at a leisurely pace. It was almost as if there were some sort of magic at work. Almost as if Merlin really was a sorcerer.

I wandered through the dense greenery in the direction that I believed Avalon was. The air carried a warm spring breeze, and I started to feel uncomfortably hot in my thick tunics and armor. I heard rushing water and I gravitated toward it, my mouth yearning for water. The sound turned out to be generated by a thin stream running over smooth, flat stones. I cupped a bit of the cool water in my hands and lapped it up. Then, hoping that the patrol was still involved with the map and the planning out of the day, I proceeded to follow the stream.

It fed into the Avalon as expected, and like always, the view was breathtaking.

The weeping willow trees groped at the glassy surface and not even a ripple disturbed the meditative state of the lake. The smooth, white pebbles crunched under my brown boots that were now muddied from the stream bed as I crept forward to the water's edge. My hand desired the fresh and serene touch of the body of water before me.

"Who might you be?" a calm, female voice asked softly. The voice was like honey and whipped butter mixed together, soothing and thick and smooth.

I turned toward the direction of the voice. It was a girl with a grass satchel loosely hanging from her wrist that was covered in light blue knotwork patterns like Merlin's tattoos. She was clothed in a flowing white dress that seemed to fall over her body such as a waterfall might. It was the same dress that the other girl I had met on Avalon had worn, though it looked much better on the girl who stood before me now. She looked fuller, the flows and waves of the dress falling over her in a satisfying way, unlike on the thinner girl I had met who had looked almost scrawny. Delicate, thin, golden waves of hair that fell to her waist added to the impression of the beauty of the girl. They shaped the pale and full outline of her face. Full pink lips led up to a shapely, straight nose and her eyes took my breath away. Her eyes were the exact color of the lake, to the exact shade, and their almond shape gave a thoughtful, yet fiercely intense gateway into her mind. I had never been in love in my life, but I was now.

As I walked toward the girl in awe, I realized that she was much shorter than me. I felt very large standing only a few feet away from her, the top of her head only reaching my chin. I very much enjoyed this sudden burst of masculinity.

"Please answer me," The girl said, and cocked her head at me as if confused at why I was looking at her so intently instead of answering her question. I realized then that she was not only a creature with voluptuous beauty to be admired but also a human being who wished to converse with me.

"My name is Arthur," I said, forcing myself to stay articulate, but carefully analyzing every curve and color in her body and hair.

She continued to cock her head at me, seemingly examining me as in-depth as I was her. "I thought people such as you that wore garments of iron had more names and titles and silly things such as that?"

"Well, I…" I had to stop for a moment to rip my mind away from memorizing her figure to remembering common things like where I was from. "I do…"

"Please tell them to me," she said. Concern began to form in her fearless eyes as she watched my inability to process reality.

"I am…I am from Cadbury Castle in Camelot," I said. And then without thinking about my audience, "I am the son of King Uther Pendragon."

"Are you going to kill me then?" she asked and sighed, looking at the ground. She did not let me speak. "I suppose Nimue was right…I should have stayed on the island instead of exploring. *Oh please, Goddess, give me charm.*"

She bowed her head and waited for me to attack. I figured this was the time to explain my position and how I thought that this girl was the most beautiful thing I had ever seen. Well, maybe not the latter.

"I am not here to kill you," I told her. "I think my father's policies are unjust and I choose not to follow them."

"You are his only son though?" she asked, as if she was confused about how I could not be completely loyal to my father when I shared his blood.

"Just because I was born to him does not mean I agree with him," I said, almost irritated. I was tired of people believing that I was a certain way because of who my father was. "I did not choose my father."

I found it odd that I did not know her name and we were already talking about who my father was and how he defined me.

"I suppose that is true," she answered and furrowed her brow as if she were looking into my mind. "It was rather rude of me to assume that you would be like him. I apologize."

I nodded and we just looked at each other for a moment. I forced myself to look away from her body and to the lake. I desperately wanted to know her name, but I did not wish to be presumptuous.

"My name is Viviane," she said finally. Her eyes were scanning me up and down as if she were checking to make sure I was not really planning to attack her.

I had heard the name Viviane before. Merlin had talked about her a great deal more than he had talked about any of the other girls on Avalon. They must have been good friends.

"A pleasure to meet you," I said, lacking any other words to say. I stuck my hand out for her to shake.

She just looked at the hand and cocked her head, "What are you doing?"

"Well, I thought we could shake hands," I said. Until now, I had thought that it was a common ritual that people did and did not need explaining.

"Why?" she asked suspiciously.

I just looked at her for a moment.

"Oh!" she said as realization struck her. She literally giggled. "That is one of those silly things that Romans and Britons do when they meet!"

I continued to look at her strangely. I finally brought my hand back to rest at where Caliburnus hung at my belt.

Her eyes suddenly widened when she caught sight of the sword. She just stared at it. I stared at her.

I was not the least bit scared of Viviane, even through her obvious strangeness, as one might expect. Rather she intrigued me. I was strange myself, and that commonality between the two of us further cemented my growing attraction to her.

I pulled my sword out of its scabbard and handed it to her without her asking. I could tell that she wanted to look at it, and since she was from the same place as Merlin, she was undoubtedly connected to it and interested in it in the same way that he was. Viviane analyzed the sword slowly and carefully, looking at every design and detail engraved on the hilt and the blade. Then she looked at me for a few moments. I admired obvious intelligence that shone through her eyes and the way that I could tell her mind was working to come to a conclusion about the sword and me.

Then, to no one in particular, she began to rant, "I told Nimue that I needed to come to shore today! I told her! And there she was, not believing me and thinking me foolish to the point where I had to run away to follow my senses! And look what I have found! I have found our protector! He who is to save us! I found Caliburnus and her sacred wielder!"

I was not so sure what she was talking about, but I had a feeling it was about me.

"Who is Nimue?" I asked her.

"You can hear me?" she asked. She had practically yelled. Of course I heard her.

"Yes."

"You see on Avalon people cannot hear me," Viviane explained. "They just turn their heads away when I think."

I wanted to say, *Or maybe they can hear you and they ignore you because they think you are insane. That is alright though, I am insane as well. In fact, I believe that I travel thousands of years in the future every time I fall asleep.* Instead, I replied with a simple, "Oh."

"Merlin always understood me when I thought," she said thoughtfully. She sat down on the white pebble beach. I did as well, the rocks digging slightly uncomfortably into my legs. "He understood lots of things about me. I wish that he had not left to…well, I suppose he left to look after you."

It was my turn to cock my head in confusion. She continued to "think," this time directed slightly more toward me.

"A few days ago he left saying something about it having to do with his purpose which is to help our protector. Then he took the ferry to shore and I have not heard from him since, although I have seen him in my visions. I see him with our protector. I know he is doing what he needs to do. I hate my visions you know. Too much time spent in the future than in the present. They always come when I am swimming or collecting herbs, never when they are supposed to, when I want to use my sight."

Once again, I had become hopelessly lost in her rant seemingly about nothing. I recognized some things that she was saying, and I knew that she could have been spouting precious information that was crucial to my future and I would not have had the slightest idea.

"Sometimes, I feel like I spend too much time in the future and not enough in the present," I muttered. I felt I needed to inject a personal quo of my own in order to remain an active part of the conversation

"How is that?" she asked curiously.

"It is complicated," I told her, not wishing to elaborate. We met each other's eyes for a brief moment, and I felt as if we were inside of the other's soul.

"Oh, alright," she said. Then she picked up a stone and put it into her satchel. "I am very sorry that I have confused you."

"How do you know that you have confused me?" I asked.

"I know things about people." Indeed she did.

I sighed loudly to cover the awkward gap in conversation. I looked at my sword, sitting in Viviane's lap. I wanted it back, but she seemed very possessive of it at the moment. She just looked out to the lake and stayed like that, saying nothing.

I realized then, that I was actually supposed to be somewhere that was not here at Avalon with Viviane. Lionel was likely worried about me. Soon enough, some of the men might come looking for me and then I would have to contend with the fact that some of them were vigorously loyal to my father, and may try to kill Viviane for her obvious devotion to the Old Ways.

"I think that I must leave," I said and stood up. She grabbed my wrist and I craned my neck around to look at her, her touch startling me.

"No," she said, with her hand still tightly gripping my wrist and her eyes locked in deep contact with my own, "your men have not even thought of your absence and will not think of it until they are ready to leave and Sir Lionel completes a head count. They will not be ready to leave for another hour. Two horses were carelessly tied up and escaped into the forest causing a delay."

My eyes widened as I looked at her in shock. How she had known all of those things about the group of men that I had come with? Maybe that was what she was talking about when she spoke of the visions that annoyed her so very much.

I pulled my arm away from her, "How did you know that?"

I noticed that my tone of voice was more curious than alarmed.

"I had a vision when I touched you," she told me. "And I am sorry that touch scares you so much."

It was oddly comforting to know that Viviane knew a few of my innermost thoughts and feelings. I would not feel the slightest bit comfortable with anyone else invading my mind, but with Viviane it seemed alright. Even though I had only known her for a few minutes, I felt completely at ease with her. She made sense. Her insanity, although strange, also made sense. Everything about her screamed safe, and I wanted to have her in my arms. I wanted to carry her back to Cadbury Castle and keep her in my chambers. Viviane would understand me. I knew it. She would understand my *here* and *there* predicament, she would sympathize with my troubles with my father, she would never say I was mean, she would understand my honesty and my outlook on life. I needed to have her in my life.

"I like you," I said simply. It had probably sounded stupid, but I meant it like I had never meant anything else. I would have said *I love you* if not for the intimidation factor of those three words.

"I like you too," she replied with the same firmness that I had felt in my voice. She meant it as well.

And this simple declaration of admiration lifted my soul from the bottom of Hades where it had shattered when the board had been pulled from under my mother's feet. This person that I had met only minutes ago was like golden fire in my veins, pulsing through my body, giving life from the ends of my fingertips and warming my core. I felt a heat that was completely theoretical lick at my feet and brush up my trousers, melting my armor, and raising my hair all around my head. My heart was ablaze with orange light.

She had set me on fire.

Chapter IX
Arthur

I think that the worst decision I have ever made is telling anyone about there. It does not matter whether it is in America or Britain; either way, it was terrible judgement on my part. And as I stare back at my younger years, I have no idea what I thought to gain from telling anyone. Maybe it was attention, as my father quite firmly believed. Or maybe it was that I was quite certainly insane and because I was insane, I did not know to not tell others. I think it was because I was lonely, so utterly lonely. I had no one to commiserate with, none that I knew who were like me: stuck between two places, both almost unheard of by the other.

The thing that I found the most peculiar about peoples' aversion to believing me, or even pitying me, was their complete lack of sympathy in this area compared to everything else. People were so emotional and tolerant toward most everything else— especially American people—except when I mentioned *there*. I very much regret telling those I did about *there* for this reason. I believed that they would try to help me, or at the least feel sorry for me, but instead they told me that I was making it up. That the only reason I had made it up *was* for attention. Really, all I wanted was someone to talk to about it. One soul that would understand, so that maybe, maybe I would not be so alone in the bleak cross-section between two times.

I never intended to tell Ty about *there*; I wanted to keep our friendship pure, without supernatural pollution or non-American aspects. Also, judging from his demeanor, he seemed as if he would not understand. He would probably just think I was kidding.

After our mishap with the high schoolers in the general store, I decided that I needed to learn more about American culture in order to not stand out too much. I was determined not to make such a fool out of myself again. I searched a list of all the acceptable contractions in the English language on my laptop, and I found out that "pot" was actually a drug called marijuana, which was green leaves that had the ability to deplete people's awareness through being a depressant.

It was not as hard to adapt to American culture as one might think. Because it was all around me, it was almost a forced immersion and I realized that I was probably trying harder not to fall in step with the culture than I was trying to become involved with it. I found that as soon as I let go of my "different" origins while I was *here*, I fit in better too.

I had fewer worries *here*. I had no imposing kingship, no terrible father, no dead mother, and no constant pressure to be the best and most adept at all the things I did. I was just Arthur. Not *Prince Arthur of Camelot, Heir to the High King of Britain. Not Arthur who is not good enough to carry the Pendragon name. Not Arthur, the poor boy who was probably cursed by a pixie at birth and is now so completely insane that he will likely lead our country into a state of turmoil and ruin.*

I liked *here*. I liked America. It was more suited to my thoughts and my interests I suppose. Even though I knew that no one would ever come to understand or believe my insanity of *here and there*, I still felt much more comfortable *here*. I was not a failure. In fact, I often received the best scores in the seventh grade in pre-algebra, and the coach had asked my foster parents to sign me up to play football year-round like Ty did and they had let me. I could do my drawings instead of being lectured by Father Patricius about my lack of ability in Latin. This was where I belonged.

Not to say that there were not things I liked about *there*. I liked Lancelot. After all, he was my best friend. I liked that people were less particular about things. If you happened to accidentally do something imperfectly, it was generally forgotten, although that could just be a characteristic of my nobility and therefore my rank-given respect. I suppose if you misused someone's title, such as calling them an Earl when they were a Duke, they might be fairly upset, but in America, as I found out from Ty, if you called someone colored or Negro instead of African-American or Mexican instead of Latino, people would be very offended. And none of these titles were really even titles. They were just an extremely complicated system to be "politically correct".

*****

Colorado Springs, America, 2009

My seventh grade year finished out fine. Uneventfully, if you will. I made A's in all my classes, and I went out for track and received second place on our team in the shot put. I even turned in one of my drawings, one of a bright blue house with white trim and a metal roof, to the school art show fundraiser and someone bought it for twenty-five dollars. Band went well and I signed up to play again in eighth grade. I enjoyed most of the members' company because most of them seemed more focused on school than trivial things.

I found out that Miss Adams did *not* whack her students with a stick based on the number of tallies they had, unlike Ty and Helix had led me to believe. Rather, the number showed up on the bottom of your report card at the end of the year along with a note from your dominant teacher about your behavior. I had three tallies and the Ector's seemed proud of this, even though I had still obviously been caught misbehaving three times which meant I had been imperfect. Although, compared with Ty's whopping sixty-two marks, I suppose I could not complain so much.

Summertime in America was two things: hot and dry. Or maybe that was just Colorado. *There*, summertime was warm and soft, and it smelled of dew, honey, and sweaty men. *Here*, it smelled of freshly cut grass, untempted air, and food sizzling on a barbeque. American summer was like a fast-moving train that began its journey the day school let out and found its destination when the new school year began. While on this journey, everything moved so quickly yet so lazily that it seemed as if time had stopped in an unannounced dimension where one day faded quietly into the next and nights were like long blinks of wide eyes.

*****

Camelot, Britain, 646

I went back to see Viviane every other day after our first meeting.

The day we met, the patrol had eventually gotten itself back in order, however by that time it was much too late to finish the patrol without staying the night, and we had not had the proper supplies for that. So we had decided to do the planned journey the next day and headed home. Kay and Bedivere had said nothing to me on the way back. Lionel had noticed this but had said nothing to either of the two parties.

Lancelot and I decided that Merlin should live in a very tall, unused tower at the western end of the palace. We had always called the tower the Wizard's Tower after all. This was because the only things that lived in it were rats and some unusually large spiders and my father always said that people with magic were no good. The three of us went up the tower's long, spiral staircase one day with brooms in hand. We swept away all the cobwebs and dust and unknown, dead, furry creatures.

Gawain, we found stumbling out of the city tavern during a trip into town on a journey to find a new belt for Lancelot.

"Is that...?" Lancelot asked me as we meandered along the dirt road, every so often leaping out of the way of trampling horse hooves.

I squinted to get a better look. As I mentioned before, it seemed my eyesight was not as good as others. As we came closer, a dark mass began to form into a shock of wavy black hair. Light skin began to mold into chiseled features and deep black eyes. The oversized black tunic that he always wore flowed around his body like water. A silver dagger glittered at his hip. I wondered where he had gotten it.

"Gawain," I affirmed, and we walked quietly up to his side.

Gawain said that the owner of the tavern had offered him a room in exchange for his help around the facilities and retrieving things. Gawain had agreed and had been staying in the inn for a good month and a half, since my father's men had taken back Cadbury Castle that awful night.

We told Gawain about Merlin and he did not seem as interested or enthusiastic about us meeting a Druid as one may have thought. In fact, the only thing he really seemed interested in talking about was himself. Apparently, he had slain a griffin with only the dagger at his side, which he had stolen from Saxon invaders. The men in the tavern had been so amazed when Gawain had regaled them with his tales of valor. A thirteen-year-old boy slaying a griffin was a most impressive story. It was all I could do to keep my mouth shut about how I had killed a dragon the year before. When I was only *twelve,* I might add.

As for Viviane.

I cared about Viviane more than I had ever cared for anyone in my life. She felt like the breath in my lungs and the blood in my veins. What I continued to fight for, to live for, was to please her. To simply talk with her, or stare at her beautiful face and vibrant body was all I wanted.

"What is living on the Isle of Avalon like?" I asked her one afternoon as we sat on the white pebbled shore together and stared out into the misty abyss of the lake.

"It is very quiet," she said thoughtfully and cocked her head in the way that she always did. I smiled at this. It had been three months since we had first seen each other and we had learned each other's habits fairly well. "People do not like to talk so much."

"Oh." I looked out at a weeping willow tree that was gracing the surface of the water with its drooping branches. I wondered if maybe they only did not like to talk to Viviane because of her strangeness. I felt that people did that to me sometimes. "I am sorry."

"It can be very peaceful…" she trailed off, almost having said her piece as a question. "What is it like living in that big castle?"

"Well, I…" I played with a stone in my hand and then threw it out to the lake as hard as I could, "there are too many people, and they all expect too many things from me. They also…I think they think that something is wrong with me."

"I think I know what you mean." She gave a half-hearted smile and gazed out to the island and her home. "You know Arthur…I," she looked at me very closely, "I do not think anything is wrong with you."

I grinned and tried to force my smile down and look serious. It did not work so well, however, and her thoughtful features melted into happiness as mine had done.

"In fact, I think things are quite right with you," she told me. Her foggy blue eyes met mine. I lost myself in her eyes. I wanted to wrap my arms around her and bring her into my chest and hold her. I wanted her to be mine so I could be with her forever.

I settled on grabbing her hand and savoring the way its coolness was absorbed into my own much bigger palm. It was like electricity, her touch. Great flashing bolts of white lightning jolting up through my fingertips and the lines on my palm, all shooting at light speed to my heart, heating my core and bringing strength to my muscles. All from holding her hand. If only more could happen.

The same day that I had held Viviane's hand, Lancelot, Merlin, and I brought our supper of bread, cheese, and watered down wine, all wrapped in a cloth, to the palace gardens.

We sat down in a small grassy area that was hidden with overgrown bushes. Lancelot spread the cloth and the food out, and I ate hungrily.

"You do know that training was canceled today for that trial, right?" Lancelot asked me as he observed the amount of food I was scarfing down.

"Mhmm," I said through a mouthful of bread, "I ran six miles today."

"Where to?" he asked. I had not told them about Viviane, instead always finding excuses to scamper off to Avalon, such as training being canceled.

"Avalon," I said absentmindedly and took a drink of wine from our shared wineskin.

Merlin scowled at me, "What were you doing there?"

"Visiting someone," I said simply.

Merlin continued to shoot nasty looks at me. He asked, "And who, on Avalon, would be willing to commune with *you*?"

I felt the sudden urge to put him in his place. I remembered his adoration of her. "Viviane."

His eyes flared with anger. "As if Viviane would even consider spending time with the son of Uther Pendragon."

It was my turn to expel my wicked glare upon Merlin.

Lancelot defended me, "You know it is not his fault."

Merlin said nothing and continued to silently curse me with his eyes.

We ate silently for the rest of dinner. Then we went to our respective chambers and processed the events from the day.

I lay in bed and stared up at the white canopy above me. A chill ran through my body even though it was summer and I pulled the furs and wool blankets past my stomach and my chest to my chin.

I thought about Viviane. I wanted her to be here with me. I wanted her to be with me forever.

*****

Near Colorado Springs, America, 2009

Riding down a raging river on a plastic circle inflated with air from my lungs was a new experience altogether.

Ty, Helix, and I had all managed to get thirty dollars from our parents, my foster parents, and we had gone down to the big department store and purchased black and red inner tubes. Then Miss Marion had driven us down to the mountain river in the woods and had told us to make sure not to hurt ourselves. She changed into a lavender swimsuit, set up a blue lawn chair, slathered herself with suntan lotion, and set out to sunbathe with a couple other women who were supervising younger children playing in the shallows of the river.

"Are you guys sure this is a good idea?" I asked, clad in my green swim shorts. I looked tentatively at the flowing water, holding the inner tube in the crook of my left arm. The hot Colorado sun beat down on my bare back and I enjoyed the golden light upon me. Swimming in the still waters of lakes and pools was one thing, swimming against the current of a river was something completely different.

"'Course," Ty assured me, "been doing it since I was six."

That sounded like when Ty told me that he had broken into the graveyard thousands of times.

"He's right, Arthur," Helix agreed. "We'll be fine. Long as you can swim, you'll be okay."

I could swim, but I still was not sure of myself. The current looked awfully fast and the water awfully deep.

"Come on," Ty said to us and stepped into the shallows of the river. I swallowed and followed him and Helix up to my knees. I set the inner tube on the surface and it was pulled with the current so I had to hold it tightly. The current tugged at the blonde leg hair that had developed on me, and I shivered for a moment even though the water was not cold and the air must have been above ninety.

Ty and Helix began to walk further out into the water while I stayed with my feet planted. I was afraid that the current would knock me over and sweep me away. Then I would be forced under the cool liquid and the world would slowly begin to fade above me as I gradually was unable to breathe. The thought of wading any farther out scared me.

"What are you waiting for bro?" Helix called to me.

Arthur, you tackled the leader of the Saxons. You have fought with some of the best soldiers that have ever lived. You have killed a dragon for goodness sake! Granted, all of that was there, *but the point remains, you can get the heck out in that river and you will not die!*

"Coming!" I called out to him.

I began to wade out. I shivered again as the water rose above my hips and over my navel. Thankfully, I had grown an inch or so in the last month and I stood a bit taller than the two other boys, so when the water came to their necks, it only came to the top of my chest.

We held the inflated plastic rings in front of us. I asked, "How do we get up on them now?"

"You just gotta jump," Ty informed me, and with that, he sprung up from the bottom of the river and landed on his stomach on the side of the ring. We both laughed at his funny appearance. I grabbed the inner tube to keep it from being pulled away while he situated himself.

"You get up next Arthur," Helix commanded me. For some reason his command bothered me slightly. I said nothing of it.

"Okay," I answered, and I jumped up and grabbed the opposite side of the ring while Helix held it for me. The sunbaked plastic was hot on my abdomen in contrast to the cool water.

Then Helix jumped onto his own ring and we were at the mercy of the current. Fear shot through me. What if we were to collide with those sharp rocks on the other shore? What if we were tipped over and something like a branch were to hold us underwater so that we would not breathe? I tensed as I ran through the various bad possibilities in my head. While I did this, Helix and Ty screamed in excitement as the river hurled us like a great self-propelling road.

I held on tight to the thick plastic of the inner tube and kept my eyes wide, ready to fend off any possible dangers.

After we had been riding for about seven painstaking minutes, I asked my companions, "Where do we get off?"

"Just up here!" Ty yelled to me and pointed to a shore that looked as if it were covered in gray sand. "Then we can go again! This time with stunts!"

"Yeah…" I looked at the water that was carrying me quickly forward.

"You just gotta jump on off!" Ty informed us as he hopped off into the water.

I took a deep breath and slid off the warm plastic. The coolness and thickness of the water shocked me, and a jolt went through my body as I was completely submerged. My hair flowed all around my head. I had to get to the surface. I could not breathe. I struggled with frantic movements to reach the surface. I caught the inner tube and I panted. My hair was slicked down the sides of my face. I was alright.

We all kicked our inner tubes to the shore and I sat on the dry, gray sand for a few minutes, sighing. I decided I did not like the water.

Chapter X

The Darkling Forest, outside Camelot, Britain, 646

Summer in Camelot, unlike in America, went by like any other season; it just happened to be warmer. The same patrols were run, the same training exercises, the same terrible Latin lessons, the same war. Each day fading into the next like shades of gray drawn with the side of a pencil. It was all the same, that is, until the annual August capture the flag exercise.

Capture the flag was a game that my grandfather had brought over from Rome and it had become a traditional training exercise. We either played it in the forest just north of Camelot or the troops commandeered the palace and played throughout the towers. In August, we played it in the woods because it was usually nice and sunny out and, therefore, we did not have to worry about things getting ruined.

So, we all headed out to the forest, all thirty-two of us. That was all the men and boys of Camelot who were not off fighting in the war. Lionel and Kay were the captains. That was how desperate we were for men. Kay was second rank in fighting. If it had been up to me, I would have chosen Kay's friend Bedivere to be captain, at least he was sometimes nice to me.

Lancelot and I stood next to each other with the other twenty-eight boys under the cool shade of the trees of the forest. Kay and Lionel stood in front of the group holding their metal staffs in front of their bodies. Kay stood with his chin up, looking quite haughty. The worst part was that it seemed as if he were looking straight at me, almost as if to say, *I am better than you Arthur. Look, I am captain and you are not.*

Lionel announced the rules of the game and how he and Kay would pick who would be on their teams. Then he offered Kay first pick. As predicted, he chose Bedivere and Bedivere went to stand next to him. I had a looming feeling that Lancelot and I would be picked close to last, or worst of all, on separate teams. So, surprise struck me when Lionel called my name first.

I walked to his side and he smiled at me and patted my shoulder which was now only a couple inches below his own.

The picking continued, and Lionel did pick Lancelot, thank goodness. I would not be alone. Towards the dwindling end of the supply of boys, Lionel picked someone named Perceval. I had never met Perceval before, even though he looked about my age. Maybe his father had gone to fight in the war and he was being fostered here in Camelot. That was a common occurrence.

Once everyone was picked, the teams followed their captains to their respective bases to collect capes and banners in their team's colors. Lionel's team was yellow, so we all put on an ugly, urine colored cape, and were given time to socialize while Lionel formulated a strategy.

The yellow base was basically a large stone bowl with jagged sides making up the edges. Moss lined everything, blending it almost completely with the forest. Crevices in the jagged sides made storage areas for spare weapons, food, and other supplies. Lancelot and I sat down with our legs crossed, alone in a corner watching the men mill around and struggle to fasten capes to their shoulders.

Perceval walked up to Lancelot and me. We just watched him, calculating. We both stood up as he approached.

"Hello," he said. I noticed that he was two inches taller than me, and that bothered me.

"Hello," I replied, tilting my chin up ever so slightly.

"My name is Perceval," he said, not knowing that I already knew his name. "I figured I had best introduce myself to you since you were first pick."

"Ah," I said as if I knew exactly what I was doing.

"So what is your name?" he prompted me, obviously annoyed at my lack of niceties.

"Arthur," I told him. Then arrogantly, "Arthur *Pendragon*."

"My lord," he bowed his head slightly to me. Lancelot elbowed me in the ribs. Usually, I would never use my title to make myself look better; I just felt a bit insecure around Perceval for some reason.

"Mhmm," I replied. Lancelot elbowed me again and I punched him in the arm. "Nice to meet you, Perceval."

"We better go get our capes," Lancelot motioned to the boy who was handing out the atrocious yellow capes. "Coming Perceval?"

I saw Perceval smile at Lancelot's including him. Usually, it was me who introduced new people to our friendships. This bothered me too. Part of it may have been self-doubt. I was afraid that if Lancelot made another friend, then he might not be friends with me anymore. But that was silly; I must keep these thoughts out of my head.

We each received a cape from the light-haired boy who was handing them out and Lancelot fastened mine and Perceval's. Lancelot was always the best with clips and ties. The yellow, as predicted, looked dreadful with our brown tunics, but it was Lionel's color, so we had to cope.

"Gather 'round!" Lionel yelled to all the boys at the base.

We formed a semicircle around him to listen to the strategy that he had decided upon.

"We are going to be almost exclusively defensive," Lionel explained, "so we will have almost everyone guarding the base. Three of us will be invading the blue team and retrieving their flag."

"Who will be the three on offense?" a large, stocky boy asked. I knew that his name was Alb, and that he was incredibly strong even though he was only fifteen.

"I was just getting to that," Lionel explained. "Arthur, Perceval, and I will be the offense. The rest of you will be the defense."

I looked at Lancelot and he shrugged. Perceval was grinning at me. *Oh, joy.* All I could think of was that Perceval was going to screw it up. After all, how much experience could he have if he had just come to Cadbury Castle?

Lionel went on to give everyone their posts. Perceval and I walked up to where Lionel was standing and stood next to him. After Lionel finished speaking to everyone, he turned to us.

"You are fine being offense, right?" he asked us.

We nodded.

"Great!" Lionel clapped his hands together. He seemed to have caught on to my slight aversion to Perceval and was smiling nervously. "I thought the three of us would be a great team. Perceval works mace, Arthur sword, and me staff. That way we can be diverse."

I shrugged, "How do you know Perceval?"

"He is my brother," Lionel told me. I looked at the two of them. Lionel's tan skin and curly blonde hair, Perceval's short, dark straight hair and pale skin. Lionel was average height for being twenty-one, but Perceval was as tall as Lionel and he was probably only thirteen or fourteen. They looked nothing alike.

I just looked at Lionel and raised my eyebrows.

"Adopted brother," Lionel clarified. "My father was good friends with his. When Perceval's father…passed, he went to live with my mother in Cornwall where I am from."

I nodded, processing the information. When Lionel's mother had died a couple of months ago, Perceval must have been forced to move to Cadbury Castle. He had probably gotten here only about a week ago which explained why I had not seen him before.

We sat down in a small, three person circle on the mossy stone ground and Lionel explained the strategy he had come up with to us.

I would sneak in through the back of their base and grab the flag while he and Perceval came in from the front to cause a distraction. Once Perceval and Lionel got free of the tiff they would likely be in with Kay's men, I would trade the real flag with Lionel for a blue tunic. Lionel and Perceval would then hide in a small cave that they knew about way in the back of the forest where Kay would probably not have anyone on guard. Then, when I had the attention of the blue defense, I would climb a tree with the flag and wait the night out. When all the men had gathered around the tree to wait me out, Lionel and Perceval would slip back to our own base undetected, and thus, win the game.

When Lionel finished explaining, Perceval and I nodded in understanding and submission and glanced at each other as if we were sizing the other up.

We heard the *dong* of the silver bell call out over the forest signaling the start of the game. The rest of the boys went to their posts around the base and around the bright yellow flag that stood in the center of the stone bowl.

"Ready?" Lionel asked us.

"Ready!" Perceval said cheerfully. I glared at him. People should not sound that cheerful.

"Mhmm," I answered and patted Caliburnus at my side. I noticed Perceval had a large, mounted, metal mace in his left hand. He was left-handed as well, such a surprise. Left-handed people only added to the lack of structure and uniformity of the human race. I suppose one could say that variation was good, and I agreed in terms of race and personality. However, when there were right- and left-handed people it made it so that some things had to be made two ways and that was just plain inefficient.

Lionel nodded, still gauging my demeanor, and stood up. "Do you have the things you need?"

"My sword," I answered, drawing it from its scabbard.

Perceval held up his mace.

The mace was bronze, which was quite interesting, most often steel or gold was used. The Greeks used to make their weapons out of bronze. Maybe he was Greek and it had been passed down to him. That would make sense based on his very dark hair and fair skin.

"For Britain," Lionel chanted softly.

"For Britain," Perceval echoed.

I said nothing.

Britain was my father's country.

Sprinting through greenery while the world blurred around you and adrenaline turned your blood into liquid energy was a most amazing and horrifying experience. I loved it. All I felt was clean, thick, refreshing air filling my lungs and being expelled through my mouth in wheezes of sticky panting. I knew that sweat formed on my arms and soaked through my tunic, but it felt like raindrops with the air rushing by my running figure. My cape flew behind me like an ugly yellow banner, proudly displayed in a show of defiance. The blue flag was bunched in my left hand which did not hold a sword. It felt wet. And sticky.

Urine.

They had pissed on the flag.

My eyes searched my surroundings for Lionel so I could pass the contaminated flag to him. The smell caught up to me and it burned my nose hairs. My dislike of Kay increased dramatically due to his disgusting battle strategy and his inherent lack of hygiene.

I saw a flash of yellow behind a thick sycamore tree and I aimed my sprint toward it, knowing that it was Lionel who was waiting for me.

I handed him the soiled flag and he nodded to me, shoving the blue tunic at me and immediately sprinting off in the direction that I had been running. I doubled back, holding the tunic so the blue could be seen, listening carefully to the trampling feet of Kay's men running after me.

I looked rapidly around me for a decent climbing tree, anything with broad low branches that I could pull myself up on without too much trouble.

I saw it: a huge field maple tree with an immense amount of lush green leaves and thick branches showing that it was healthy enough to hold my weight.

I jumped as high as I could and thankfully caught the lowest branch, my fingers straining to wrap around the rough bark. I used all my strength to pull my body up with my arms so I could hook my leg around the branch and pull up to a seated position. From there, I carefully stood up, supporting myself by leaning against the trunk and grabbed the next branch which was at chest height. I pulled myself up to a standing position on that branch and looked down. I was only about ten feet off the ground. The branches were more tightly woven up here and the tree would be easily scaled from here. I looked up and saw a place where I could comfortably sit and wait for either one of the blue team to climb the tree and harass me or for Lionel and Perceval to win the game.

I heard the sound of boys panting and feet pounding against the forest floor. I tried my best to quiet my heavy breathing from my sprint, but it was still audible.

"I saw him go this way Bedivere!" I heard Kay's voice say in frustration. "I swear I saw him!"

"Well, he is not here!" Bedivere said back. "You probably just imagined that you saw him."

"I do not imagine things!" Kay said harshly. I could almost picture him smirking. "Although he certainly does. I swear that boy does not have his head on straight."

I gritted my teeth and gripped the branch I was holding harder. I wanted nothing more than to draw my sword and run some sense into Kay.

"Probably from the witch he has been lying with," Bedivere snickered.

My chest was so tight I thought it would burst open and my stomach churned with hot lava. Rage pulsated through my body and I twisted awkwardly trying to compensate. I wanted to yell and swear and fight them. Talking about my insanity was one thing, I had grown used to that since my terrible decision to tell about my American escapades. Talking about Viviane, whom I had only held hands with, as a witch that I merely saw to sleep with was something completely different.

I accidentally broke a slim branch from the tightness of my fist. My eyes widened nervously and I sat completely still.

"Bed' did you hear that?" Kay asked quickly, hearing my sound.

"I did," Bedivere answered.

"It had to be Arthur," Kay breathed.

I hoped with all my heart they did not look up.

They looked up.

"Get down from there!" Kay yelled at me. Then, catching a glimpse of the blue fabric, "And give us back our flag!"

"The flag you *pissed* on?!" I questioned angrily. One, because of frustration. Two, to give Lionel more time.

"Well, we thought it would keep you away!" Kay said spitefully. "I suppose you do not notice though after the filth you have been in company with! What was his name? Merlin?"

"Shut up, Kay," my voice was incredibly low with my anger, my voice deepening in general, and my fight to keep high-pitched cracks out of it.

"Do we need to shoot at you?" he sneered at me. "Give it up, you have been caught! Now give us back our flag!"

"I have not been caught until I give up! And I have no intention of doing so!" My anger invaded my senses. "Unlike you with that dragon!"

"You bastard…" Kay glared daggers at me.

"What dragon?" Bedivere asked, curious.

"You say one word and I swear—" Kay's words were cut off as a flash of orange and yellow light cascaded into our vision like a waterfall.

The leaves of my tree caught fire and I heard an ominous crackling sound. Tongues of flame licked up at me and I felt their heat through my tunic.

I had no choice but to jump.

So jump I did.

To my surprise, I felt a body cushion my fall, and arms, a leather tunic, and the hardness of a metal staff pressed against my body.

Kay had caught me.

A giant flaming bird appeared out of the fiery mountain that had once been my hiding place. Its pastel orange and yellow wings must have spanned ten feet, and red and blue feathery tendrils of fire made up its long tail. The body of the beast was sheer, burnt golden light, burning our eyes with its bright glory. The bird was like a sunbeam cascading into a dark room, although the room was not dark, and the sunbeam was too much.

159

"Phoenix," I heard Bedivere whisper softly as Kay pushed me away from his body, feeling the need to cement the fact that he still did, in fact, hate me.

I carefully drew Caliburnus from its place on my belt and held it weakly in front of myself. The bird's eyes were fiery balls of light like on the Fourth of July *there*, they were bursting in my eyes, hypnotizing me with their silent explosions.

I looked at Kay. He was frozen at the sight of the magnificent creature. I kicked his shin and his reflexes managed to function and he kicked me back, then moved his metal staff defensively in front of his body. Bedivere clutched the staff of his spiked mace to his chest.

The bird's eyes continued to stay fixated on us as if we were an extremely interesting form of entertainment. One wrong step and it would expel waves of fire upon us. How could we fight it if it could incinerate us in seconds?

Its powerful wings flapped less and it landed on two thin, crimson legs. The leaves around it caught fire and others roasted and turned to a dead brown color.

"What do we do?" Bedivere asked without taking his eyes off of the phoenix.

I waited for an answer that Kay was not going to give.

Bedivere was asking me.

"W-well," I gauged our surroundings; broad trunked deciduous trees, a brownish green forest floor, and— I listened carefully. I heard the faintest trickling of water in the far distance. A tiny stream, maybe our one chance of not being burned alive like heretics and witches.

I looked in the direction of the sound of the water and thought quickly. My thoughts raced like a thousand horses, all edging the others out in order for the chance to receive first place, to be the winner.

Water put out fire, I knew that much, and that was why my interests had been immediately sparked when I heard the stream. I also knew that water could be absorbed. One time in physical science class in America, we had done a lab project in which we tested the absorbency of water with different materials by measuring how far the water rose on the material when one end was inserted into a glass. We had used a dry cloth as one of the materials. The blue decoy tunic was still clutched tight in my left hand; *it* was made of cloth.

"On my count of three, we run," I whispered, having apparently assumed the leadership role in our threesome of nerve-wracked boys.

They both nodded to me and, despite the fear welling up in my throat, I felt a sense of pleasure come from their subordination and respect for me.

"One…" I pointed toward the sound of the stream so they would know which direction to run. "Two…" I took a deep breath, preparing myself for the pounding sprint I was about to do. "Three!"

And then we ran. Adrenaline fueling our legs that were hitting the ground like horses galloping into battle. Our arms pumped with every step we took as if we were boxing some invisible being that stood a few feet out of our reach.

The river was closer than I expected. I did not even stop to make sure that the phoenix had followed us. I cast the dry tunic into the tiny stream and shoved it under the light flow of water with the toe of my boot. Once I was satisfied that it was thoroughly sopping with liquid, I picked it up, incurring a waterfall down the front of my tunic that cooled my hot chest.

I turned back in the direction from where we had come. The phoenix stood, as expected, watching us, almost as if it were curious of us rather than as if it had a violent desire for our deaths.

Without another thought, I threw the wet tunic on the great bird's side and it sizzled like raw meat on a hot griddle. The phoenix cawed the most brilliantly terrifying sound I had ever heard, and its eyes flashed pure white as the flaming feathers on its side were doused, revealing exposed pink skin. My opportunity had arisen.

I lunged forward while the phoenix still screamed in pain at the wetting of its flame, and I plunged my sword into the skin that had been made visible after the disappearance of the feathery fire.

I expected some sort of blood to gush or ooze out onto my sword and myself as had happened with the dragon when I pierced its armor, but none did. With a great burst of blinding white light, the phoenix's body was lifted into the air by some unseen force and my sword fell to the ground. Then the body exploded into gray ash like the eruption of a volcano and a small something fell to the burnt ground.

I tucked my still clean sword back into my belt and looked at Bedivere and Kay who were staring at me in awe. They were standing in the stream as if it would have saved them from the flames of the phoenix.

I looked at the small something that had fallen to the ground when the body had exploded. At first glance, it looked like an orange marble. I picked it up and felt its surprisingly heavy weight in my palm. Dim orange and red light swirled around inside the sphere. Its exterior felt like warm glass and I was afraid that if I dropped it, it would break and whatever was flowing inside of it would scatter, seeping into the ground to rain upon the roots of the trees.

"Arthur I—" Bedivere stepped toward me and dipped his head down ever so slightly so I was taller, "I am sorry I ever doubted you."

Kay just nodded curtly. To me, that meant so much more than Bedivere's words. He was acknowledging that I was worthy of his respect, that we might one day even be friends and get along and consider each other's thoughts and ideas like allies instead of adversaries.

We all heard the bell ring loudly. The game was over. Lionel must have gotten the flag back to our base.

I just looked from Kay to Bedivere and back again, trying to decide what to do. Finally, figuring that I was still in the position of leadership I said, "We best go back to the meeting place then."

"Yes," Bedivere agreed.

I tucked the spherical object in the side of my breeches under my trousers and we began to walk in a quiet line of three back to the central area halfway between the two bases. When we were just a few minutes from emerging into the area crowded with blue and yellow clad boys, Kay spoke to me.

"Arthur."

"Yes?" I answered.

"You should train with Bed' and me sometime. You might get better practice than with Lancelot."

And even though he was completely degrading my best friend, it still made me smile. Maybe I was finally going to be accepted by people that were not misfits among most of the palace community. And for that I was happy.

Chapter XI

Colorado Springs, America, 2009

Eighth grade was really no different than seventh grade.

We received different teachers and different classes and things, but the general structure was still completely the same aside from the fact that now my daily schedule went band, biology, algebra, language arts, history.

"Hello!" Mr. George boomed as he shut the door to his classroom.

Nobody responded. The entire class just stared at the tall, bald man in anticipation for him to start class for the first time.

"You have a seating chart!" he said enthusiastically.

The entire class groaned. Seating charts were the worst because you might get put next to someone who never paid any attention, someone who paid too much attention, or someone who smelled.

I looked at Ty, who shrugged. Language arts was the only class that we had together, and it was terrible that now we might not even be able to sit together. We walked to the side of the classroom and stood against it with the rest of the students waiting for our new seats.

I looked around the room anxiously for anyone that I could hope to be seated next to; someone with whom I could get along. There were a few boys from the football team that looked tolerable. The rest of the people in class either annoyed me or did not register as positive or negative in my mind.

If I Could Tell It

The worst part about middle school was that everybody knew everybody. This might not seem like a detriment because you knew the names and personalities of the people in your classes, but it also meant that everyone also had an established niche in the school pecking order, something I found out was very real after a year in America. Even though there were not official ranks like in Britain, there was a very obvious social hierarchy at school. Especially with the girls.

With girls, it was not about who was the prettiest, the smartest, or even the wealthiest that had the most power; it seemed that whichever of them was the meanest triumphed. I found this incredibly interesting. Whichever girl could manage to exclude and emotionally knock down the most other girls won in some twisted way, perhaps choosing which six got the privilege of sitting at the center lunch table. At the moment, this girl was Claire Woods.

I mention this because Mr. George put me right behind her in our desk rows.

Even I had to admit that Claire was pretty. And even though that was not a contribution to her rank in the girl hierarchy, everyone still noticed. She had perfectly straight, caramel colored hair that fell just below her shoulders and had sharp blonde streaks at the bottom. She was model thin, which I ordinarily would not have appreciated if not for her face. Her face was sharp and cunning, yet with feminine softness, set into perfect, tanned skin. She always dressed quite suggestively as well, which only contributed to this perception. Her hair always smelled of overly ripe strawberries, as if she bathed in jam.

She was also mean. Incredibly mean. I did not like her one bit.

In seventh grade, Claire had taken a picture of a girl named Phoebe, who had apparently "stolen" her boyfriend, in the locker room with no clothes on and sent it to our entire seventh grade class. Then she had shown it to the principal and told him that Phoebe was sending nudes to all the boys in our grade and needed to be punished. To top it off, she had posted on her Facebook account that she had heard Phoebe was pregnant and that was why she had left school. Phoebe did not come back to Carmel this year.

I almost admired the strategy it took to pull something like that off. However, in my opinion, the social hierarchy of girls in middle school was much more complex than it probably should have been. I was very glad I was a boy.

Behind me there was a new boy whom Mr. George introduced as Kaiden Brockelle.

Before he even sat down, I could tell he was a little too full of himself. Perfectly cut, short dark hair sat on top of a pale face completely covered in freckles. Tight lips resided under an upturned nose and dark eyes that confidently scanned the class.

"The first half of the year we will be studying sentence structure and doing book groups," Mr. George announced with fervor. He was diving straight into the material, unlike the other teachers who wasted quite a lot of time introducing themselves and their teaching methods. I liked that he was going quickly into the curriculum, but I did not like how overly enthusiastic he was.

He passed papers to each of the rows and we all received one. "This is your syllabus. I expect it signed and returned by the beginning of next week. I suggest you actually read it before you and your parents sign it."

"We are going to start with sentence structure," he explained, "but first I want you to get to know the people around you for a few minutes. *Around you.* That means don't get out of your seat."

I rolled my eyes at his inefficient explanation.

166

I felt a tap on my shoulder and I quickly spun around to face Kaiden who was staring at me expectantly, a little bit like he was watching a zoo animal. "Hi."

"Hi…" I said with a curt wave. I resisted the urge to roll my eyes and turn back around. I needed to make some allies in this class besides Ty and the few boys that I knew from football.

"My name's Kaiden." He smiled at me.

I obviously already know what your name is because the teacher just introduced you to our entire class. Are you completely stupid? "Arthur."

"Do you know Helix?" Kaiden asked. "I started going to his church, he said one of his friends was Arthur."

I nodded.

"What's your favorite class so far?" he asked me. Now he was just trying to make conversation.

"Algebra," I answered laconically. I decided to try and stay as quiescent as possible in order to get him to stop talking to me.

"I think I have geometry at the same time you have algebra," Kaiden said, thinking for a moment. "I saw you coming out of Mr. Jefferson's room when I came out of Mrs. Henry's."

"Okay," I said, keeping my brevity.

After a few more moments of awkward conversation, Mr. George put a sentence on the overhead projector and told us to diagram it.

We had done sentence diagramming last year in language arts. I was never very good at it. For some reason, the patterns displayed in grammar were never as easy to understand as the patterns in math.

After we were all done, Mr. George came around to check our work, and no surprise, he said mine was wrong and suggested I ask someone for help. Kaiden immediately tapped me on the shoulder.

"I can help you," Kaiden said. "I got it right."

I wanted to tell him to shut up and never talk to me again because he was seriously beginning to piss me off, however, Mr. George was standing right next to us and had suggested I find some help.

"Okay, thanks," I said as good naturedly as possible through gritting my teeth.

After Kaiden had helped me, it was time to leave for the next period and he lined up right behind me at the door. I could feel his breath on my neck. He needed to back off.

"Hey, Arthur?" he asked.

"Yeah?" I said without turning to face him.

"If you ever need help with algebra, I can do it."

I had to use every single self-respecting fiber of my being not to backhand him at that very moment. How dare he insult me like that? Where everyone in the line could probably hear too! What have I done to deserve this leech?!

"I don't think so," I said sharply and shook my hair out with a little jerk.

Obviously, I was not the happiest when he sat down at our table during lunch. Or when he proceeded to be a part of my friend group every day from then on.

Football started up again after a couple days and I was even better this year since I had been playing on the club team with Ty all summer long. We won most of our games, all except one when most of our players were out sick with the stomach flu.

I went to school every day as I should and I did my homework and I practiced my trumpet and I went to football practice. I had lots of friends, and *frenemies* (Kaiden). My hobbies and my schoolwork came easily to me, therefore, life was easy. Or as easy as life could be when I was constantly wondering about the purpose of my existence in America and about things that were happening *there*.

I was always thinking, waiting, predicting that something to do with *there* would happen *here*. Something, *anything*, to explain it all. To explain either why I was insane or why I was apparently time traveling every single night of my life while I slept. Nothing came though, nothing ever came. One day was just like the next. I was constantly in a state of hopefulness. Hope that something in my life would finally make sense, anything to explain my otherworldly thoughts and existence.

*****

Arthur

I won the sword event in the winter solstice tournament when I was thirteen.

To the crowd, it seemed that my father congratulated me, was even proud of me, perhaps appreciative that I was his son. But that was only to the crowd. The few times that I spoke to him after were only when he called me to ask me what had gone on with the patrols. Lionel had been sent off to war in September and he had convinced my father to appoint me to organize and set up the patrols. It was a bittersweet goodbye, mine and Lionel's. He had been almost like the father figure I never had over the previous summer, teaching me about the ways of the world and helping me through the crisis of my mother's passing. I had a feeling that he would come back though. Somehow, I just knew. We would be together again and, someday, he would advise me on my most important decisions.

My like for Viviane turned into love.

I still craved to one day hold her and be a complete part of her existence, to be impossibly close. Now it was something different though, something powerful. I just loved to be with her, to talk with her, to simply sit next to her on the shore of Avalon and gaze into the lake. She was so blissfully unique, so absolutely wonderful. She understood me, made me feel valid. I even told her about America and she did not tell me that I was making it up. She did not tell me that I was insane. She merely considered it and said that she was sorry that I was forced to go through with it but that there must be some reason that I would quite probably find out eventually in my life.

*****

The Lake of Avalon, Britain, 647

I went to her the night of my fourteenth birthday and we sat and stared as the sun cast its auburn glow, masked by the dull mist, upon the lake.

"Arthur?" she said to me as she laced her thin fingers through my right hand that was considerably bigger than hers.

"Yes?" I asked.

"Nimue says that she is going to die soon."

I had found out that Nimue was the current Lady of the Lake, and that she was Viviane's mentor on her way to becoming the next Lady of Avalon. Nimue had also meddled a bit in my conception. When my mother was still married to Morgain's father, Gorlois, my father fell in love with her from afar. When Gorlois had died in the war, my father saw it as a chance to go after his wife. With Nimue's help, he had disguised himself as Gorlois and had gone into the manor at night before my mother found out about the death of her husband. Using a magic charm (my father, being a hypocrite and using magic even though he killed people for it) I was conceived when my father, disguised as her husband, convinced her to sleep with him. Four months later, once my mother was well aware of her pregnancy, my father summoned her to Cadbury Castle where he explained the whole story and married her. Now, Morgain resented Ygraine for allowing Uther to take advantage of her so soon after Gorlois's death in my father's war.

"I am sorry," I said, frowning. "I suppose that means that you are to become the Lady of Avalon now."

"I suppose it does," she sighed. "I wish that we could run off into the forest and not have to worry about our responsibilities anymore."

"Me too," I agreed and gave a harsh little laugh. Oh, how much I wanted that.

"Someday you are going to be king, Arthur," she said abruptly, "and I am going to be the Lady of Avalon."

"Someday," I whispered. Then cynically, "I doubt soon though. My father will never leave me his land willingly. He thinks that I am an insane idiot."

"But if you are to be king and I am to be the Lady of the Lake..." Viviane leaned against my side and fireworks went off in my head. I carefully put my arm around her, feeling excited, yet as if I were walking on eggshells, as if one move too far and our relationship would be destroyed. "Well, the High King of Britain and the Lady of the Lake are always enemies."

"It will not be that way with us though," I told her firmly. "Viviane, I..."

I had to think about what I was about to say carefully, too carefully. I meant it with all my heart though. I could not break my passion.

"What is it?" she asked sweetly.

"Viviane, someday I want to marry you."

"Oh, Arthur..." My heart dropped from my throat to the pit of my stomach. "Arthur..."

I looked at the ground with a sudden, great interest.

"I want that too." Her eyebrows were furrowed and my heart was lifted even though I knew that she was not

171

finished speaking. "But I cannot be your queen. You know that."

"Why not?" I asked, more frustrated than anything. My perfect future of having a wife that understood me was crumbling into dust like a brick dropped onto cement from five thousand feet.

She just looked at me and we locked eyes for a long while, my arm still around her. Then she looked away to the lake and I stared at the side of her head

"I think you know why not," she said finally.

I swallowed and threw a milky white pebble out to the lake in hatred at my realization that I did, in fact, know why not and that it was, in fact, a good reason.

"Arthur," she moved a lock of blonde hair out of my eyes, "someday you will marry a beautiful woman, and you will love her so much more than you love me. You will be happy."

I shook my head as if in disbelief. I loved Viviane, and I loved her because she understood me so well. I did not believe that I would ever find another female such as her, such that understood my predicament of *here* and *there*, such that appreciated my unique ideas and perceptions of the world around me.

"Will you still visit me?" she asked me softly, in a barely audible whisper. "Now that you know this."

"Yes Viviane, I will."

As much as I wanted Viviane's approval, to know that she thought me a worthy husband—the approval that she had failed to give me—I wanted her company even more. Even being at her side was breathtaking, talking to someone with whom I could finally indulge my deepest secrets. Even if I knew that it would not last.

*****

Colorado Springs, America, 2010

The unavoidable buzz of high school began in late March and became more and more prominent as the school year came to an end.

The high school, Harrison High School, was about a ten minute drive from the Ector's house and our school had toured it a couple of days ago to see where we were going and which classes we might want to take.

I had decided to take a drafting class and dropped band the moment I had seen the list of all the elective classes. It was almost exactly like my drawings and then I would learn how to actually make things that could potentially be used to instruct a builder. Plus, it counted as a math and art credit and could be used to apply for college scholarships.

I also decided that I would take Latin.

Of course, I hated Latin. However, because of the painstaking and terrible lessons *there* with Father Patricius, I had become almost fluent in the complicated language. Therefore, I figured it would be quite an easy class for me.

I finished filling out which classes I was planning to take and signed my name at the bottom of the sheet. Then I folded it in half and walked down the stairs. I set the orange paper on the kitchen counter for Miss Marion to sign and began to walk back up to the stairs. As I was leaving, Mr. Ector came into the room and immediately saw me.

"Arthur," he said to me and jerked his chin over toward the living room, "talk with me for a bit."

I nodded and followed him into the living room. I sat down on the couch and he sat in his recliner across from me. I was a little nervous around Mr. Ector, so I made sure to have especially good posture in front of him. I knew that he was in charge and was the master of the house I lived in *here*.

I looked at him expectantly, waiting for him to say his piece.

"Arthur," he said my name thoughtfully, as if feeling the way my name tasted on his tongue, "you have been living with Marion and me for a year and a half. That's a pretty long time in your life."

I bit the side of my cheek. I desperately hoped that this was not what I thought that it was. I knew that foster parents in America were generally temporary, as soon as the couple or family decided that their foster child was no longer right for them or they were tired of taking care of him or her, they simply passed them on to a new couple who would then take care of them. I had a terrible feeling in the pit of my stomach that I was to be "passed on" from the Ectors.

"Yes, sir," I agreed respectfully. I suppose that I was rejected by my own blood father *there*, why not by someone who I was not even actually related?

"Well, Marion and I think that it is time we had a conversation with you about it, or rather, I have a conversation with you about it," he explained. He furrowed his eyebrows as if thinking about how to phrase something.

"Yes, sir," I said again. Then looking down, "I understand."

"You do?" he asked, confused. "Did Marion already talk to you about this?"

"No, sir," I told him, "I just…"

"Do you not want us to adopt you?"

Adoption? That was not what I was expecting. Not at all. I was expecting him to gently tell me that they were giving me back. Adoption was something completely different. The fact that they wanted to discuss it with me meant that they accepted me. That maybe a family actually wanted me. And I realized that that was what I wanted as well. I wanted a family. Even after the destruction of my family *there*. It had been over a year since Morgain caused the death of my mother and I had barely spoken to my father in the months that followed. I was in dire need of support in my life and Mr. Ector was here handing it to me in the form of adoption papers.

"Yes, sir!" I said, uncharacteristically enthusiastic. I tried to force down my smile and my overly excited manner. I needed to be stoic and monotone. Strong. "I mean, I would like that very much, sir."

He smiled happily and nodded to himself. Then he stood up, having received the answer he was wishing for, and patted my shoulder. "I'm glad, Arthur. I really like you."

I swallowed my saliva and smiled. "Thank you, sir."

I resisted my *there*-given urge to bow to him and just sat on the couch for a minute after he left. I gave up trying to swallow down my grin and let it take over my face. I had a family again, a family that wanted me, perhaps even loved me. And the funny part was, because they did not know about *there* (and never would), they would never know just how much their adopting me meant. They would never understand how they had lifted my heart from the darkest depths of Hades to the base of the heavens. But what matters is that they did, and I knew.

*****

Cadbury Castle, Britain, 647

I found out I was to fight in the war when I was fourteen.

Of course, I always knew the day would come. It was unavoidable really. A fact of life that I had accepted. One day, I would be sent off to fight in my father's war and there was a fifty percent probability that the men would bring my body back on a long piece of fabric held together by sticks. And whether I died or not, my father would still have in his mind that I had failed.

It was June in Camelot, and since the rain had stopped its perpetual battering of the ground, we could train in the sunshine of the yard and admire the beauty of the flora on long walks through the forest. Viviane and I took to taking walks instead of only sitting by the lake. She always told me of what the things in the forest represented and why the Goddess had apparently placed them there. It really was interesting, learning about the complex rituals and belief system of the Druids and the Old Ways. It was a very strange way of looking at things, but then again, I believed that they should be able to follow their own beliefs, unlike my father.

While I was eating breakfast alone in my chambers, my father sent a message boy to summon me to his throne room. I looked up from my porridge a moment and motioned for the boy to speak. He told me my father's message, and I filled my mouth with porridge to avoid talking for a moment. He stood there, awkwardly, waiting for me to dismiss him.

"I will come," I said finally. Then I waved my hand toward the door. "You are dismissed."

The boy bowed and left, and I decided to finish the very large amount of food that had been brought to me very slowly in order to prolong the amount of time until I would have to speak with my father. Eventually, no matter how slowly I ate, the food still disappeared, and I no longer had an excuse to stall.

As I stood, I found myself with an uncomfortable pressure in my stomach; I had not realized how much I had eaten in order to avoid my father. I clutched my aching abdomen and walked to my wardrobe where I pulled on a bright blue, semiformal tunic over the thin undertunic that was draped over my body. Austin had not come to me today because he was visiting his aunt who was sick in Tintagel for a few weeks, and I had requested not to have any other servants attend me.

I looked at my reflection in the window behind my table. The back part of my hair was sticking almost straight up from the way I had slept, and my part was in a lopsided zigzag. I flipped my head down and back up; now all of my hair looked messy, almost like a show of rebellion to my father who had a certain dislike for my hair, the same with the rest of me.

I slid Caliburnus that was hanging from my bedpost into my belt. Its weight comforted me and reminded me of Viviane whom I loved. It made me confident, as if I could face whatever danger or hardship, almost as if Viviane were by my side.

"Father." I tilted my chin up as I threw open the large doors to the throne room, completely ignoring the guards who were supposed to open the doors for me. "You have called me to your presence?"

"I have," he affirmed haughtily, glaring at me from his throne. I noticed that the women who seemed to follow him were not attending him today.

I stared at him. It was he who had called me and he who would explain his reasoning.

"How old are you now?" he asked, looking up to the ceiling as if the answer were there. "Sixteen? Seventeen?"

I felt my mouth twitch. My father did not even remember how old I was. I growled, "Fourteen."

"Ah," his eyes rolled back dramatically and eventually his steely gaze fell back to my face. "I suppose that is old enough."

"For what?" I said it low and monotone, somewhere between angry and careless.

"Oh…" he had to think on this for a moment, as if remembering what he had eaten for supper the night before. "Well I am sending another squadron of men to the Saxon grounds and I figure you best earn your place in Britain."

I continued to stare blankly at him. His words that he was sending me off to war had not quite registered in my mind yet. It was masked by my anger for my father.

"I am also sending Halpin's boy...Kay? Yes...Kay I believe," he thought for a second, "and his foster brother Be..." he paused again.

"Bedivere," I finished his sentence for him, condescendingly, "their names are Kay and Bedivere."

"Yes..." My father's face turned into a look of confusion for a brief moment and then back to a fierce glare. "I also want that heretic friend of yours out of my palace, and that boy, Lionel, brought here."

Perceval and Lancelot. I had almost completely forgotten about Perceval in the past few months. All my time had been consumed with my frequent visits to Avalon, and I often skipped group training and fought by myself.

"Is that all?" I asked, giving him my steeliest glare.

"I want you to tell those boys to have supper with me tonight in the dining hall. We will discuss the war and when you will be leaving for it then."

"Yes," I said, defiantly not using any title for him, even *Father.*

He decided not to pick a fight with me over it. He just sighed and I turned to leave.

"And Arthur," I spun on my heel at the sound of his voice, "I had better not hear of you going to Avalon to see that witch again."

"Who told you about Viviane?" I growled. The only people who knew about her were Lancelot, Merlin, Kay, Bedivere, and...

Gawain.

I had told him about Viviane that day when we had met him at the tavern and he had been bragging about all of the beautiful girls that were constantly trying to seduce him. Now, I realized that my petty bragging back had been an incredibly stupid decision. If only I could have been mature enough to just calmly nod and not let Gawain's bragging get into my head.

"Oh…" my father tapped his temple as if thinking, "some *friend* of yours from the city."

A friend indeed. I looked at my father with beams of pure hatred shooting from my eyes.

"And just in case you find the desire to go back to her or any other girl, just know that if I hear of you slinking around with someone who you are not to marry that she will be killed."

I swallowed and looked straight into my father's pale blue eyes. "Farewell."

And then I left.

Immediately after I left my father's throne room I speed-walked through the palace corridors to the stables where I saw a big black stallion impatiently stamping its hooves. I quickly undid its reigns which were tied to a post in its stall and led it out into open area of the stables. My father's master of horses was also off at war so I knew that there would be no one to check the stables to see that the horse was missing.

I pulled a saddle down from its pegs on the wall and situated on the horse's back, then I hoisted myself up, took a deep breath, and kicked the stallion's flank as hard as I could. I needed it to run as fast as its legs could manage. I needed to get to Viviane. I needed to ask her to marry me once and for all before I went off to war. I needed her to be mine.

Chapter XII

The Lake of Avalon, Britain, 647

I tied the stallion to a willow tree on the shore of Avalon, near where Viviane and I generally met, and sprinted out across the white pebbled beach to the water where the tiny, icy waves lapped at my boots.

"Viviane!" I called across the lake. My voice became strained, "Viviane! Lady of Avalon I summon thee!"

A ripple appeared about thirty feet from the shore. I stared at it as it became the exact shape that a stone makes when you cast it into a still, glassy pond. The figure of a girl made of water rose out of the ripple, and the water melted away to reveal Viviane, whom I loved, treading in water that must have been at least thirty feet deep.

"Viviane," I breathed as I looked upon her wet golden hair and her wet white dress that clung to her body perfectly in every way.

She only looked at me and began to swim toward me, or rather wade on the ground beneath the surface that was really only water, her magic allowing her to stand in the currents like no one else might hope to do.

She came about six feet away from me, still in the water, and looked at me.

I knew that she had now become the Lady of the Lake. Not because she had told me, but because of the way she looked, the silvery glow that she gave off, her serious and strong expression. Confidence now flowed off her like a waterfall and wrapped her like a warm cloak. Her eyes shone with health and wisdom. It was like she had been born again.

"Arthur," she said in a firm, yet smooth voice, "what is it that you are so concerned with?"

"I am going to fight in the war," I said quickly. "And my father forbid me from seeing any girl that I am not going to marry. So if you say that you will marry me now then we can still be together. Please, Viviane."

"Arthur, we already had this conversation," she said with just a hint of irritation in her voice. "My place is here, at Avalon. I am the Lady of the Lake now."

"But Viviane, do you not love me?" I asked. I looked her in her eyes. Staring her down. Forcing the answer out of her.

"I do love you," she said solemnly, "but I love Avalon as well. I was born to love Avalon."

"I know…" I trailed off. She walked closer to me, her dress trailing in the water behind her. "I just thought…"

She looked me straight in the eyes then. Our vision in a perfect, uninterruptable balance. The world might end and our gaze would not be broken. I was not aware of what was happening, just of her form standing across from me; her face that was only inches away from mine; her sweet breath that smelled of honey and dew; her absolute perfection.

And then she kissed me.

She kissed me for what felt like ages. Years of bliss passing through her lips to mine. Those years that I pictured when we would be married. My kingship was no longer a reality. There was no war to which I was to be sent off. *Here* and *There* were only *Now*. It was just like she had said, we were living in the woods, alone and together. Never having to speak to another soul besides the other again. Just like I wanted. My fantasy fulfilled.

She moved back to two feet away from me and I let out a quiet sigh of satisfaction. All I wanted was to pull her close and kiss her again. And again. And again.

"Arthur, I have something to give you," she said quietly, "before you go off to fight."

"What is it?" I asked while I fought off the overwhelming urge to grab her and pull her into me.

"Come," she commanded and grabbed my hand forcefully.

She dragged me by my hand out into the water and I planted my feet when the surface of the icy liquid came up to my neck and my tunic was flowing weightlessly around my body. I was still afraid to swim in such deep water.

She dove into the lake and completely vanished for a few seconds. She had to have swum at least ten feet away from me underwater by now. I shivered as the water caressed my legs and I felt my clothes no longer tight on my body. It was a dreamlike, sickening feeling; as if I were sinking away from reality. Or maybe that was just Avalon.

Then I saw silver glinting across the water. The silver grew into a blade, the blade of a sword. With it came a golden hilt and then a pale white hand, Viviane's hand. The hand of the girl I loved.

I suppose she was not a girl anymore for she was the Lady of the Lake. She was a woman. And yet here I was, still a boy.

The hand continued to rise, giving way to the rest of her arm and then a mountain of wet blonde hair that she threw back out of her face as she rose out of the water so that her dress was revealed. Viviane kept rising out of the water by some unseen, supernatural force until it was only her legs and the skirt of her dress under the surface of the glasslike, gray lake.

Then she came toward me, the brilliant sword still in hand, raised above her. It was shining like a star above the dull, monotonous colors of Avalon. She reached me and her face looked like the most powerful thing I had ever seen. So impossibly fierce yet wise. As if she knew well beyond her thirteen years of life. And she did.

She cupped her free hand on my cheek. It was cold and felt almost as smooth and icy as the water that she stood on. Then, she brought the sword down and turned it so that the blade was held vertically between her eyes.

"Arthur Pendragon," she said. "Future High King of Britain. Our protector."

I wet my lips and swallowed, staying completely silent, watching each move she made with absolute interest and nervousness.

"You have taken Caliburnus from the womb of the earth and you have proven your worth to me, the Lady of Avalon, the Lake of the Goddess," Viviane went on. It seemed that she was no longer looking at me but at something that was invisible hovering just in front of my face.

She brought the sword down to tilt against my forehead. The cool blade somehow felt comforting against my skin. Natural, as if it were meant to be there.

"This is the sword Excalibur," Viviane told me, keeping the blade of the large sword against my forehead. "It is the most powerful sword in Britain. It has the power to kill anything."

I swallowed and waited for her to continue.

"This sword belongs to you," she said. "It has belonged to you since it was forged by dragon fire and it will belong to you until the day you die and it is cast back into the lake."

I had no idea what her ominous words meant, but I listened solemnly and watched her glimmering eyes with the utmost interest.

She held the sword out across her hands then, the flat of the blade resting delicately in her small hands. She motioned with her body for me to take the brilliant sword and I did.

As soon as I took the sword in my hands, I felt a wave of euphoria wash over me. It was pure bliss, as if warm, golden light had taken hold of my nerves and adrenaline was being pumped into my veins at a gallon per second. The golden hilt was comfortably cool against the rough callouses of my hands and its weight was perfect. I felt as if I could take on anything. Anyone.

Viviane took Caliburnus out of my belt and threw it into the lake as far as she could. I did not care. Excalibur was mine.

She raised her hands and brought them to my temples as I breathed deeply, indulging in the feelings that Excalibur was forcing through my body. I bowed my head to her.

I felt her kiss my forehead gently. Then she softly pushed me away from her and I let my gaze linger on her beauty.

Her fingertips grazed mine as I let the sword drop to my side.

"I love you Arthur Pendragon," she told me solemnly. "I shall not ever forget you."

"Viviane…" I tried and reached out to touch her hand again. But there was nothing for me to touch. She had vanished into the mist.

Viviane was gone.

Chapter XIII

Cadbury Castle, Britain, 647

L ancelot and I walked to supper together that night.

We walked through the castle corridors to the dining hall silently, each of us knowing the exact reason that we were going. The imminent fate with which we were faced.

We met Kay and Bedivere at the doors, their faces just as grim and melancholy as ours. Perceval was inside already, always the pleaser of our masters. I wondered if he knew yet what the meeting was for. Probably. We all knew that this day would come.

"Where did you get that sword?" Bedivere asked curiously as we stood outside the room, prolonging the time before the war became a part of our reality.

I just looked at him for a second. Then my gaze shifted from face to face around the small circle the four of us had made. I trusted them. They were my brothers.

"Viviane gave it to me."

Each of them nodded respectfully. They no longer made fun of my love for Viviane. In fact, none of them really made fun of me at all anymore. They held me in a higher respect than they did when we were younger. Maybe it was because of my incredible swordsmanship and skill in fighting. Maybe it was because of my future kingship. Maybe, as Viviane had once said, it was because of the aura about me.

"We should probably go in," I said authoritatively. I opened my mouth to say more, maybe words of encouragement, but there was nothing more to be said.

I led them, single file, into the large dining hall. The ornate, vaulted ceiling seemed to glare at us with disapproving eyes as if it thought we deserved to be forced off to war.

Perceval was sitting to the left of my father as expected. That was where my mother used to sit. I swallowed, thinking about her.

I sat down to the right of my father and Lancelot sat down next to me. Kay and Bedivere sat down next to Perceval.

My father cleared his throat loudly and we all looked in his direction, neatly folding our hands in our laps. I rested my palm on top of Excalibur's pommel.

"You know why you all are here," he began. "Arthur must have at least managed to tell you that much as I told him to."

I breathed deeply and counted to ten in my head, desperately trying to keep my temper under control. I knew that the anger he was putting on my shoulders was really only the anger from the death of my mother.

"He did not need to tell us that you were going to force us o—" Bedivere started angrily. I heard Kay stomp on his foot and he lowered his chin in submission. "I am sorry your majesty. I have spoken out of turn."

My father ignored him. "You are here so that we may discuss your placements in the war against the Saxons."

A male servant came and filled our goblets with wine and I drank thirstily in a desperate attempt to lose a part of my consciousness. I knew it would not help though. it was much too watered down. The king wanted us to stay alert. I noticed, however, that his cup was being filled from a different pitcher.

"I think that all of you will be our leadership on the front lines," he said casually, as if he were discussing flower placement in the palace gardens. "My old master of patrols...Lionel, is there. I believe that you are all acquainted with him, yes?"

The five of us looked at each other. It had been so long since we had last seen Lionel and we all missed his comforting smile and mentoring. At least the war meant that we were going to see him again.

"The morning after tomorrow you shall depart from the palace with thirty men from the city. You will go straight to Lionel who will get you accustomed to the living situation and the tasks at hand. The next battle will be fought one week from tonight."

Servants brought platters of mutton pies, rosemary bread, and sugared carrots. All foods that I loved. I suppose that the kitchen staff had thought of me. The smell was tempting, but I could not bring myself to eat and I saw that the others could not either. The pits that had formed in our stomachs were already too heavy.

My father shrugged at our lack of appetite and began to eat. With his mouth full he spoke, "Arthur will be leading this battle."

I looked up from the untouched plate of food that had been served to me. I felt the boys' gazes on me.

"I will?"

"As much as it frightens me, you are going to be king someday. Stop sounding so surprised," he commanded me. He muttered, "Unless you get yourself killed on the first day."

I felt my eyes widen. I was going to be leading hundreds of men into battle. This was the most responsibility I had ever been given and it was an immense amount of responsibility.

"Yes sir," I said without emotion.

"You had better not cost me the war," he said harshly. His fierce glare met my own and our eyes locked.

"I shall not."

He looked away first.

*****

If I Could Tell It

Colorado Springs, America, 2010

"Arthur!" Ty yelled at me as I accidentally tripped over his foot and brought him down to the weight room floor with me. "What the heck is wrong with you?! You've been even more of a klutz than normal today."

"Sorry," I muttered, "I'm not really sure what's going on with me."

Of course I knew what was going on with me. I was going off to war. And I was the one leading the troops.

"Well fix it. Man, I can't deal with you knockin' me down every five seconds," he said, irritated. "Com'n, save that for the field."

I shrugged and reached to put away the weight clips I was using.

"That's it for today boys!" Coach Knox said loudly. "See you all Thursday night!"

Summer weight training for high school football began a few weeks ago and Ty and I both made the JV team. We were the only freshmen not on C team too.

I looked down at my sweaty, white T-shirt and neon green basketball shorts. It said 'Harrison High School Panthers' in big black letters across my chest. I determined that I could wait to take a shower until I got home and motioned for Ty to follow me out of the weight room.

We walked alone through the empty school to the abandoned cafeteria. Our sneakers clicked on the linoleum flooring and we walked silently out the door to the outdoor eating area.

"My foster parents are going to adopt me," I told him as we emerged into the hot, dry Colorado air.

"That's sweet man," Ty said and smiled at me. "That why you've been so weird today?"

"Um…yeah." I needed a cover story. "I guess."

"Okay," he agreed, we began to walk through the parking lot. "This must be a big deal for you."

189

"Kinda." We ducked the chain that blocked the parking lot off from the normal road for the summer.

"Are you ever gonna tell me about where you came from before here?" Ty asked presumptuously.

"Well…uh…" I trailed off. I had to think of something quickly. Or maybe I did not. I had been close friends with Ty for almost two years now. If I could trust anyone in America with my secret it would be him. I took a deep breath. "It's a long story."

"Well, it's three miles to our neighborhood, so I got time," Ty said and shrugged his broad, dark shoulders.

"Well, I mean…" I searched my mind for any way that I might not sound completely insane. "I'm not really from here," I smiled to myself at my word choice.

"Yeah. I got that," Ty said. "Come on, you can trust me. I'm your best friend. What'd you do escape from juvie or somethin'?"

"This is going to sound really strange," I prefaced. "In fact, it's probably the weirdest thing you've ever heard."

Ty laughed, "Oh believe me, no matter how crazy your story is or what you've done, I'll bet I've heard worse."

"Okay so…" My mind told me this was a terrible idea and to make up some story about escaping from juvenile detention for Ty, "you're going to think I'm totally insane."

"Look, man," Ty said, beginning to get irritated, "just tell me. I can take it."

He asked for it. You have to just tell him the truth. He is your friend; he will not tell you that you are insane like everyone else. Lancelot is your friend and he does not believe you, but at least you can talk to him about it. Stop being afraid Arthur. That is weak, just tell him.

"So every single night when I'm going to sleep, I don't actually go to sleep. I go to the year 647 in medieval Britain where I'm kind of a big deal, I'm the king's son and I'm about to go off to war and lead this huge battle against the Saxons. I have no clue how I started coming here. All I know is that I lived in medieval Britain my whole life and when I was twelve, I started coming to America in my sleep. It's been happening for the past two years now and I don't know why."

I clenched my teeth and looked at Ty. I braced myself for a look of disapproval and the words I heard all too often: *Arthur you are insane.*

He looked confused for a second. Then his mouth formed a grin, and then he laughed. He laughed for a good minute and a half as we walked down the side of the road. I just confessed my deepest, most inner secret and he was laughing at it as if it were the funniest thing ever.

"You're tellin' me that—" He tried to stifle his laughter so he could get words out. "That you're King Arthur? Frickin' King Arthur? Man, you're hilarious! How long did it take you to come up with that story? Musta' been all through weights. Ha!"

He kept laughing and I smiled awkwardly. My mistake was made now, there was no taking it back now.

"Good cover story, huh?" I said, pretending that I actually had made all of it up. That was my only option now.

"Best I've heard," Ty said, still laughing. "But seriously man, where are you really from?"

"Tennessee," I said, thinking of the first state that popped into my mind. "My parents were uh…killed in a car crash."

"Oh…" he said, his voice suddenly plagued with sympathy. If only he had been that way when I told him the truth. "I'm sorry man. That sucks."

"Yeah…" I trailed off and looked at the road that was paved in pink from the Colorado rock beneath my feet.

"But King Arthur man," he started laughing again. I gave a half chuckle, hiding my sadness. "What'd you pull a sword outta a stone too?"

If only he knew.

Chapter XIV
Camelot, Britain, 647

I had always thought of myself as a leader. Dominant, the alpha, the one that people looked to for guidance in a time of crisis. Someone that others could depend on to have a plan, to give instruction. That was me. Especially in a group of people my age. I could take commands, then tell others what they needed to do in order to make the bigger system work. That was what I was good at.

I never felt more like a leader than the day I rode off to war.

I was decked in my shining, silver battle armor, my red cape with the gold Pendragon crest flowing behind me as the wind blew it back. Excalibur hung proudly at my side and I sat atop my white stallion with confidence. I felt invincible.

Kay and Bedivere flanked me and Perceval and Lancelot rode at their sides. Behind them came thirty footmen from the city that my father had ordered. Women and children, as there were not many men left, stood up and down the streets of Camelot as we rode through, cheering. Cheering me. Because I was leading.

They shouted my name proudly and small children reached out to touch my horse as I trotted by. I smiled to myself, basking in my momentary glory. The praise felt good, but at what cost? I was being praised for going to kill other people, innocent people. And I was leading other innocent people into the war to be killed themselves. It really was a stupid thing.

Suddenly, my horse reared up onto its hind legs, stopping the parade. I pulled back on the reigns and came to a complete stop, curiously looking to see what had caused this sudden halt.

"Who goes there?" I asked in my deepest, most authoritative voice. Thankfully my voice did not crack.

"Arthur, 'tis me!" It was a northern accent. One I had not heard in a couple of months. One that I did not want to hear for another couple of months.

"What do you want, Gawain?"

"I want to march with you," he said firmly.

"Gawain, we are going to war; I doubt you want to go with us," I said, irritated. I wanted to collect the last bit of glory that was being issued to me in the form of this parade. "Get out of my way."

"Arthur, I want to march with you." He was serious for once in his life. Dead serious. "I want to fight by your side."

I motioned with a gloved hand for him to continue, my horse stamped impatiently.

"You have helped me in the past, and Britain has been good to me," Gawain said, nodding. "It is my duty to fight for it. I think I may have given you a hard time in the past but know that I mean this: I can think of no one better for whom to fight."

I looked at him for a moment. I analyzed his pale face that was hidden by his perfect hair. His dark eyes were impossibly sincere.

"Well, come on then," I told him and reached my hand down to him. He took it, and I hoisted him up behind me on my horse. "You belong with the cavalry; you are my cousin after all."

*****

Arthur

After what happened when I told Ty the truth about how I came to Colorado Springs, I kept myself guarded. I knew that nobody would ever believe me when I told them, but still there was some part of me that hoped that if someone were close enough to me, they would believe me. They would not think that I was insane. They would not laugh at me.

That part of me died after telling Ty the truth.

I gave up hope that there would be anyone who could possibly understand. Except for Viviane of course. But Viviane was once in a lifetime, once in the span of existence. And Viviane was gone.

I told myself that I would never tell another soul about the strange occurrences of *here* and *there*. They would be separate. Only I would know of it, and it would never flee outside the void of my mind. If nobody knew, then nobody could make fun of me.

*****

Central British Battle Camp, 647

We reached the war camp the day before the battle was to commence. Lionel was waiting at the covered entrance to welcome us.

"Arthur, my lord." He bowed to me, which I found strange because he had always been my master. I suppose I was now his. I was the leader now.

I nodded, and he led us into the camp. I noticed that he had a curly, blonde beard now; he had not been able to shave as he fought and lived in this rugged camp of men.

As soon as I led our parade into the camp, every man and boy got down on one knee. I swallowed. This was what it was going to be like from now on.

The six of us that were cavalry (including Gawain) dismounted from our horses and followed Lionel to our respective tents.

Mine was a bright red weathered fabric that was held up in the center by a large wooden pole and was staked to the ground in a circle. I entered through a flap that was buttoned to the tent, and one of the footmen followed me in with a trunk full of my things.

Toward the back there was a wood and grass cot and next to it was a wooden bedside table. In the center of the tent was a rectangular oak table with six matching chairs around it. The flooring was a thin worn rug that was draped straight over the grass on the ground. This was to be my home for as long as the war lasted, which might very well be the rest of my life. The quarters were not very prestigious, but I knew that they were probably the nicest in the entire camp.

After I was done investigating my small living area, I walked back out into the center of the camp to look around and try to make some sort of sense of everything.

Every eye turned to me as I meandered into everyone's vision. I did not mean to be the center of attention, it just happened. The men rose as I approached and I glanced around nervously. I realized that they were expecting me to make some sort of speech.

My armor suddenly felt as if it weighed three hundred pounds when really it was only seventy-five. I took a deep breath and squeezed Excalibur's hilt nervously. I saw Lancelot and Perceval standing together with Gawain watching me expectantly. I cleared my throat and forced words to form in my mouth.

I had never had any problems coming up with words to say in front of a crowd. Public speaking had never been hard for me, as it was for many people. But when I stood in that camp, with all of those men looking at me hopefully, as if I were going to be the one to bring them out of this wretched war, it was hard. It scared me. I was only a fourteen-year-old boy who had been thrown into an impossible situation that I had no control over.

"H-hello," I said weakly, then cursed myself for beginning so unconfident. I cleared my throat again. I had no idea what to say. "My name is Arthur."

Duh! Of course they know who you are! Do not start with that you idiot! You have to sound strong! Masculine! Like you might actually not completely fail at leading them into battle!

"I believe that this war has gone on too long," I said truthfully. I praised myself for the deepness of my voice. "I think that it is time we end it."

There were nods of approval from the circle of men that had gathered around me. I sucked in air through my nose.

"I have never led so many men before," I said, praying that it did not make me sound weak and inexperienced, "so many valiant warriors. I know that many of you probably doubt my ability to do so but hear me on this: I promise that we will end this catastrophe and that we will all be able to go home, at least for a little bit. If not tomorrow, then in the times to come."

I heard a single pair of hands clapping. It was Bedivere. He was nodding as he did so. Then Kay joined in with him, then Lancelot, Gawain, and Perceval. More and more men joined in until I saw every person around me clapping. I smiled and I felt the nervous pit in my stomach dissolve. I nodded, and I could not keep myself from grinning at their approval. Never before had I felt a better feeling. It was even more rejuvenating than when I had held Excalibur in my hands for the first time.

I let out the breath that I had not realized I had been holding. These men believed that I could do it. If only I could believe as well.

*****

Colorado Springs, America, 2010

That day in America, I was a nervous wreck.

I was so nervous that as soon as I woke, I ran to the bathroom and threw up.

Miss Marion had heard me and she immediately got out of bed and helped me clean myself up. After she had me shower and brush my teeth, she tucked me back into bed and told me that I needed to stay there all day. I could not even go to football practice that afternoon.

"Did you feel sick yesterday?" she asked me as she shoved an electric thermometer into my mouth.

I pointed to the metal stick that was keeping me from answering her.

"Oh, right," she said and laughed. The thermometer beeped and she pulled it out. "Ninety-seven point eight. You don't have a fever."

I nodded. Of course I did not have a fever. I was not sick.

"Are you upset about something sweetie?" she asked me as she brushed my hair out of my face.

"Um, no," I said as I pulled the comforter up over my bare chest. "It was probably just something I ate."

"I don't think so," she disagreed with me. "You ate what Anthony and I ate yesterday. A lot more of it though."

I shrugged.

"Arthur, you've lived with me for two years now. I can tell when there's something going on," she said. I resisted the urge to roll my eyes. I loved Miss Marion as my second mother, but she knew next to nothing about me. "You can tell me."

"Really, it's nothing," I said. All I wanted was for her to go away so I could go back to sleep and hopefully wake up *there* so I could make some last minute critiques to the plan of attack.

"You haven't been drinking have you?" she asked suspiciously. "Or heaven forbid, doing marijuana?"

"No, no, of course not," I said quickly. "I don't know what's going on with me."

Miss Marion sighed in defeat, obviously realizing that she was not going to get a real answer out of me.

"Well, if your stomach feels better when you wake up, I'll make you the best pancakes you've ever had," she said and stood up from sitting on the edge of my bed. She began to leave, and I smiled. "You are sick on your summer vacation after all."

"Hey, Miss Marion," I said as she opened the door.

"Yes, sweetie?"

"Thank you so much for everything you've done for me."

"I like doing it for you Arthur," she said and smiled warmly at me. "Now get some rest."

I turned out my bedside lamp, buried my face in my pillow, and went into plagued sleep.

*****

Central British Battle Camp, Britain, 647

It was still dark when I woke up *there*. I rose from my cot and slipped a cloak over my under tunic and breeches and pulled on a pair of leather boots. I used the candle on my table as a light and walked to Lionel's tent which was directly to the right of mine.

"Hello?" I called softly.

"Hello, Arthur," Lionel's voice called back to mine, he was sitting in the dark at his own table. "Please, sit down."

I sat down where he requested and lit his candles with my own so that we could see each other clearly.

"I can never sleep the night before a battle either," Lionel said truthfully. "I just keep thinking of all those men we are to kill…they must have families too…"

I nodded even though that was not at all what I was thinking. I had never felt much compassion toward the men that we were going to kill tomorrow. I was thinking only of how we could acquire victory.

"Drink," Lionel commanded me and pushed a silver chalice toward me.

I took a sip expecting wine and instead tasted a thicker, metallic liquid.

"What is this?" I asked as I licked my lips and swallowed, trying to get the bitter taste out of my mouth.

"Dragon's blood," he said solemnly and took a draft. "It is supposed to make it so that you can kill without feeling. That might just be a myth though."

I just looked at him for a moment. I suppose Lionel's compassion was one of the things that made him so great. I never imagined that it might be a flaw. Now that I thought about it, it very well would be in a war. Someone like me could probably kill without a second thought as I did not like people that much because they did not make sense. Lionel liked people. How could he kill them?

"I do not think I will have a problem killing," I said truthfully.

Lionel sighed, "You always were different."

I did not say anything and we just looked at each other in the silence.

"What if I fail?" I asked quietly. "What if I mess up and I lead all the men to their deaths?"

"Arthur." He put his hand on my shoulder. "You are an amazing young man. I can think of no one else that I would want to lead me to battle."

"But I have never even fought before," I said unconfidently. "I am so inexperienced."

"Are the boys giving you a hard time still?" Lionel asked. "Kay? Bedivere?"

"No, they are not," I said and played with some of the melted wax on my candle.

"You will gain experience," Lionel told me firmly. "Right now, all you need to worry about is getting some sleep. You have a big day ahead of you tomorrow. We will meet in my tent tomorrow to discuss our plan of attack."

I nodded and got up from the table.

"And Arthur," Lionel said, I turned back around, "all of us have faith in you. The question is do you have faith in yourself?"

*****

Colorado Springs, America, 2010

I woke up around ten o'clock that morning and went down to the kitchen in just my shorts.

Miss Marion ruffled my hair and put a heaping plate full of fluffy golden pancakes in front of me. I drowned them in maple syrup and began shoveling forkfuls in my mouth. I realized that I had not eaten anything last night *there*, in the war camp, because of my nervousness and I was starving.

When I was finished, I leaned back in my seat and sighed. I just needed someone to reassure me that everything would be alright like my mother used to do. My real mother. I desperately wished that I could confide in Miss Marion about what I was going through, but I knew that she would not believe me. She would have the same reaction as Ty, except she might actually think I was insane.

It felt like I was stuck between two worlds. Each one was holding one of my hands and pulling, trying with all its might to keep me there. Each of the worlds was equally strong, so neither one could pull me in all the way.

Sometimes one would feel like it was winning, and I felt much more attached to it, and other times it felt as if I could not decide which one was real. That was what it was like most of the time. The lines between the real and the fake were blurred.

*****

Central British Battle Camp, Britain, 647

Lionel woke me up that morning. To my surprise, I had actually overslept, which was the last thing I expected to do considering how incredibly nervous I was to be leading the Britons into battle that day. Soon after, we walked into his tent where Lancelot, Perceval, Kay, Bedivere, Gawain, and Merlin!? were already seated around his table eating hard biscuits and dried venison.

I sat down in the seat left for me and rubbed my messy hair so it stuck straight up in the front—at least it was out of my eyes.

"Merlin?" I asked tiredly. "What are you doing here?"

"I cannot have you and Lancelot going on adventures without me now can I?" Merlin asked playfully.

I raised my eyebrows at him. Whenever Lancelot and I went on small quests to do things, he always opted not to go. "Since when has this realization occurred to you?"

"Knowing you, Arthur, you will trip and fall as you are riding in. I cannot have you dying before your kingship," Merlin said, with an edge to his voice. I knew what he was saying. He was worried about me and he wanted to help me fight.

I smiled, "How did you even get here?"

"I will let you guess," he said mysteriously. That obviously meant that he had used sorcery, and I gave him a knowing look. If he divulged the secret that he was a sorcerer, many of the men in camp would have him killed immediately because of my father's laws.

"Are you ready?" Lancelot asked me warmly. He gave me a gentle pat on my shoulder.

I nodded and took a biscuit from the steel tray on the table. It tasted like dried glue and cardboard, but I ate it anyway and took another because I knew that I would regret it later if I did not.

Lionel took a breath and spoke quietly to me, "Arthur, because you are the leader, it is your duty to come up with the basis for a plan of attack and lead this meeting."

I cringed. I should have realized that.

"What is the terrain of the battlefield like?" I asked him, trying to get at least some sort of idea of what it might be like before I started rattling off gibberish.

"It is a flat grassy meadow inside of a long valley; there are a few rocks, but they are not big enough to hide behind," Lionel explained. "We need a plan that does not require archers to be unseen. I believe that is where we have failed in the past."

"You said that the battle will be held in a valley?" I asked.

"Yes."

"What if we did not march straight through the valley and instead came over the sides?" I asked. "Or we could have a few people marching the normal route and have the rest come rushing down?"

"The sides of the valley are practically cliffs," Lionel said doubtfully. "It would be incredibly difficult to bring horses down over them."

"We could have archers on horses going the normal way." I could practically feel the wheels in my mind beginning to spin rapidly as an idea formed. "All the rest of us could come down over the sides by foot and pose a distraction while the archers on the horses at the far end of the valley pick off the Saxon's cavalry one by one. Then the archers would not need to be hidden at all. Plus, I think that a lot of our men are better with sword and spear on foot than on horseback, at least I am. We have more of a range of angles that way and we are more agile."

Everyone at the table was staring at me wide-eyed. I do not think that they had expected me to come up with a plan so quickly. I smiled to myself. I had impressed them. Then, remembering what my teachers *there* had lectured me about teamwork and not just taking over I said, "At least, if you all think that is a good plan."

Kay sat up in his seat. "That is actually a brilliant plan, Arthur. That way we could use our tournament training, you know, the work we do to get better in our individual duels."

"And it would give our footmen more of an advantage," Perceval agreed. "If we are on the ground with them it makes that angle of the force stronger and would likely make it so that less of them get hurt or killed."

"Am I late?" A lazy voice came into our ears.

We all looked in that direction. Gawain was slouching in the tent flap door frame. He looked like he had been drinking. I was beginning to regret my decision to let him come with us.

"Who is that?" Lionel asked. I realized that when I had introduced Gawain to those who had not known him on the journey here, Lionel had not been with us. Somehow, it felt wrong to say to Lionel that he was the boy I had hidden in my closet.

"That is Gawain," I said quickly before any of the other boys could say anything that would potentially embarrass me in front of Lionel, whom I greatly respected. "He is my cousin."

"Wait a moment…" Lionel said as if thinking hard. "Your cousin…Gawain…you are that boy from Orkney who went missing a few years back! Morgause's son!"

Gawain nodded as if he were proud of the fact that he had caused so much panic with his disappearance. He bowed. "At your service, my lord."

I rolled my eyes.

"How did he get here?" Lionel asked. "Uther never mentioned anything about him."

"Probably because Arthur kept him hidden in his rooms," Perceval said triumphantly. He knew he was tattling and he smirked at me; I wanted to hit him.

"It was for only three months!" I defended myself. "Believe me, that is the most amount of time I can handle with Gawain!"

"You are the one who brought him home with you from Meredith," Kay said haughtily. He had obviously gotten annoyed with Gawain over the course of our journey as well. However, he did not need to take it out on me.

"Oh, and what were we doing in Meredith, Kay?" I fired back. "I remember. *I* was killing the dragon that *you* ran from! And then lied about!"

His nostrils flared. We had never spoken to anyone else about what had happened that day.

"That did not happen!" he defended himself.

"Really?" I asked angrily. "Gawain was there! Let us ask him!"

The two of us looked in fury at Gawain who was barely standing up and looking at us wide-eyed as if afraid of the both of us.

"Uh…" he said nervously, looking at the two of us who were both seething in anger. "I-I do not want to get into the fight between you two."

"Gawain is right!" Lionel's voice suddenly pierced through our rage. He stood up quickly. "Both of you are acting like children!"

"I am not the one lying," I said arrogantly and glared at Kay, my eyes like fire.

"Arthur," Lionel scolded me, "you are supposed to be our leader. You are arguing with one of your men about something that happened a long time ago that none of us even know about. You are not doing your duty."

Kay continued to smirk at me as if vindicated. I gave him my fiercest glare in hopes of impressing my anger on him.

"Kay," Lionel began. I smirked at Kay. At least he was in trouble too. "You should not have blamed Arthur for bringing an extra man with us. We can use all the help we can get. He is an advantage for us."

"And you," Lionel's stern tone went in Gawain's direction, "are you *drunk*?!"

"W-well, I only had four cups out of that ale barrel by the well," he said, his eyes never quite meeting Lionel's.

I had to stifle my laughter and I noticed the other boys at the table doing the same.

"*Only* four cups...?" Lionel blinked. "That ale is not watered down yet! That is why it is by the well!"

I had to put my hand over my mouth to keep from laughing out loud at Gawain's stupidity.

"I know," Gawain said.

All of us looked at him awkwardly. Lionel sucked in air through his nose. I could tell he was deciding whether or not to try and argue with Gawain. He must have decided against it because he sat down and put his hand up as if implying he did not know how to deal with Gawain.

We all looked at each other, waiting for something to happen. Gradually each and every gaze shifted to me. I looked to Lionel for help, and he motioned with his eyes for me to speak.

"Anyway," I said, clearing the wayward glances and the tone that now lingered around the tent. Gawain sat down on the ground, which I found odd, but I did not question it. "Did anyone have anything more to say about my plan?"

Heads shook.

"What if our archers cannot aim on horseback?" Lancelot asked quietly. He was usually like that in a group, quiet.

"That is a risk we must be willing to take," I said firmly.

"I have something to say," Merlin spoke up.

"Yes?"

"What if the Saxons do not intend to march straight down the valley?" he asked. "Or what if they use magic and find out what the plan is?"

All of us went dead silent. We heard the tent rustle in the morning breeze. One did not mention magic. Especially not that someone could be using it against us.

"Ah, Merlin," Lancelot said softly, "I doubt anyone is using magic against us."

Merlin took the hint and shut his mouth.

"He is right about if they do not march straight down the valley," Bedivere said, standing up for Merlin, whom I assumed he had just met. "We should have at least some sort of back up plan."

"We should use the woods," Lancelot said. "We know how to use them from our capture the flag games. We can use that to our advantage. If anything goes wrong, we run into the woods and hide out until we can regroup."

"That is a good idea," I agreed. "So is it settled then? If anyone disagrees say nay."

Everyone shook their heads. I took a breath. At least now we had a plan. I felt good about the plan too. It was so unique that it just might work.

"We will meet in the center of camp, two hours past noon, to march," Lionel said solemnly. "Until then, get your things ready, prepare your body and your mind. This will be a night to remember."

Chapter XV

Central British Battle Camp, Britain, 647

The first time I took a man's life I learned two things.

One, it is much easier to fight to kill than to fight to knock someone to the ground. Two, there is nothing special about anybody.

The first thing I learned was self-explanatory, and I should have realized it before I fought. Obviously, it would be easier to fight if I could simply run someone through or slash their face rather than come up with a complex strategy to knock them off of their feet without hurting them. The second was slightly more complicated.

When I ran down the side of the valley into the battle with my men, there was no pause from our opposing side. No brief moment to assess us, or who we might be. These people that were coming at me were no longer men with thoughts and aspirations. They were vicious, bloodthirsty wolves with only the idea of our deaths plaguing their thoughts. And because of this, we too had to become wolves.

Because when you fought to kill, you did not see right and wrong, and you did not think of the life in your hands as you sliced with the pulsating sword and stabbed fingers into throats. You thought only of your two goals. Your two morals that determined your imminent success.

You must kill, and you must not be killed. And that was all that mattered.

Excalibur was slick in my leather gloves and my armor felt at least fifty pounds heavier than when I had strapped it onto my body that morning. My left shoulder hurt terribly as if my arm were about to fall off at the slightest jostle. My feet were mechanical; they did not move by my mind's accord. I breathed hot condensation that stuck on my cheeks inside of my helmet. My vision was a blur of green and brown leaves and forest terrain. I could not see details well, only enough so I did not run into trees. One step after another, one shooting pain through my shoulder after another. Even if I wanted to stop walking, I knew that I could not. My body would not let me.

Then, all of a sudden, the ground was no longer there. I was falling and for a second, because of the lack of gravity, I did not feel the pain that was coursing through my veins. I knew that at any moment I would hit the ground and the pain would be amplified a hundred times, but I still felt relieved for the brief moment I was falling aimlessly without boundaries.

Then, as predicted, I hit the ground with an immeasurable amount of force that was translated into the same amount of piercing, sharp pain. I tried to cry out, but my body would not let me. I tried to move, but I could not. Fireworks shot behind my eyelids, feeling exactly like the explosions that were going on beneath my skin.

I closed my eyes and tried to lay as still as possible. I did not care if anyone found me.

I would welcome death.

*****

Arthur

I had not dreamed in so long because of *there*. Every time I went to sleep, it was only to wake up in America. However, when I let myself go during the battle, I dreamed for the first time I could remember since I was twelve years old.

210

I was taller then I was normally, at least six and a half feet. My shoulders were broader as well, and I felt much heavier yet, at the same time, stronger. I put my hand on my cheek to feel rough stubble covering my face. I came to the conclusion that I must be older.

I was in Avalon. Literally in Avalon. My feet were bare, and icy water lapped at my ankles. Gray water stretched out in front of me while mist curled over the surface like an elaborate maze that only the priestesses on the island knew how to navigate.

I saw Viviane standing in the lake in front of me. Her white dress was in tatters, and her right eye was blackened as if someone had hit her. Her skin was so pale it looked blue, and her body that I had once thought so voluptuously beautiful was now as thin as bone.

I began to run to her, the water making it difficult to sprint. I realized that I was naked and the frigid lake was freezing my blood. After not so long a time, I felt my limbs go numb, and I could run quickly without pain.

When I reached her, it was no longer Viviane. It was a young boy, no older than ten. His skin was as pale as mine, and he had the same rolling gray eyes as me, the same square jaw. However, the hair that flowed around his face separated his looks from mine. It was wavy and as black as midnight, shining in the dull gray light that filtered through the mist down to the lake.

By some unknown force, I put my hand on his cheek. It was cold, colder than the lake, which surprised me. No living human could be as cold as that boy. As my hand rested gently on his cheek, the boy began to grow, or rather age. I saw his face mature and his hair grow down past his waist. The top of his head that had barely come to my navel was now to my neck.

Suddenly the boy, who had become a young man, grabbed my wrist. He grabbed it hard and ripped my hand away. I felt myself blench as if I desperately wanted his affection.

I looked down for a moment and then back up. Excalibur was in the boy's hand now. He wielded it as if he had never held a sword before. His grip was wrong, and I could have taken the sword away from him quite easily, especially with the strength I now had.

Then, as quick as if he had done it a thousand times, the boy plunged my sword deep into my chest. I felt him pierce my heart; it hurt so badly, but, at the same time, I felt an overwhelming wave of relief. In my mind, I heard a voice tell me that this was what I wanted. For so long this was what I had wanted, and it was finally here.

After my heart was hit, I fell back into the water. I felt the icy liquid surround my body and I stared up at the gray sky, waiting for my world to fade.

Then a spidery black darkness crept into the mist in curls and spirals it slowly took over the sky until my vision was completely gone.

I had no concept of my reality that had just ended.

*****

The forest outside the Central British Battle Camp, Britain, 647

There was heavy breathing coming from above my head. I looked up to see the silvery blade of a cavalry sword aimed at my throat.

I acted purely on instinct and immediately rolled away, wincing as my body weight fell onto my shoulder. I got to my feet as fast as I could, fighting through all the cries from my body to just lay back down and let this stranger kill me. I raised Excalibur, which had been clutched tightly in my hand since I had fallen asleep, and narrowed my gaze at my attacker.

It was a boy, a few years my senior, with no armor covering his body. He had on a long, dark brown cape and a hood covered the eyes in his dark face. His left hand, the one that was not clutching the cavalry sword, was pressed against his stomach and I saw a bit of red blood spreading like a blossom on his light brown tunic.

If I Could Tell It

He jabbed at me and I blocked easily. I could tell he did not have the training that I did.

I spun on my heel backwards and struck at his left side. A burst of pain shot through my shoulder, my chest, and down my arm. I resisted the urge to scream.

The boy barely blocked me and we held in a lock for a few seconds. Then he cried out and he used the hand that was holding his stomach to strengthen his block. We broke our lock together and stood precariously, facing each other for a moment.

Both of us were breathing heavy. We knew that we were now supposed to fight to the death. But what if we did not? Both of us were hurt, we could very well both die. What if we called a truce? What if *I* called a truce? Would my rank count in these terms? Could I *command* him to call a truce? Probably not.

I put my hands up above my head, still holding my sword in case he did not follow what I was doing. I looked him square in the eyes, trying desperately to convey my message with my expression because I doubted that he spoke English.

He looked at me, I expected in utter confusion, for I could not see his eyes which were hidden by his hood, for a brief moment. Then he copied what I was doing with his long cavalry sword above his head. He did not remove his hand from his stomach wound.

I took a breath and held it. I decided to take a possibly life-threatening risk. I dropped my sword to the ground. I told myself that I could take it back up defensively if I needed. Then I slowly pulled my helmet over my head and wiped my sweaty hair from my forehead. I hoped that I was showing him that I wished to stop fighting by putting my head on the line.

The boy dropped his sword as well and pulled his dark hood back from his head revealing chocolaty brown, unmarked skin. Almond shaped eyes almost as dark as Lancelot's gazed at me from under the mask of uncertainty that hovered above his face. I was right about his age; he could not have been more than a couple years older than I was and I was already taller than him.

I pointed to my chest with a gloved hand to motion to myself. "Arthur."

"I speak English." the boy said in a fairly high, yet mature voice.

"You do?" I asked stupidly. I should have just moved to the initial problem which was the fact that we were supposed to be killing each other.

He just nodded.

"I think we should call a truce between us," I stated professionally. "Both of us are wounded and we will both die if we fight. We can help each other. Nobody has to know."

"I agree," the boy said. He sighed as if greatly sad about something, "I am a Briton after all."

That would explain why he knew English.

"Why are you fighting for the Saxons then?" I asked him, almost suspiciously.

He sat down on the forest floor and I copied him. "I am from Ashdown, very far north. Saxon invaders killed my parents and threatened to kill me and my little sister as well if I did not fight for them. They have her in their camp right now."

"I am sorry," I said in quiet respect. "What is your name?"

"Ellion," he said, and wiped short, straight dark hair back from his forehead. "You said your name is Arthur? Are you named after the prince?"

I smiled to myself and had to force myself not to chuckle. I figured that I could trust Ellion. If need be, I could kill him at a second's notice.

"I *am* the prince."

Ellion bowed his head. "My lord, I am so sorry. I should have realized from your armor."

I laughed, "Well considering that you were about to kill me, I think we should skip the titles."

He smiled, "Good thing I waited."

"Good thing." I twirled a dead leaf between my fingers. "What do we do now?"

"Wait out the rest of the battle I suppose," Ellion said. "We cannot go out like this."

I nodded. I stared at Excalibur. I wondered what Viviane would do if she knew that I was sitting in the woods like a coward at my first battle, barely able to stand.

"Was your father a knight?" I asked him.

He shook his head. "A blacksmith."

I nodded. "What about you? Would you want to be a knight?"

Ellion smiled, "I would love to be a knight. However, I am afraid that no noble blood runs in my veins. I am as much a peasant as they come."

"So?" I asked, almost angrily. "That should not matter. If you are a worthy man, then you should have the right to knighthood."

"I wish it was that way." He sighed. "But it is not, and I have accepted the fact that I will be a smith like my father. And I will be a good one at that!"

I just looked at him. I could tell that he wanted to be a knight like I wanted to be an architect. The difference was that I had the opportunity to fulfill my dream. In America that is.

"When I am king, it will be different," I said quietly. "I am going to make it so that any man can be knighted as long as he proves himself worthy of the title."

"Can you do that?" Ellion asked half excitedly.

"I am not sure," I answered. "But I am going to try. I want to knight whomever I see fit."

Ellion nodded slowly and smiled. "I hope that you can."

I smiled back.

Then we just sat there for what seemed like an eternity, just waiting for something to happen.

I was not sure exactly what we were waiting for because if a man from either side came to our rescue then the other would surely be killed. It would be difficult to explain to one of the men I fought with that a Saxon warrior was actually a Briton and that I had made a truce with him and that he would inevitably not turn on us.

Then I had an idea. Technically, Ellion was a Briton and if the Saxons had not threatened him and his sister he would undoubtedly have been a part of the British Army and probably would have fought under me this very battle.

"Ellion?" I asked.

"Yes, Arthur?" he asked back. I smiled inwardly because he had used my name and not my title. It made me feel as if we were actually friends and could possibly have a future friendship.

"What if you come back to my camp with me?" I asked, trying not to sound quite as presumptuous as I thought I did.

"Your men would kill me," Ellion informed me. "I fought for the Saxons."

"Because you were *forced* to," I argued. "You are a Briton at heart and blood and if blood seems to matter so much in the matter of kings then it should matter for this as well!"

I let out a breath I did not know I had been holding.

"Also, I am——" I thought for a moment, deciding whether or not to bring my rank into the argument. If there was ever a right time, I figured that it would be now. "I am their prince, and I am going to be their king one day. By the virgin, if I say you can come to camp with me then you can!"

Ellion looked shocked by my sudden burst of passion and enthusiasm. Truthfully, I was too. Somehow, I just thought that Ellion desperately needed to be a part of my life. I wanted his approval, his friendship, and I was not sure why.

"What do you say?" I said a little softer, but with just as much force.

"What about my sister?" he asked, a gentle vulnerability creeping into his dark eyes. "They will kill her if they find out that I am fighting for the British Army."

"Then we will rescue her," I said. I felt a fire burning behind my eyes with passion. I knew what I wanted and there was nothing that could stop me now. "My friends and I will sneak into their camp and rescue her. I will do it alone if I must."

"Could you even do that?" Ellion breathed.

"I have slayed a dragon," I said proudly. "I can very well rescue her."

Ellion gaped at me. "You slayed a *dragon*?"

"It is quite a story," I said with a chuckle, thinking of the tiff between Kay and me. "Now we must get to my camp. They will think I am dead if I am here too much longer."

Ellion grinned, revealing a mouth of white teeth that contrasted against his dark skin. "Thank you."

"Of course," I said and put my hand behind me to hoist myself off the ground, completely forgetting about my shoulder. "Agh!"

"Let me help you," Ellion said and stood up with his left hand still over his stomach wound.

He helped me to my feet with his right hand and I thanked him.

"How did this happen anyway?" he asked me. He picked up my helmet from the ground and carried it for me under his arm. I cradled my injured arm with my other, desperately trying to alleviate some of the pulsing pain that seemed to be pumping through my nerves at an impossible rate.

"I swung too hard I guess," I said as we began to walk in what I thought was the direction of the British camp. "Then while I was fighting the man, he forced the pommel of his sword into the back of my shoulder and I heard this terrible popping sound and then I was crying out in pain. I knocked him to the ground with a final blow and then I ran into the forest. That was the plan when we got injured. I fell down that edge when I was running and I think I made it worse. What about you?"

"There was this boy," Ellion explained. "He was dressed all in peasant clothes, but he had on the cape of a nobleman and he was walking very strangely."

"Gawain," I said and laughed slightly. I felt my face fall. "You did not…kill him, did you??"

"No," Ellion assured me. "But I scraped his face up a little with my mace."

"Good," I said. "He deserves a few scrapes on his face."

Ellion laughed. I told him about our meeting and what Lionel had done when Gawain had walked in on us.

"What is the name of your sister?" I asked when our laughter had died down.

"Elaine."

Chapter XVI
Central British Battle Camp, Britain, 647

"Everyone, this is Ellion," I said as I stood in front of the bonfire which all of the men were sitting around and drinking ale. "He is going to be joining us."

I adjusted the cloth sling that was supporting my shoulder for the time being. I looked around carefully to make sure that no one was going to challenge me about my decision to invite Ellion into camp. I nodded slowly when I was sure that everyone was alright with it, granted I had not told them that he had formerly fought for the Saxons. I judged that the lie was alright because I trusted Ellion and he was technically British and therefore right to fight with us.

We sat down on the hard, dusty ground next to Lancelot, whom I had told the whole story to as soon as we had gotten to camp. He handed me a worn metal cup filled with lukewarm ale and as I took a long draft, Lancelot patted my thigh. I looked at him.

"Good job my friend," he told me. "Your plan worked."

"What do you mean?" I asked.

"You did not hear?" Lancelot asked.

I shook my head. I had no idea what he was talking about.

"We won the battle," he said happily. "Thanks to you and your idea."

"Did…did they surrender?" I asked. A shred of hope worked its way into my mind.

He shook his head, "No, but only one of our men was killed today, and when we sent a scout to look at the damage done, there were over seventy Saxon bodies on the field."

"Really?" I asked, surprised.

"Yes," Lancelot said. "Arthur, any doubt you might have had should be gone now."

I nodded solemnly and looked into the fire, continuing to drink my ale in silence.

"Y-you!" a slurred voice ruptured my thoughts.

I looked up quickly to see Gawain, practically tripping over himself with drunkenness. He wore only an under tunic and breeches with his oversized cloak mostly covering his body. I looked to his face for the scratches that Ellion had supposedly given him. They were there as he had said. They resembled the wounds of a giant bear or lion claw raking across the soft, fragile skin of the face.

"Y-you are the one th-that gave me this," Gawain spit at Ellion. He moved his cup in front of his face for emphasis, but only managed to spill most of his ale down the front of his undertunic. "You are n-not-t British! You are a-a Saxon!"

"No, I am not," Ellion said crisply and stood to face Gawain. "I *am* British, from the village of Ashdown."

"Then why-why were you—"

Lancelot and I stood up together. I cupped my hand over Gawain's mouth so he would stop talking.

"I think you have had a bit too much ale Gawain," Lancelot said loudly, in case anyone had been eavesdropping and were assuming things that they should not.

I jerked my head in the direction of Gawain's tent and I heard Lancelot begin talking to him in soothing tones, leading him slowly toward his place of rest.

"I apologize for Gawain," I said as I sat back down next to Ellion. "He frustrates all of us quite frequently."

"Not all of your friends can be as perfect as Lancelot," Ellion said with a slight laugh.

"What do you mean?" I asked him as we watched Lancelot help Gawain into his tent.

"Never mind," he shook his head. "Thank you for letting me be here."

"This is where you *should* be," I said forcefully. "And I promise that we will get your sister…I just need to talk to Kay and Bedivere about it."

Ellion nodded and sighed sadly, "She is all I have left of my parents."

I looked at him for a second. Then I said softly, "My sister killed my mother. My father hates me."

I thought about what I had said in the long moments that it took Ellion to respond to me. I almost wished that I were in Ellion's position, to love my family so much that I wanted my sister back to remember my mother and father. I think I had almost felt that connection with my mother, but never with my father. My sister was evil: pure, terrible evil. And I did not know why.

*****

Colorado Springs, America, 2010

I was forced to run errands with Miss Marion after football practice, which I had to sit out of because of a "bizarre shoulder injury" that Coach Knox just could not seem to figure out. Miss Marion insisted that I go with her to pick out new sneakers for school instead of going home, *and* she made an appointment to have my shoulder looked at by a doctor.

It never ceased to amuse me how superficial, selfish, and utterly unaware American people were.

There, where I was from, I was fighting for my life. I was organizing plans for men who did not know if they would even wake up the next morning. Men whose families did not know if they would be able to afford supper the next day or clothe themselves properly. Even I, the highest rank in the wealthiest class of all of Britain, was still fighting for survival, maybe not in the same ways, but I was still fighting for the survival of my people, the mere avoidance of death.

Here, where I had come to be, I had my adopted mother fussing over whether I should trim my hair short or get blue or red sneakers. And *here*, I was not even in the wealthy class. *Here*, I was average. My new family obsessed over having every possession be the most perfect, luxurious item. It was the expectation that was embedded in the minds of American children from the day they were born: *I deserve that.*

And why, might I ask, was this the common morale amongst my peers in this day and age? I was afraid that I already knew the answer because I too had been beguiled by this plush culture. It was because we could. We bought the nicest things because we could. We bought *everything* because we could. Because we did not need to worry about the basic goal of survival. However, was it because we had far surpassed the man who fought for his life and whose family could not afford supper, or was it just because we had become a selfish, entitled people?

We had begun to drown in our own greed like a thirsty man in water. People had wanted with such lust for so long to be able to live in luxury as the American people now did, yet when we achieved this, we were just as, if not more, unhappy as the peasant people *there* who lived with next to nothing.

"Arthur, can you read that to me?" Miss Marion asked as she searched for her wallet in her purse while we were waiting in line at the doctor's office.

"Um…" I squinted at the electronic message board above the receptionist who was talking on the phone. "No. The print is too small."

She found her wallet and looked up at the board with me, "You really can't read that?"

I shook my head, "Nope."

She looked at me closely for a second, as if she were trying to look into my mind.

"What?" I asked.

"I am going to make an optometrist appointment for you while we're here," she told me, biting her lip.

"A what?"

"I want to have your eyes examined," she said and began to face the receptionist who had just gotten off the phone. "I think you might need glasses."

"I do not need glasses," I informed her

"Quiet, Arthur, I am trying to have a conversation," she said sternly.

I rolled my eyes. She had, out of the blue, told me that I needed to get glasses and then expected me not to talk to her about making the appointment.

"Go up to the pediatric clinic on floor two," the receptionist informed Miss Marion. "During his examination the nurse will test his eyes to see if we need to make an optometrist appointment. If he needs one, then we might be able to make one for later today."

I let air out loudly through my mouth and Miss Marion gave me a look. I suddenly decided to become very interested in a poster on the bone structure of a human knee.

"Thank you," she said to the receptionist and ushered me by my arm to the waiting area.

We sat down in rough, cloth chairs and I examined the stack of magazines on the small square table next to me.

"What was that about?" she asked me, tapping my bicep.

"What was what about?" I responded. "I just don't think I need glasses."

"You interrupted me and then rolled your eyes at me right in front of that lady," she scolded. "What's going on?"

"Nothing," I said, half irritated that she thought something was wrong with me.

"I can tell something's wrong," she said. "You seem on edge. Please just tell me what happened."

I looked at Miss Marion for a moment. She was the closest thing I had to a mother. A mother almost like the one that Morgain had taken away from me. The mother who had somehow managed to curtail my father from hating me as much as he did. The mother who had loved me. Morgain had ripped her away from me like she had cut the rope I was hanging by from a cliff.

"*Nothing*," I said again. "My shoulder just hurts."

"Arthur Ector?" a nurse opened the door and asked sweetly.

I nodded, and Miss Marion and I stood up and followed the nurse through the door.

I failed my eye examination.

Well, the nurse felt the need to say that I did not *fail* it; it was only that I was different, but I knew that was only the American disposition speaking. She then scheduled an optometrist appointment for right after the appointment for my shoulder, which meant that I had to sit at the medical facilities for another hour and a half, which I hated. All of the unfamiliar, fake, chemical smells made me uncomfortable, and all I wanted to do was run out the big doors at the end of the building and not come back.

"It looks like you dislocated it and then shoved it back into place…" Dr. Halverson said as he examined my shoulder.

He had had me take my shirt off and then took my heart rate before he began examining my shoulder. I sat patiently on the table and dutifully did as I was told as he felt my body and checked me over. Secretly, I had to hold myself back from pushing him away as fast as I could. His touch, any stranger's touch, made me nervous. It was uncomfortable and I just wanted him to stop.

"Do you have any idea how this could have happened?" he asked me.

I looked at Miss Marion who was sitting in a chair and raking her eyes over me and the doctor as if trying to extract the most amount of information possible from the situation. "Football practice probably."

"But you don't know exactly *when* it began hurting?" the doctor asked suspiciously.

"This morning I guess," I said nonchalantly. "It really doesn't hurt that much. I don't even know why my coach made me sit out."

"Coach Knox said you could barely run and you couldn't catch," Miss Marion interjected. "Don't try to downplay it. You don't need to be tough here."

I just looked at her for a moment. Obviously, I needed to downplay it. I had no cause for the injury. Unless I wanted to tell the doctor that I actually was fighting in a war that happened to be happening in medieval Britain.

"I know," I said, calculating. "It just feels a lot better now."

"Well, that tends to be a good thing," the doctor said, running his hands like feathers over my skin from the bottom of my shoulder blade to my nipple. "Does your chest hurt at all?"

I shook my head.

"That really doesn't give me very much to go on," he said, distraught.

He gave Miss Marion a long knowing look and then turned to his computer. He began typing very quickly and occasionally looking back at me from over the top of his reading glasses.

"I am going to prescribe you some pain medication that you can pick up at the pharmacy downstairs," he explained. "If it continues to hurt, I want you to come back in and talk to me about it, and please, if you do come back in, be more descriptive."

I nodded, and then Miss Marion ushered me out of Dr. Halverson's office.

*****

Central British Battle Camp, Britain, 647

After I woke, I meandered over to Merlin and Lancelot's tent which was directly to the left of mine.

They were sitting upright on their cots and talking with only breeches on and sheepskin covering their legs.

"Can I talk to the both of you about something?" I asked as I came to stand between their two cots.

"Of course, Arthur," Lancelot said and patted the bed beside him to signal me to sit down.

I complied and turned to face him and Merlin. "There is a problem with Ellion."

"I already told Merlin," Lancelot said quietly.

I sighed. On the one hand, Lancelot's telling Merlin made it much easier for me because now I did not have to tell him, but on the other hand, it made me a little sad that Lancelot seemed to be growing closer to Merlin than to me. I suppose that was only fair though; I had not been spending as much time with him as I used to, what with the going to Avalon to see Viviane and training with Kay and Bedivere more frequently. It still bothered me, however. Lancelot and I had been best friends for as long as I could remember, and even though we were still close, he was beginning to get closer to others as well and that was only natural.

"I wanted to ask you if you might know what is wrong with my shoulder," I told Merlin. I needed to stall for a few moments before asking him a favor as big as raiding the Saxon camp.

"Come here," Merlin commanded me.

I walked to him, and he brushed his fingers over the cloth that covered my left shoulder and my arm. I looked at Lancelot and raised my eyebrows at him as if asking him what Merlin was doing. I felt a slight tingling everywhere that he ran his hands over. The tingling spread to all parts of my body and gave me an inherent sense of nervousness that proclaimed something supernatural going on.

"It is dislocated," Merlin said simply. "You must be in a great deal of pain."

"I guess," I said; it had been hurting, but not so much that it was unbearable.

Merlin let his hands wander over my shoulder once more. "It seems it was dislocated more than once yesterday." He frowned. "Like it went back into place and then was ripped out of place again."

I swallowed. That must have been from my fall down the ravine in the forest when I ran.

"How do you know all of this?" I asked him.

"I just do," Merlin said, looking down.

I set my glare on him. "They taught you at Avalon."

He gave the slightest incline of his chin that I could still make out as a nod. "There are lots of things I can do that you need not know...not yet at least."

I decided not to interrogate him about it, thinking that it would only cause another bout of Merlin's sarcasm and judgement toward me. "Can you fix it? My shoulder I mean."

"It is going to hurt," he said, and we made eye contact for a brief moment.

"I can take it."

"Oh, I am sure you can," he said sarcastically.

Then he gripped my forearm and mounted his other hand on my chest. I braced myself for the expected pain and then he jerked my entire arm up and toward my body.

I yelled with the sudden pain that jolted through my body with a thousand lightning bolts at once in red shades of shooting pain. Then all of it suddenly lifted and all I felt was a dull ache pulsating through my chest and arm.

I looked at Merlin. "Now what?"

"Now you be careful and do not dislocate it again," Merlin scolded me. "Unless you enjoy what you just felt."

I nodded. "You ought to become a physician."

He shrugged. "And deal with people like you all day?"

I rolled my eyes and looked at Lancelot. "Amazing that you can spend so much time with him."

Lancelot just gave me a half-hearted smile. Helpful.

"Actually," I began, "there is another problem as well."

"And that is?" Merlin asked, almost condescendingly.

"Ellion has a sister in the Saxon camp," I explained, choosing to ignore the slight edge in his voice. I rubbed my shoulder when I felt it pulse in a soft pain. "One of the reasons I convinced him to come with me was by saying that I, and possibly my friends, would go to rescue her. If they find out that he has come to our side, they will kill her."

"So, you want us to help rescue her?" Merlin asked, raising an eyebrow.

"Yes," I said truthfully.

"Why can you not do it by yourself?" he asked sharply. "I thought you were the big war leader now."

I ignored Merlin and turned to face Lancelot. "What do you say?"

"Arthur, going into the Saxon camp is a really bad idea, especially after our success yesterday," Lancelot informed me. "They would kill us the moment they saw us."

"But we have to help Ellion," I argued. "He is British. We have a duty to help his sister."

Lancelot sighed and found a sudden interest in the ground beneath his cot. "Let me think about it, Arthur."

"Please think quickly my friend," I said to him. "I hate to think of what they will do to her if they find out Ellion is going to fight for us."

"What are you doing?" I asked Kay when I walked up to him, Bedivere, and Perceval shooting arrows at a target that they had painted with deer blood on an oak tree near the edge of camp.

"What does it look like?" Kay replied with an edge in his voice.

I took a breath and rolled my eyes at him, forcing my temper down into the pit of my stomach. I clenched my fists.

"Never mind," I shook my head and began to walk away.

"Arthur, wait," Bedivere put his hand on my right shoulder, "what did you want to talk about?"

"Nothing worth dealing with that coward," I said, glaring at Kay who turned to face me.

"Says the one who ran from the battlefield," Kay said with a mean smirk. "Your shoulder does not look so bad now."

"Merlin fixed it," I said through gritting my teeth. "It was dislocated."

"Oh?" He turned to the makeshift target and let loose an arrow, I silently rejoiced when it missed the center by at least a foot. "To me, it just seems like you are taking after that king of ours."

"Excuse me?" I felt my short fingernails dig into my palms. I tried to force my feet into the earth as the rage coursed through my veins like a raging river. It felt like my stomach had turned into a volcano with the roiling anger.

"You heard me." He narrowed his eyes and his thin lips formed a smile. "You are exactly like Uther. Running from battle while men lose their lives for you. I cannot wait for your turn at running our country. I think I would have almost preferred Morgain."

That was all it took. Words. Words that should have run off my back like raindrops.

My body jerked forward and my hands made hard contact with his chest. He stumbled a good five feet back and then regained his balance.

I stood with my feet planted and gave him my fiercest, most steeled glare. I felt completely justified in shoving him.

"When I got here, I found out my father was dead!" Kay came back at me, running with all of his might. He yelled, "This is his fault. At least I can be proud to carry my father's name with me! Are you proud to have Pendragon blood?!"

I punched him hard in the nose. I felt his warm blood run onto my fist, and I closed my eyes. I did not want to do this. Kay was more or less my friend, but more importantly, he was my ally, more than my ally, my teammate.

I felt pain explode in my jaw. It made my rage turn white hot like a firecracker. My survival instincts began to fuel my moves. The years of training began to shape my actions. The training to kill.

The pain in my jaw immediately went numb. The world blurred. All I could see was the direction of where my rage needed to be expelled, to a single target. I had one goal, one motive. I needed to kill him. He represented everything I hated about my family;

everything that I was afraid I could not achieve. He had turned into even more than that. He was my insanity. He was whatever force that caused me to go *there*. He was Lancelot telling me that I had drank too much at supper when I told him. He was my father who laughed at me, Ty who was amazed I could make up such a story.

I spun on my heel with every burning fiber of my being. My fist drew a perfect circle around my body and my mind, at a thousand miles per hour, appreciated it for a moment. I loved circles because of their reliability, their perfection, the things that the world would never have. The reliability that would never come in my life. The perfection that I wanted so much and that always disappointed.

My fist collided with the side of Kay's head so hard my hand went numb. He fell to the ground.

The world was still blurry. I could not make out anything. I could not hear any distinct sounds. Voices on top of voices formed a dull hum in the back of my mind.

I fell to my knees. Guilt came over me in a tidal wave. My vision was a mess of green grass and dusty earth. The pain in my jaw returned as an aching, stinging mess of pain. I tasted blood in my mouth.

I looked down to see Excalibur hanging from my belt. I drew it from its scabbard and looked at the blade. It glinted in the dull sunlight. Its clarity formed in and out of my vision. I shifted it to my left hand. I raised up my right hand next to it. That was what I had used to hurt my comrade.

I ran the blade along my palm and stared at it, expressionless, as a stream of blood ran down my wrist. The pain felt good. I deserved it.

Then a dark hand grabbed the hilt of Excalibur and ripped it from my grasp.

I fell onto my back and stared at the gray, seemingly cloudless sky. Faces came into my vision. Lancelot, Merlin, Bedivere, Lionel, Ellion.

Then it all spiraled out of my view and turned to velvety darkness.

*****

Colorado Springs, America, 2010

Sadly, Miss Marion was right; I did need glasses.

After the optometrist had tested my eyes with various devices that looked like something my father might use to torture criminals, they concluded that I needed glasses.

I sullenly followed Miss Marion down the hall where we picked up my prescription for the glasses we would order from the boutique within the hospital and then to the pharmacy where a person in the long white lab coat gave her an orange bottle with tiny white pills that I was instructed to take whenever my shoulder was bothering me. I knew now, after Merlin's consultation, that I would not need them *here*.

I tried the best I could to keep *there*'s events from the night before out of my mind. I woke up and had breakfast with Miss Marion and Mr. Ector before he went off to work. He gave me another lecture about how childish my hair looked and how much I needed to cut it. I just nodded respectfully, unwilling to sacrifice my hair that I knew was a thing of masculinity *there*.

After breakfast, I never changed out of the sweats I had worn to bed because Miss Marion called Coach Knox and told him that I was not going to be at football practice that day.

By two in the afternoon, I sat sulking at my desk playing a video game on my laptop with my headphones on. I had died for the fourteenth time in a row when I finally decided I needed to exit the game for a bit before I threw it across the room.

I stared at my desktop screensaver for a good five minutes before eventually opening the Google search bar.

I typed 'Sir Kay' into the search bar and clicked on the 'Go' button. The little wheel spun for a moment and then a bunch of old paintings and drawings showed up under images.

The first written part under the line of images read:

'In Arthurian legend, Sir Kay is Sir Ector's son and King Arthur's foster brother and later seneschal, as well as one of the first Knights of the Round Table—Wikipedia'

I frowned. Kay's foster brother was Bedivere. Sir Ector...Mr. Ector. Mr. Ector was my foster father.

I typed 'King Arthur' into the search bar, searching for an answer. The reality that always came up, my supposed past, never seemed plausible.

'King Arthur is a legendary British leader who, according to medieval histories and romances, led the defense of Britain against Saxon invaders in the late 5th and early 6th centuries AD.—Wikipedia'

I suppose that was true. I decided not to dig any further into what certain legends said I was going to do *there*.

I tried 'King Arthur and Sir Kay'.

I chose the third site down.

'Sir Kay is always described as King Arthur's seneschal (an official in charge of domestic arrangements in the medieval household and overseer of the servants). He is usually shown as boorish, mocking, and cruel. In a number of romances, Kay's insults inspire the hero to prove Kay wrong by undertaking a quest. Despite his rude character, Kay holds...—Pace University.'

I thought about this for a moment. "In a number of romances, Kay's insults inspire the hero to prove Kay wrong by undertaking a quest." Kay insulted me all the time. The closest definite thing I had done to a quest was slaying that dragon when I was twelve, and that was

233

inspired by Kay and his arrogance. The legends seemed to know everything about me.

"Are you still playing video games?" Miss Marion's voice startled me, and I felt a jolt go through my body.

"Y-yes," I said, closing the laptop quickly.

She set a plate of chocolate chip cookies and a glass of milk next to my arm on my desk. "I made cookies."

"Thank you," I said and spun around in my chair to look at her. I took a bite of a cookie and through my mouthful said, "they're good."

She nodded and ruffled my hair. "I *am* sorry about your shoulder. I'm just trying to do what's best for you."

"I know," I said and smiled. "But really, I'm fine. It was just a one time thing."

"Arthur, were you looking at pornography when I came in?" she asked with a stern look.

"What?" I exclaimed. "No! Of course not! Why would you think that?"

"Because you closed the computer really fast." She tapped her foot against the carpeted floor quickly. "Like I said, I'm just trying to do what's best for you."

"I know," I said again. "I was just looking up some stuff."

"What kind of stuff?" she asked. She sat on my bed.

I growled inwardly. I just wanted her to leave so I could finish my research about *there*. I knew one excuse that seemed to always work.

"About my parents."

"It's not bad for you to want to look at things from before you came to us," she said as a concerned look slowly spread across her face. "You just never talk about it."

"Nothing to talk about," I said quickly. "You and Mr. Ector are my family now."

She smiled and rubbed my shoulder, then began to leave.

"Miss Marion?" I asked before she could get out the door.

"Yes?"

"Do you know anything about the Arthurian legends?" I asked her.

"Like the sword in the stone and the Holy Grail?" she replied.

"Um, yeah."

"I did a project on it when I was your age," she said. "I was always more interested in the legend of Robin Hood though because my parents named me after his wife Marion…I guess it makes sense that you would want to know about King Arthur then…"

I just looked at her awkwardly.

"Anyways," she said, "what do you want to know?"

"Do you know anything about a character named Kay?" I asked, looking at her very carefully.

She looked up, trying to think. "All I can remember is that he was one of the Knights of the Round Table."

"Knights of the Round Table?" I asked, trying to look into her mind. Whenever I did my King Arthur searches I usually stopped after about ten seconds because it freaked me out too much. I had read about the table somewhere.

"Yeah," she said. "He had a round table where he and all of his knights sat."

"Interesting," I said.

"I need to go check on my other batch of cookies." She kissed the top of my head. "I'm glad you're taking an interest in history."

If only she knew.

I turned back to my desk and took a sheet of paper from the stack that I had stolen from Mr. Ector's printer. I took out my compass—the big one—and drew a circle around a point I had marked with my pencil.

I took the red notebook that I had used for some of my drawings and started listing names.

- Lancelot
- Merlin
- Perceval
- Lionel
- Bedivere
- Gawain
- Kay
- Ellion
- Me

Nine names. Nine names of the men and boys who had fought with me *there*. Nine was a square number. I liked that. The square root of nine was three.

Beneath the names, I started to write numbers.

9 names
$\sqrt{9} = 3$
$9 + 3 = 12$
$3^2 = 9$
$12 + 2 = 14, 14/2 = 7$
7 is the fifth positive prime integer
$3 + 2 = 5$
$14 - 5 = 9$
14 relates every number I have derived from 9
<u>14</u>

I took the edge of my protractor and drew a diameter line through the center of the circle through both sides. Then I calculated that in order to divide a 360-degree circle into fourteen sections, I needed to make each section 25.71 degrees wide.

I measured 25.71 degrees from the diameter line of my circle, drew a line, and continued to measure 25.71 degree sections around the entirety of the circle until I had fourteen equal sections. I marked the chords (lines across the circle) at each of the intersections of the line and the circle that I had drawn with my compass with my pencil.

I calculated the midpoints on each of the chords in the sectors and marked a line from each up from the edge of the graphite circle. I calculated the sum of the interior angles from a fourteen sided nonagon and found out that each obtuse angle would be 154.29 degrees.

I drew tangent lines from each of the sector points that I drew, making sure that it intersected the midpoint lines at roughly 154.29 degrees.

After I drew each of the fourteen tangents from the section points of the circle, I held the paper I was drawing on up to the light.

I had never drawn anything even remotely like the fourteen tangent circle, but somehow it felt familiar to me. It seemed that it would become important, but just not yet.

I folded the paper in quarters and then in half so it made a small, pocket-sized rectangle. I stood up and shoved it into my bed table drawer where I kept a flashlight and a tiny notebook with an attached pen. Miss Marion had put it there as a "dream journal." Too bad I did not have dreams.

I would worry about what my drawing meant another time.

Chapter XVII

Central British Battle Camp, Britain, 647

I opened my eyes to find Perceval's face inches from mine. Immediately, I tried to get up and we bumped foreheads.

"W-what are you doing?" I asked, sitting all the way up.

"I told you he was not dead!" Perceval yelled to seemingly no one.

"Who thinks I am dead?" I asked. I ran my hand down the back of my head and brushed twigs and dirt out of my hair.

I looked straight ahead to see Kay, Bedivere, and Ellion looking at me nervously. The last time I had seen Kay he had looked dead, laying on the dirt as if he would never move again. That was why I had tried to hurt myself. The guilt had been overwhelming.

"Nobody thinks you are dead," Bedivere said with a fierce look at Perceval. "I just said that you *looked* like you were dead."

I stood up and walked towards them. I needed to at least try to make things right. "I am so sorry Kay. I did not mean to hurt you."

"I am fine," he said through his teeth. I saw a dark purple bruise forming on the side of his head through his ear length, sandy hair. "Are you?"

"Yes." I brushed off my trousers. "Before I...blacked out, I saw Lancelot, Merlin, and Lionel. Where are they?"

"They were never here," Perceval said. "Ellion and I were just watching Kay and Bedivere shoot. We did not tell anyone about the fight or what you...did...after."

"Good," I said, letting out a sigh of relief. "Lionel does not need to know."

I saw my sword in Ellion's hands. I walked up to him, and he handed it to me. He said nothing.

"I need to talk to you," I told Kay, raising my chin up to tell him that I wanted to leave.

"So you can hit me again?" he asked. "No thank you."

I gritted my teeth and looked at him with the most superiority I could muster. "As your commander."

Kay and Bedivere exchanged a long look as he followed me toward where the camp met the edge of the forest. I stopped walking when I was sure the others could no longer see us or hear us.

"What?" Kay asked when I stopped. "You shoved me first. And that thing on your hand, you did that to yourself."

I glanced at my hand. They had wrapped it in cloth torn from a tunic to stop the bleeding. I needed to remember to thank whoever had done that.

"What do you have against me, Kay?"

We made eye contact for a long, long while and I dared him with my eyes to speak first.

"I *hate* him," Kay whispered.

"Hate who?" I asked, trying to match his tone.

"Uther Pendragon."

I said nothing for a moment and then I spoke, ever so softly, "So do I."

"He killed my father." A tear ran down his face and across the scab from the battle that was beginning to form. "And he slept with my mother."

"How do you know that?" I asked skeptically. Then remembered that I was trying my very hardest to be sensitive.

"Bedivere told me yesterday." He looked at the ground. "He found out from the maid."

"I am so sorry," I said. "If it is any condolences, I am sure I feel the same as you."

"How?" he asked, shaking his head. "How could you feel that way about your father? You are his blood; blood means more than anything. You know that."

"Maybe it does not." I stared down at the beautiful hilt of Excalibur. "After my mother died, he told me it was all my fault. Then he started drinking…and…and sleeping around with other women."

Kay nodded slowly and asked, "Arthur, why are we here? Fighting for that wretched man?"

I looked up at him. "We are not fighting for him. We are fighting for Britain. We are fighting for all of the people who depend on us to keep them safe. We are fighting for people like Ellion, whose parents were killed by Saxons and whose sister was taken hostage. We are fighting for them."

"Ellion told us about his family…" Kay trailed off. "He said you were going to try to form a rescue party for his sister."

"I am," I agreed.

"Then let me be your first man," Kay said and held out his hand.

I took it and smiled. "Thank you, Kay."

We turned and began to walk back when he spoke, "Arthur?"

"Yes?" I replied.

"Good thing you did not hit me as hard as you thought you did."

When we got back to where the others were still watching Bedivere shoot at the painted target, I told them that Kay was going to come with me to help rescue Ellion's sister. Perceval and Bedivere both agreed to come; however, much to his dislike, I told Ellion that he could not come in case any of the guards recognized him and found he had committed treason.

After they had agreed, I went back to Lancelot and Merlin's tent to ask them what they had decided.

"Kay, Bedivere, and Perceval are going to go with me," I told them, sitting at their makeshift table. They had not been outside their tent that day because, as Lancelot had said, *Kay and Bedivere would bully them*. I told them they were acting like wimps and that I would tell Kay and Bedivere to leave them alone.

Lancelot just glared at me. "Not everyone goes through life not caring what people say to them."

I ignored his comment and persisted in trying to convince them to come with me. "Are you really afraid? We fought against them in battle yesterday and we won. Rescuing one fourteen-year-old girl should not be that difficult. She is younger than you!"

"I will go," Merlin said. "The men in this camp are beginning to act like animals. I would love a chance to get out."

"Thank you," I said to him, then set my gaze on Lancelot. "Come with me, my friend."

"Fine, Arthur," Lancelot said. "Fine, you win."

I smiled, "Just think, someday you may be known as a hero: Sir Lancelot the Valiant."

The six of us gathered at the north end of the camp, close to the valley in which we had fought.

We sat cross-legged in a circle, which made me happy, on the grass. We had opted not to wear armor because it was loud and we could not move as fast if we had to make a hasty escape that required an ample amount of agility.

"Perceval," Bedivere said sternly. I noticed that Bedivere had taken a sort of brotherly approach to Perceval since he had arrived. I suppose it made sense because Bedivere was three years older, at seventeen, and both his and Perceval's forte in battle and tourney was mace. "You had better not tell Lionel about this. Or anyone else for that matter."

Perceval shook his head enthusiastically, "I swear I will not."

"Say it," Bedivere said. "I do not want this to end up like the dead deer."

"What?" I asked. I had obviously missed a story.

"Long story short, Perceval cannot keep a secret from Lionel," Bedivere said without moving his gaze from Perceval. "Say it."

"I promise I will not tell Lionel about what we are doing," Perceval said, sitting on his hands. He looked like a child. That was something that bothered me about Perceval; he oftentimes acted younger than he was. Immature. I cannot stand immature people.

"May I speak now?" I asked.

Nobody else around the circle spoke, and all their gazes fell on me, so I assumed that was their way of giving me the floor.

"Ellion said they were keeping his sister, Elaine, in the main Saxon tent where the leaders are. He said something about their highest-ranking leader being a woman," I told them. "I say we locate where the main tent is and enter the camp from there so we have to travel less in the open. We should have two people enter from the back, nearest the forest, two from the sides, and two from the front, more as a distraction than anything."

Nobody made a move to interrupt so I continued.

"The two that come in from the front should be the biggest, loudest, and most sturdy; the ones that can hold off the longest without backup," I said. I made eye contact with Bedivere. He was as tall as Perceval and was the broadest of us. Hopefully, as I grew that would change. "The two from the sides should be the quickest and most agile, the best fighters. If anyone were to take the leaders on an individual basis it would be them…"

I trailed off and let my gaze travel to Merlin and Lancelot.

"The two that come from behind should be the quietest, the smallest, and look the least threatening. They will be the ones to ultimately take Elaine from the tent and back into the forest." I bit my lip and fingered the hilt of my sword. "Now, unless anyone has any other ideas, we need to choose who will go where."

"They should go from the back," Bedivere said, pointing to Merlin and Lancelot. "Least threatening?"

"Poor choice of words," I said when Lancelot gave me a look.

"Then you had better go from the front," Merlin told him. "Loudest one."

Bedivere glared at him and tension rose within the group. I felt it like poisonous gas polluting our team and I bit my lip, frantically trying to come up with a solution.

"Kay should be from the side," I said. Forming an alliance with one of them would be a start. Positivity strengthens. "He is a good warrior."

Kay bowed his head in quiet gratitude.

"Perceval and I are left," I told the group. "One of us needs to go from the front and one from the side."

"Perceval and Bedivere both fight with a mace," Kay said. "We should have more of a variety from each angle. Arthur should go from the front."

I looked down and picked at the leather on my boot. What Kay was suggesting was not part of my plan. I wanted to fight the Saxon leaders and prove that I was not a coward who ran away from battle. If I could do that, I would redeem myself, both in my eyes and in the eyes of my men.

"I agree," Bedivere said. "A sword and a mace will have more variability then two maces."

"Perceval is bigger than me," I interjected.

"Not really," Bedivere said, looking at the two of us. "Do you not want to fight beside me?"

"Of course I do," I told him. I suppose redeeming myself would have to wait. "I would be honored to fight by your side."

"Good," Bedivere said.

"So, it is settled then?" I asked.

All the boys nodded.

"We should leave now," Kay said, "before the sun sets."

All of us nodded again and I stood and waited for them to copy me.

"What are you doing here?" I saw Lionel walking toward our circle.

Bedivere and Kay made nervous eye contact.

"Hunting," Kay said. He looked at Lionel, almost as if challenging him.

"This late?" Lionel asked skeptically. "With this many of you? What are you hunting for? Dragons?"

Kay and I exchanged a look.

"Deer," I said. "We are hunting for deer. They come out at this time of day."

"Really?" Lionel asked. He looked straight at me. "With your battle weapons? Those must be some deer."

"Must be." I bit the inside of my cheek.

"Perceval?" Lionel asked, staring straight at him. "Are you actually hunting?"

I saw Bedivere's fist in the center of Perceval's back. I stared at him. Perceval looked from Kay to Lionel and back again.

"We…" I gave Perceval my most steely glare. "We are going hunting…for deer."

"Are you sure?"

I stepped toward Lionel. "Sir, I was sent here to lead these men and that is what I intend to do. I mean you no disrespect, but if I say that we are going hunting for deer, then we most definitely are going hunting for deer."

"I trust you, Arthur," Lionel said. He set his gaze on Kay and Bedivere. "It is them I do not trust. You know that they strung up the organs of a dead deer in Lancelot and Merlin's tent the other day?"

So that was the dead deer story. Bedivere shoved his fist into Perceval's back and Perceval squirmed uncomfortably.

"I do now, sir," I said. "However, I am not one for childish antics. We are simply going hunting. Now, let us go please."

Lionel and I made fierce eye contact for a few moments and I inclined my chin ever so slightly as a show of confidence.

"I hope you are successful."

Then he strode back into the center of camp.

"Do you remember the plan?" I asked, peering through the bushes at a black dyed, burlap tent flap.

"We remembered it the last hundred times you asked," Kay said sarcastically. I resisted the urge to explain to him that I had obviously not asked them a hundred times. The most I could have asked them without it being my only speech would have been about ten times and I know that I had only asked around three times.

I glanced at him and then back to the tent.

"You ready to run?" I asked Bedivere.

"Ready when you are," he replied and raised his chain mace up so I could see.

I gave him a thumbs up with my left hand and he looked at me strangely. I forgot that thumbs up were from *there*. "Sorry. I am ready."

He nodded and we crept to the outer edges of the group behind the bushes, me on the left and him on the right.

We looked at each other and I jerked my head up. Then I held up my left hand with three fingers extended, then two…then one…then we ran.

I sprinted around the side of the large black tent with my sword held out in front of me until Bedivere and I reached the front. We expected to meet a horde of Saxon soldiers that we would have to fight off. Instead, we found it completely deserted. There was not even one guard outside the leaders' tent.

I looked at Bedivere and lowered my sword down to my side. He returned my gaze with a confused expression. I put a finger to my lips and crept toward the entrance to the tent. Still, there was no reaction. Complete silence haunted the air, devoid of human noise pollution.

I extended the blade of Excalibur to the tent flap and the afternoon sun glinted off the metal. I lifted the flap and jerked my head toward the entrance to tell Bedivere to enter with me. As quietly as we could, we stepped through the threshold of black fabric into the quarters of our enemy.

My boots felt no carpet or artificial flooring covering the ground. Instead, we were greeted by lush, springy grass. It seemed impossible that grass would grow so healthily in such a dark place because plants needed sunlight to thrive; I had learned that in my middle school science class. The only way it would make any sense would be if the grass was fake, however, that was only a thing of *there*: American falseness.

I heard a soft scraping sound and suddenly the tent was flooded with daylight. I raised my sword to the source only to find Kay, who had sliced through the side of the tent to enter. We nodded to each other in silent acknowledgement. A few moments later, Perceval entered in the same fashion.

The four of us very slowly walked toward a table covered with an oversized red cloth in the center of the tent. As we came closer, I saw that an unlit yellow beeswax candle in a steel holder was set on top of the table and an audible squeaking sound could be heard. A mouse perhaps?

Then I heard the tent flap at the entrance lift. All of us swung around with our weapons poised to kill as we had been trained for all our lives.

My blood was on fire from the adrenaline shooting through my body. It felt almost as powerful as the rage that fueled my movements in my fight with Kay. I felt invincible. I could take apart whatever it was that was about to attack. I both hated and loved the feeling with an improbable mix of fear, excitement, and pleasure all combined into a powerful potion that was coursing through my veins. I was set to kill, completely of emotion and not of mind.

There was nothing at the entrance. It was only the wind that caused the flap to stir. I sighed and felt my heartbeat peak and begin its descent back down to only a bit above normal keeping my mind and body awake and aware.

We turned back toward the table clothed in red and continued to creep closer to it, cautiously glancing around the dark tent, not knowing what to expect.

When we reached the table, I stood facing the candle. It looked as if it had never been lit before because the wick was white and the wax unmelted. The holder was plain, smooth steel and had no markings. I glanced back at my comrades and waved my hand over the candle just to see what would happen.

A tiny orange flame arose from the wick as soon as my hand hovered above it. I flinched in surprise at the sudden reaction and looked straight over the table into a very pale face. Gray eyes, so similar to my own, peered back at me with malice brewing within.

I stared into the face of my sister.

Chapter XVIII

Central Saxon Battle Camp, Britain, 647

"Morgain," I breathed.

I had so many feelings. So much hatred. So much rage. Such an urge to kill. Violent thoughts took over my mind like a plague. All I could think about was running Excalibur through her black dress, into her chest, through her skin, her flesh, piercing her heart. I pictured the way it would feel. The way my sword would lodge in her. The way I would twist before pulling it out.

"Hello, Brother," she said. Her eyes glimmered, filled with malice. A smile formed across her thin, red lips.

I started to raise my sword, but all too quickly, she raised a straw doll close to my face. She squeezed it and I felt my body involuntarily constrict around me.

"My name is Morgana now," she whispered, still squeezing the doll. "I do not want the name Ygraine gave me."

I could barely breathe; my words were tight in my chest, but I wheezed them out, "Y-you killed her."

"Yes. I did," she smiled again and looked at the ground. *"Edcennan of hê ofsêon sê, mâl fæge feyweorðan caru."*

I looked at her, not knowing what she was saying. It was a language I had only heard a few times. Sometimes Viviane used to speak it when she would go off on her rants and Merlin would occasionally say a word, mostly curses.

The straw doll began to glow a dull green and my vision began to take on the same greenish hue.

If I Could Tell It

The world began to spin. It began to spin as if I were turning in circles, but my feet remained planted solidly to the grass beneath me.

Scenes began to play out in front of my eyes. First, scenes of battle:

It was midday. The sun was shining brightly overhead. I felt the weight of my battle armor on my shoulders. My boot crunched on something and I looked down. I was standing on top of a body, a Saxon warrior. Blood streamed down his chest and an arrow protruded from his breast. My boot had broken his ribs and his chest had caved in from my weight. I was shocked and I immediately stepped off of the cadaver. I stepped back onto another man. He let out a low moan and I tripped in shock. I stumbled backward and fell onto something soft and wet. Another body, this time the spilled innards of a man's stomach.

I tried to yell, but my voice seemed to not be working. My head tilted sideways and I saw the rest of the battlefield. It was filled with bodies like the ones I had fallen on.

Then the sky turned a piercing green and the world began to spin again. Solid ground was under my feet. The cold hilt of my sword was in my hand. I was gripping it tightly.

I felt that my shoulders were broader and I was much, much taller. It was like the dream I had had when I fell in that first battle before I had met Ellion.

I was facing Lancelot, looking down at him from my height. He was older now and he had a short mustache covering his upper lip.

I was yelling at him in a very deep voice in words that I could not quite make out. His eyes were full of sorrow and remorse. I wanted to scream at myself to stop yelling at him. He looked so sorry, so sad.

Then I shoved the blade of Excalibur through his stomach, firmly, with absolutely no hesitation.

The sky turned green again and I was standing at the balcony where my father stood at executions. I was holding the hand of a girl no older than sixteen. She looked up at me with shining gray eyes. Tears were streaming down her face.

I looked down at the executioner's block to see a large board with a naked man nailed to it by his wrists. I stared at the scene intently, as if I wanted it to happen more than anything else. I raised up my hand and brought it down—a signal.

A man in a black hood took out a pair of pliers. He took the naked man's hand and pulled out his thumbnail. Then he took the nail and shoved it deep into the man's bare chest. The man screamed loudly. Then the man in black took a small vat of hot tar and poured it over the wound caused by the nail. The screams of pain were the most terrible thing I had ever heard.

The girl at my side whimpered and cried even harder.

"How can you do this?" she screamed. "How can you be this terrible?"

The sky became laced in hues of green and then the world spun me to a battle. A battle in the dead of night. It was raining and I was standing in a valley.

The boy from my dream walked up to me. We faced each other for a few moments and I felt tears form in my eyes. I took off my helmet and reached out my hand to him. I knew that I desperately wanted the approval of this boy.

My hair was wet and slicked against my forehead and I wiped it away, looking sorrowfully at the boy. His glare remained as cold and cruel as stone.

"This is what you always said you wanted," he said ruefully.

Then he plunged his sword into my chest.

I stood facing the unlit candle. It seemed to laugh at me, its wick as white as ever and its beeswax completely unmarked. I looked over the table at Morgana's face which was quickly fading into the darkness. She smiled at me one last time and put one finger to her lips.

Then she was gone. I heard the wind blow against the tent flap like it had before and there was no trace of her.

"Arthur?" Kay asked me. "Are you alright? You seemed disoriented for a few moments."

I shook my head out forcefully. "Yes. I am fine."

He nodded and stared at the candle.

"Where are Merlin and Lancelot?" I asked, realizing that they had never come into the tent.

"Probably decided they were too afraid at the last moment," Bedivere said with an edge to his voice.

I decided not to ignore him.

I lifted the red cloth up to reveal the underside of the table, and a very scared, small, blonde figure.

I reached my hand out to the girl and tapped her shoulder. She turned around so I could see her face and the tears streaming down it. She had big, blue green eyes and quiet features that were set into a pale, pretty face. Her blonde hair seemed to reach her waist and fell in soft waves behind her body.

"W-who are you?" she asked nervously. "Have you come to hurt me?"

"We are from the British Army," I told her and knelt on the floor so my eyes were level with hers. "Are you Elaine?"

"Y-yes," she sniffed. "Did you find Ellion?"

I nodded. "He is already back at our camp. We have come to rescue you."

She nodded and looked up at me hopefully. I extended my hand to her and she took it. I helped her out from under the table.

She stood with her shoulders sunken as the four of us took in her appearance and she adjusted to her surroundings.

She had on a dress that looked as if it had once been a plain white gown but was now streaked with gray soot and torn to tatters. Her face was also covered with soot and was smeared with her own tears. She had a red mark across her face as if someone had hit her. Still, through all of her worn and dirty appearance she somehow still looked beautiful in an innocent, virgin way.

I saw Bedivere whisper something to Kay, most likely about the looks of Elaine and I shot him a glare.

"You are Elaine then?" Bedivere asked her, moving his brown hair from his forehead.

She nodded and looked at him nervously.

I slapped Bedivere across the arm. "We need to get her back to camp. She has clearly been abused."

He nodded curtly and took a long look at her before moving back a step.

"We need to go now," Kay said, nervously looking back at the entrance. "I think I heard footsteps."

We began to walk toward the tent exit when I stopped just before any daylight could reach us. "What about Merlin and Lancelot?"

"They will catch up," Kay said. "We need to go *now.*"

"What about no man left behind?" I asked.

"Since when do we live by that?" Kay asked. "It is better for at least some of us to escape than no one."

I just looked at him. That would need to change. There would need to be a code of sorts.

"Arthur," Perceval said. I noticed this was the first time he had spoken since we had arrived. "Kay is right; we need to leave while we have the chance."

I looked down at the ground. I needed to make a decision, and fast.

Lancelot was my best friend. He had always been there for me. He was the very first person I had ever told about *there*, and even though he did not believe me and did not talk about with me, he had at least listened. That was more than I could say for everyone else I had tried to tell. Except for Viviane of course.

"I am going to look for Lancelot," I told them. "Come if you will."

It was too bad that I never got the chance to search for him.

Over thirty Saxon soldiers were waiting outside the tent for us. Front and center were Morgana and the man who had aided her in the murder of my mother; the man with long dark hair and dressed all in skintight deer hide.

Morgana was smiling knowingly at me, reflecting back on our time together in the tent which nobody had seemed to have noticed but me.

"You were right," the man said to Morgana in a thick Saxon accent. It was obvious that English was not his first language and that he was only speaking it for our sake. "British soldiers."

"Not just any British soldiers, Setanta," Morgana said with a playful lilt to her voice. She inclined her chin ever so slightly. "My brother."

"Oh, I remember him, Morgana," Setanta said grimly. He scowled at me and his amber eyes seemed to bore into my mind. "He was the hero."

I stopped thinking—only reacted.

I flung myself forward, Excalibur extended. I was practically itching to kill. I craved the feeling of sliding my blade into human flesh, picturing the life ebbing away from this person that I had complete and utter control over. I craved that power, *needed* that power. My urge was only one part revenge for my mother; the other two parts were the need for power.

I was stopped by an invisible force when my sword was only two feet from Setanta's chest. He had put his hand up and suddenly, I could no longer move. Magic. He was using magic against me. Merlin was right.

"Silly boy," Setanta said calmly. I noticed that his speech pattern was like that, very calm, as if nothing ever went wrong for him. Now that I was this close to him, I saw a scar that ran across his left eye to his nose. His left eye did not seem to work quite right either. It was a creamy, off-white color with seemingly a million red lines through it and his pupil had drifted down to the bottom of his eye. I doubted he could see well out of it, if at all.

253

"You cannot hurt me, especially with only your mortal weapons."

"Believe me," I snarled. I struggled with all of my might. The invisible force wavered and I was released. I flung toward him. "I can hurt you."

I had barely grazed the deer hide of his tight tunic when I felt the impossibly painful constriction of my body that I had felt in the tent with Morgana before. I fell to the ground. It was like being pressed with an unimaginable force from all angles everywhere on my body, in my blood. She was holding the straw doll again.

"Do not underestimate him," Morgana said, taking a long look at Setanta. "He has been granted the sword Excalibur."

"By whom?" Setanta snarled, exasperation haunting his voice. "He is dirty!"

"Viviane," Morgain said. "She found a certain liking for him."

"Of course it was Viviane," he sighed. "She knows nothing. It is a wonder the Goddess chose her to be the Lady of Avalon."

I tried to choke out that he was wrong, but Morgana only squeezed the doll harder.

"What should we do with them?" Setanta asked her finally. Morgana looked straight at me and squeezed the doll even harder. It felt like my body would implode and stop functioning altogether.

"We let them go," Morgana told him. "We give them back their friends and we let them go."

"Morgana," Setanta said, "you must not be thinking straight."

"I am," she said smoothly. She smiled at me with malice again. "I have done what I needed. Arthur has seen what he needed."

Setanta looked carefully at Morgana and she raised her chin to him. Her long black hair tossed in a breeze that whistled by us. Then he turned and said something in Saxon to his men. They brought forward a very thrashed and beaten looking Lancelot and threw him down next to me. He breathed deeply, trying to catch his breath. I still lay in pain, my body squeezed by a force not my own.

Soon after, Merlin walked through the crowd by his own accord, unharmed. Before he left the cluster of men, Setanta gripped his wrist.

"Son of Taliesin," he said to Merlin, making fearsome eye contact, "make no mistake: you are committing a terrible act against your Goddess and your ways. This is treason."

Merlin held his gaze for a few moments and then simply pulled away from his grasp and went to stand above me.

"Leave," Morgana commanded us. She threw the doll down to me and immediately the pain surrounding me was lifted. I fell limply onto my back, feeling my muscles relax at long last. Merlin picked up the doll and tucked it inside his cloak.

Setanta commanded his men in Saxon and they all walked in an unorganized formation into other parts of the camp. My sister stayed and stared at us. Lancelot, who had gotten to his feet, helped me up off of the ground.

"My brother," Morgana said to me. Her eyes met mine and I sensed false security teeming within her. "You have done me a favor."

Then she vanished, her form withering away like smoke into the breeze.

The six of us made seven walked in a single file line out of the Saxon camp while the sun set and painted the sky in colors of orange and pink.

Merlin led.

When we got back to camp it was dark. Ellion and Lionel were waiting at the north end of camp from where we had left.

"How was 'hunting'?" Lionel asked me, sarcasm was dripping from his voice.

I ignored his comment and walked past him, brushing his shoulder.

"Arthur!" he said sternly. "I spoke to you!"

I looked back and glared long enough to see Kay tell Lionel something that immediately softened his expression and silenced his harsh words.

I turned and continued to walk toward my tent solemnly without a glance back.

As soon as I got to it, I collapsed in my cot and closed my eyes, not even bothering to take my clothes off or even my sword from my belt.

I needed to get out of this place.

Chapter XIX

Colorado Springs, America, 2010

Putting on my prescription glasses for the first time was like seeing the world clearly for the very first time. It reminded me a bit of the moment after a complex algebra equation is solved and the answer is suddenly made clear. Although, without the clarity of the glasses, it was difficult to see that there even was an equation.

The degrading of vision somehow reminded me of the morale displayed by most people. It had been reduced so slowly and yet at the same time so far that by the time we received the chance to correct it we did not realize how far south it had gone.

I wondered if this was the case with my father. I wondered if at one time he had been a good man. I hoped that he had. I hoped he had treated my mother well when they were young. And I hoped that what happened to him would not happen to me.

I thought that Miss Marion forcing me to get glasses was a scheme of stupidity, but as soon as I looked through them I quickly changed my opinion. Seeing clearly was something I needed to do even if it required a crutch to do so. I decided that I would wear them.

"You look so smart!" Miss Marion said as we sat in the parking lot of the ophthalmology sector of the hospital. I just looked at her for a moment. She cocked her head at me and I rolled my eyes and blew my hair out of my face; it fell on the black, plastic square rims of the glasses.

"You need a haircut." Miss Marion commented.

"No, I don't," I replied. "My hair is fine."

"Arthur, I don't want to fight with you about this anymore. You look like a mess with your hair unkempt," she told me. *How opinionated.* "You can keep it long, but you have to at least make it look purposeful."

I looked at her sideways. "I will cut my hair myself."

She looked at me and sighed, "Why do you hate getting your hair cut so much?"

"I don't know," I lied. Of course I knew why. I left my hair long and unkempt because *there* it was a sign of manhood in the Old Ways. If I cut my hair *here*, then it would transfer *there* and that was not something I wanted. "I just don't."

She sighed again and started the car. "You better have done something with it by tomorrow."

"Fine," I said. I did not have a plan yet, but I was sure that I would come up with one soon. "Where are we going now?"

"Your drafting teacher said you needed more tracing paper, right?" she asked me. "We should probably get that sooner than later."

"I guess," I said and tapped my knuckles against the plastic glove compartment box of the car. "Oh, I forgot to tell you I need to stay late after football practice tomorrow to help Ty with geometry."

"Just because you're in high school now doesn't mean you don't have to ask permission." Miss Marion scolded.

I rolled my eyes. "Can I stay after practice to help Ty with geometry?"

"Sure," Miss Marion said. "Thank you for asking permission."

"Yes," I said and looked down at my watch. Already six-thirty.

"Can we get paper tomorrow morning?" I asked her. "Harrison's just a few minutes away from Walmart."

"Why do you need to get home so bad?" she asked suspiciously. "Do you have a girl you need to email?"

"Um…" I said. I felt myself blush. The fact that she thought I had found a liking for any girls at my school somehow amused me. "I'm hungry and I want to eat dinner."

I knew that Viviane had told me that we would never be able to be together, but I still had a shred of hope in the back of my mind. I loved her and I knew I would always love her. Even *here*, in America, in this foreign land, I loved her. I loved that she was so unlike all of the superficial American girls at my school. She did not care if I was on the football team or if I was taller than six feet or what my shoes looked like. She understood me, and she understood *there*. That was an impossible quality to come by, and I knew it would be exceptionally difficult for me to ever find another woman that I felt so strongly for, if I could find one I felt for at all.

"It's getting toward the end of September, Arthur," she said suggestively. "Have you thought about asking anyone to homecoming?"

"Not really," I told her. I would have asked Viviane to homecoming. "Should I?"

"It might be fun." She turned onto the street that led to the house. At least I would get to eat after the interrogation. "What about that girl that you always talk to after your games?"

"Katie?" I asked. She came to every JV game with two of her friends and sat on the bleachers with all the parents and watched. Afterwards she would always come and tell me how well I did and ask me about random things. "She kind of freaks me out."

"She just likes you," Miss Marion said and pulled into our driveway. She opened the garage, parked the car, and turned it off so all the blue lights faded away. "Her mom's in my book club. She seems nice."

"Why would she like me?" I asked her. "She doesn't even know me."

Miss Marion looked at me in the dim light of the cement garage. I looked back at her and cocked my head in confusion. I blew my hair out of my face when it fell in front of the new glasses.

"Maybe she wants to know you," she told me.

"Why?" I asked. It made almost no sense for a complete stranger to want to get to know someone else for absolutely no reason. As far as I knew we had no commonalities except for the fact that we were in the same geometry class, even that was a stretch. I saw her get a D on a test once, suggesting that she obviously was not adept at mathematics like I was.

Miss Marion made a sound somewhat like a growl at me, "Just think about it. You might regret not going to your freshmen homecoming when you're older."

"Don't think so," I muttered as I got out of the car. "What's for dinner?"

"Anthony's on his work retreat in Denver and I ate with my friend Peggy before I picked you up at practice," she explained, "so whatever you want."

"Great," I said under my breath and walked from the garage to the kitchen to scour the pantry in order to find something that I deemed worthy of consumption.

After I ate a meal of the eclectic variety, I wandered up the stairs to my room where I turned on my computer and opened the game I had gotten a few days ago.

The game was based on the air battles of World War II and after my pilot crashed for the fourth time I exited out of the application and stared at my screensaver. It was just a sketch of the unit circle that I had downloaded from Google images, but it still comforted me to look at its perfection, at all of its angles that were drawn by computers and devoid of all human flaws.

I did not think that the problems in the world were caused by people. I thought that they were caused by humanity. The entirety of human imperfection. Of every single thing that we did wrong. It infuriated me sometimes.

Or maybe it was just because of the war.

Because when I closed my eyes, my mind was consumed by human disaster and ruckus. By the inanimate people who seemed to only be fighting to be killed. These people who I was leading into battle to be killed. I led them like sheep to the slaughter. I barely even knew why anymore. And yet, I felt bad for these people who contributed to the human imperfection that had been my insentient nemesis for as long as I could remember.

*****

Arthur

My name is Arthur Pendragon and I am fourteen and a half years old.

I have killed more men than I can keep track.

I have a scar for each of them, if not on my body then on my mind.

*****

Central British Battle Camp, Britain, 647

"Lionel," I told him as I sat against the boulder in the middle of camp, "we cannot keep doing this."

"I know." He sat down next to me. "Every man and boy in this camp has been injured if they are not dead."

"What are we going to do?" I asked him. I picked up a fallen, brown leaf in my hand and squeezed it until it made tiny flakes in my hand.

"What can we do?" he replied.

I did not say anything. There was nothing we could do. Battle after battle passed. Some we won and some we lost. It did not really matter what the result was: men still died on each side, so I suppose we lost them all; every one of the seventeen battles in which I had fought. It seemed like more than that. Every week we fought once, sometimes twice.

I never saw my sister again after we had taken Elaine back to camp. I suppose, as a woman, she did not fight in the battles. She must have just sat in their camp and practiced her witchcraft. Or maybe she conspired with Setanta while their soldiers fought. I never seemed to see him on the battlefield either. If I had seen him, he would have already been dead.

"I am going to the river," I told Lionel and stood up. He held out his hand and I took it and pulled him to his feet.

"At supper then?" he asked.

I nodded and walked in the direction of the small stream that had formed when the rain had started in early September. We called it the river even though it was only a muddy, five-foot-wide stream and barely had a current. It was the closest thing we had to a valid water source since the real river ran red with blood from the battles.

I sat on the stream bank and looked at the brown water and the tiny ripples that formed. The forest floor had turned shades of orange and red since autumn had arrived. Ordinarily, I would have admired the fiery colors with which the world had been graced. Viviane would have enjoyed it.

Viviane was my first love because she believed me.

If I Could Tell It

This was the conclusion I had come to after careful analysis of the possible reasons why I could have felt so strongly for her at such a young age. I knew that we would never marry; it was only desperation that caused me to ask her. I was so incredibly desperate for anyone to believe me. I craved the validation that came from talking with someone about *there*. I craved the validation that came from someone knowing my full truth and not thinking that I was completely insane. I craved it so much that I would take it even from someone who was almost undoubtedly insane herself.

Even though I knew the reason, I still could not stop myself from loving her.

I drew Excalibur and stared at it in my pale hands. Tiny red and white scars ran across my hands now, callouses lined my palms.

In America, they said that men should be proud of their battle scars. I was not. It seemed I had a scar everywhere on my body. I had one across my back from when a horseman's cavalry sword cut through my chainmail while I was on foot. I had one near my collarbone from where an arrow pierced my flesh. I was so fortunate to not have been hit in a place where serious injury may have been inflicted. My stomach was shredded by a man with metal claws instead of a hand. I had streaks across my face from when a man had dragged his mace across my forehead to my cheek. Bloody blisters lined my feet from boots that were too small for me. My thigh had stitches from a shallow wound by a long knife.

It was a miracle and a wonder that I was not yet dead or so injured that I could not fight.

I remembered Miss Marion's words *there* about my hair and I took one lock of my mane and held it up so the sunlight caught in it. *Here*, at war, my hair was a bit greasy and tangled, however, that was only to be expected. I took Excalibur and cut about an inch and a half off of it. It fell to about my chin when I let it go. I proceeded to cut the rest of my hair to about that length then and I pushed it back, away from my forehead, so it was out of my face for the most part. Then I slid my sword back into its scabbard and stood to go back to camp.

On the fourth step I took, I heard a faint giggling and I immediately looked across the river to the source of the sound. All I saw was a bit of white fabric that quickly disappeared from my vision. I crouched down and crawled behind the bushes on my side of the river, listening to the giggling that was accompanied by a few soft whispers. I heard footsteps in the marshy earth, and I listened as hard as I could to give myself a clue as to whom it might be.

The footsteps stopped and I peered through the fern I was behind to see two figures, a girl and a boy, that had just sat down on the streambank. The girl was very obviously Elaine, because of her white dress, pale blonde hair, and the fact that she was the only girl in the entire camp. At first, I suspected the boy to be Bedivere because he had said that he found Elaine beautiful and was always trying to get her to wander off with him. However, when I looked closer, I saw that the boy was much too thin to match Bedivere's broad figure. His coloring was also much too dark and he had a shock of dark, glossy hair that seemed to flow around his head perfectly. He kissed Elaine on the cheek, and she smiled and kissed him back on his mouth, wrapping her arms around his neck as if he were her lifeline.

I looked away to the leaf covered ground for a moment. I wondered how Ellion would feel about one of the men kissing his sister like that. He was so protective of her; he would be furious with whomever it was. I felt bad for Ellion. At least he had finally found his true forte in fighting. He was an excellent archer and he had killed many Saxon warriors helping us with bow and arrow.

Elaine pulled away first and I could finally see who her partner was.

It was Lancelot.

*****

Colorado Springs, America, 2010

"Katie?" I asked as she began to walk down the bleacher steps after the game finished. She had been sitting with her two friends whose names, I learned, were Jeanette and Sabrina. "Can I talk to you?"

"Um, sure," she said, jerking her chin toward me and grinning at Jeanette who ran her hand through her shoulder-length, curly brown hair. She walked onto the field and smiled at me nervously.

I pushed my sweaty hair off of my forehead and looked her up and down quickly. It seemed that every day she came to one of the games she wore a tighter, more revealing shirt. That interested me. Her philosophy seemed to be that the sluttier she made herself appear, the more I would be interested in her. That did not make much sense to me. In fact, the sluttier she made herself look the more I shied away from her. It intimidated me. If I liked the way she looked, that meant that other boys at school and on the football team liked it too. That also meant that if I did want to ask her out, then I would have competition. And, because I was not even sure if I liked Katie, the competition aspect did not entice me at all.

"Do you want to go to homecoming with me?" I asked her. I figured that Miss Marion would pressure me to go one way or another, and Katie did not completely annoy me.

"Yes!" she squealed excitedly. That did annoy me. I had asked her if she wanted to go to the dance with me, not offered her a million dollars or a full ride to Stanford.

"Great!" I said, forcing excitement into my voice.

She embraced me. I felt myself flinch. I hated it when strangers touched me. I hugged her back and counted to six before she let me go.

"Sorry, I think I'm a bit sweaty," I told her when she pulled away, my jersey practically wet with perspiration.

She laughed a very high-pitched giggle and then said, "It's okay."

"So, I'll see you in geometry then?" I asked her as I started to head back to the direction of the locker rooms.

"Yep!" she said happily. "You have my email too. We can write!"

I nodded with a plastic smile on my face, then turned away and felt my expression quickly melt into a comfortable glare at the ground.

I wished she were Viviane.

Chapter XX

Central British Battle Camp, 647

Four months.

Four months of the infinite doldrums of battle. Four months of killing. One month of my knowing of Lancelot and Elaine's escapades in the forest. One month of Ellion's ignorance.

It felt like longer, much longer. October was so cold that year it felt like winter had come too early. The first snow fell on our camp on October twenty-third, and even though it was only a half an inch of powdery dust it still meant trouble. Trouble meaning that we were in for a long, cold winter of frost and deep snow.

*****

Colorado Springs, America, 2010

Homecoming was terribly American.

So revoltingly superficial and bright while still charming in an egocentric and disgustingly unregimented way. That was America. And that was the homecoming dance.

Two weeks before the weekend of the game and the dance, Miss Marion took me to be fitted for a tuxedo.

I very much did not enjoy the experience.

Once we entered the shop—which was filled with shirts and pants and jackets all on matching metal racks—a short, skinny woman came up to Miss Marion and me to help us. A musty smell haunted the entire place and it made me feel like I was about to sneeze at any second.

The small woman led us to the back of the shop into a small room and told me to take off my sweatshirt, which I did uncomfortably because I did not have a T-shirt under it. Then, the woman proceeded to measure me seemingly everywhere: my waist, my hips, around my thighs, my shoulders, even my neck. It was incredibly uncomfortable for me because, as I have already expressed upon, I *hated* it when strangers touched me.

After the woman, whose name turned out to be Mrs. Gaffer, had measured me, she made me try on several white shirts, pairs of black slacks, and black jackets. Once she was satisfied with my opinion, she brought me a black vest and a bow tie and put those on me too. Miss Marion fawned over my appearance and she and Mrs. Gaffer pushed me out into a hall full of mirrors so I could look at myself.

I pushed my glasses up on my nose and stared at myself.

In my opinion, I looked ridiculous and I felt uncomfortable. Neither were things that I enjoyed. I would have much preferred to wear the gaudy tunics that I sometimes wore for festivals and feasts in Britain. However, this was the normal attire for these kinds of things in America and I knew that I needed to wear it in order to successfully fit in, so I did.

On the night of the homecoming dance, Ty's mother came to my house to pick me up before we went to get our dates.

I had on the tuxedo that Miss Marion had rented me and shiny black shoes. My hair was slicked back with gel so it stayed out of my face and my glasses sat on my ears in between strands of strategically placed hair. I had a box holding a white and silver corsage for Katie on my lap.

"Thank you for driving us, Mrs. Douglas," I said respectfully to Ty's mother.

"'Course, Arthur," she replied and looked back at us. "I'm happy to."

"They better look hot tonight," Ty whispered to me from across the seat. "Especially yours. With boobs like that, you're a lucky man."

I smirked at him and thought about telling him not to talk like that, but instead, I just went along with it. I had learned that sometimes it was better to do that than argue.

"We're here," Mrs. Douglas said and pulled into Katie's driveway.

Ty and I got out of the back seat of the car and meandered up to the front door where we rang the doorbell. Katie and Jeanette answered the door together.

If there was one word to describe the two girls tonight, it was bright.

Katie's dress was a strapless turquoise, with diamond-like gemstones covering her chest and back. It was positively stunning.

The impression that the dress gave me was positively overwhelming to my young male system. I almost entirely forgot about everything for a moment, completely caught up in the looks of a girl I was not even attracted to.

"Arthur?" Ty asked, snapping me out of staring at Katie. "You good?"

"Yes!" I said quickly, then to Jeanette and Katie, "Both of you look very nice tonight."

"Thanks," Katie said, grinning. She moved her curled hair out of her face and we watched Ty take Jeanette's hand and walk to the car. "You look nice too, Arthur."

I smiled cautiously and watched her look at me hopefully. She was waiting for me to hold her hand. I took a breath and blinked my eyes for a bit longer than normal. I told myself that everything was alright and that even if I did not like Katie I could still hold her hand; it was not harming anyone. It might even feel good.

I took her hand and she looked up at me flirtatiously through her eyelashes. I ignored it and led her to the car.

I had never really had a problem with dancing in the past—the past meaning Britain.

My mother had all of the boys learn some of the traditional dances during our training, and the girls all learned from their mothers. She had us learn because before feasts we used to have a few musicians play in the banquet hall and there would be dancing. It was really quite fun while it lasted. The steps were easy to learn, and I always found that I could handle them with ease. After my mother died, however, we stopped having those dances and we barely ever had feasts either.

When I become king and the war is over I plan to have feasts all the time and dancing before them too. Everyone seemed so much happier during feasts and the day after. Maybe it was because people could enjoy themselves and not worry about other things, or maybe it was because of the excessive drinking. Either way, I did feel like it was beneficial to the entire kingdom to have social fests such as that.

However, those dances would not be like the homecoming dance.

I expected some sort of tradition or even one organized dance. That was not the case at all.

Really, it was just a large dark room with blaring music that was filled with elegantly dressed high schoolers all trying to do highly inelegant things to one another.

"Are you having fun?" Katie practically shouted at me over the roar of blasting rap music and obnoxiously singing teenagers.

"Um..." I trailed off for a moment. She probably did not even hear me begin to answer her. Of course I was not having fun. I was miserably pressed up against the warm bodies of strangers who seemed to be controlled by the overwhelming beat of the music. I could barely make out anything because of the darkness and the flashing lights. It was literally one of the worst positions I think I have ever been. "I guess so!"

Katie just nodded silently and gave me a half-hearted smile. I returned it and shut my eyes for a brief amount of time, trying to find a fleeting moment of peace in the chaos that surrounded me. I opened my eyes again to find that the music had switched to a slower pace. Boys and girls began to press their bodies close to each other, swaying softly to the music. Katie looked at the floor and then up at me expectantly.

I looked at Ty who was practically pressed against my backside. Jeanette was holding onto him tightly and he set his chin on her head and held her to his chest.

Katie took my looking at Ty and her friend as an opportunity to attach herself to me. She leaned her head of soft curls onto the front of my pleated shirt and I cringed when I saw her face smudge a bit of tan makeup onto the pristine white fabric. The soft turquoise skirt of her dress flowed around my legs and my feet and I had to make an effort not to step on it. I put my hands on her waist and gritted my teeth together as we moved back and forth.

I was miserable.

*****

Central British Battle Camp, Britain, 647

Five months.

At the end of the fifth month, November, I was stabbed in the gut by a man in a black cloak with two long, curved knives. I had to miss a battle because Merlin said the wound was too deep for me to fight. He insisted on staying with me to take care of the wound and we sat alone in my tent while the snow came down outside.

I lay in my cot with bandages and poultices in a menagerie over my abdomen while Merlin sat in a chair above me. He watched me while I slept and he fed me and talked to me while I was awake, changing the dressing on my wound every so often.

"Merlin?" I asked him while he mashed some combination of leaves in a wooden bowl. I tried to prop myself up on my elbows and cringed from the pain that shot through me.

"Do not try to get up," he commanded me and gently pressed my chest down with his hand. "What is it you want?"

"Why are you here?" I croaked.

"I suppose now is as good of a time as any," Merlin muttered. "Do you remember what I said when you took Caliburnus from the stone?"

"You called me a dirty blooded Roman and insisted that Lancelot had done it instead of me," I recalled. I added, "And I am only a quarter Roman, I am Pictish and my mother was Druid and highlander."

Merlin just looked at me for a moment and proceeded to spread the mashed leaves on the open wound. It stung and made my stomach pulsate in pain and I felt a quiet strangling noise erupt from my throat. "I said that I was meant to guide you and to protect you." He slapped my hand away when I tried to touch my stomach.

"What do you mean?" I asked.

"For as long as I lived on Avalon, which is as long as I can remember, I have been groomed to be our protector's guide, the guide to whoever could pull Caliburnus from the stone," Merlin explained. "Your guide."

"Guide to *what*?" I asked, confused.

"I am not sure yet," he said quietly. "To being king, I presume."

"Like an advisor?"

He wrapped me in the cloth bandage again and secured it with a pin he had made from a twig. "I do not know, Arthur."

I just lay back and stared at the red tent ceiling. I could hear the softest drifting of snowflakes on it. Merlin took the wineskin and poured water into my mouth. I drank, and then settled into the cushion that my head was on.

"Did you love her?" I asked after a veil of silence. "Viviane?"

I expected him to question my statement or ask what I was talking about, but he did not. He merely said, "We are too young to find love, Arthur."

*****

Arthur

Merlin was right. We were too young to find love.

But then, at what age are we truly old enough? Love blinds us, or rather, likeness blinds us. I really did believe that I loved Viviane for a while, and then I realized that it was only desperation. The problem is that we cannot realize we have not fallen in love until we have fallen out of it.

However, can age bring us this wisdom? This knowledge of whether we are in love or not? Would I have felt any different about Viviane if I were in the same position when I was twenty?

In America, it almost feels like navigating courtship and girls is easier because of how much more accessible it was. In America, we were encouraged to form temporary relationships with the purpose of abolishing them within a short period of time. And, while this did seem rather silly, it made everything less permanent. The short relationship I had with Katie seemed fake, like a page from the book of somebody else's life. The time I spent with Viviane felt explicit, certain, and most of all, real.

*****

Central British Battle Camp, Britain, 647

Six months.

I healed and fought in three battles in December. We fought knee-deep in snow which was rather difficult. Not as many were hurt because it was so hard to fight effectively.

Winter solstice came and went. There was no tournament in Camelot. There were not enough men to compete because of the war.

Lionel and one of the other older men went to one of the nearby villages and bought back two barrels of wassail for us to drink because of the occasion. That was the first time I think I was truly drunk. In Britain, unlike in America, everyone drank some kind of alcohol at supper but never before had I just continued to consume the warm liquid until I felt my senses droop into a rather sedentary state where I did not feel like I had to think about the war or anything of importance.

The next morning, I felt terrible, but it was almost worth it to forget everything for one night.

*****

Colorado Springs, America, 2010

It was my third Christmas in America and I had most certainly developed the warm and superficial love of the sweet, plasticky holiday that was so prominent in the minds of Americans.

I remember one day Miss Marion drove me home from club football practice near the beginning of December and the entire house smelled like the cinnamon candles she had set all about the house. It was a comforting smell, warm; however, at the same time it reminded me of winter solstice feast *there*, like we used to have when my mother was still alive and I lived in Camelot. Cinnamon, and other nice spices, were sort of a status symbol *there* so my family always had an excessive amount of it, especially around winter solstice. In our food, our ale, our candles, even our perfumes reeked of spices. I reminisced for a moment about when my mother used to embrace me and cover me with her cloak when it snowed. She smelled just like the Ectors' house did now. Instead of feeling happy for the warm, Christmassy smell, I felt tears begin to well in my eyes for my mother. I shook my head out for a second and then let my familiar glare take over my face. I could not afford to feel sad about anything, neither *here* nor *there*. I could not afford weakness.

"Are you okay Arthur?" Miss Marion asked me as she caught me glaring at a red candle as if it were the object of all my woes.

"I'm fine," I said quickly, "…just tired."

She gave me half a smile, "We're going Christmas tree shopping tomorrow."

"Fun." I tried to smile back at her, but I assumed it appeared just as weak as it felt. Decorating trees was also a winter solstice tradition that the British and the Germans had adopted as a Christian tradition. When I was nine, my mother, Lancelot, and I had gone out to the roads with some strands of preserved flowers and strung them over the bare branches of the weeping willows at Avalon. Part of the lake had frozen over that winter and Lancelot and I had quite a time experiencing ice skating for the first time in history. My mother had sat on the bank and applauded us as we fell on our tailbones time after time.

I missed those days.

Chapter XXI

Central British Battle Camp, Britain, 648

Seven months.

Food became almost nonexistent in January. For this, we fought no more battles. I remember feeling hungry all the time, my stomach feeling like an empty cavern inside of my abdomen that would never be full again.

We ate all of the hard biscuits that we had been saving and the dried vegetables. Bedivere caught a deer early in the month and it was the only one that we got through January. We shared it amongst the fifty-two men in the camp. It seemed like a lot of men but compared to the original one hundred and forty-eight that had been in the camp when I had arrived, we were just sad.

We ate the seven horses mid-January.

We were literally starving, digging in the ground hoping to find worms and insects to eat. Perceval had the idea to trek to a village that was nearby, but his plan quickly evaporated as soon as we realized that with the snow being several feet deep in places, it would be near impossible to clear a trail. Just as we began to approach the end of the month, Lancelot, Ellion, and I cut up an old pair of leather boots and some deer hide leggings and burned them over a fire. We ate pieces of the clothing and shared with the other men.

A cavalryman, Sir Jameson, who was just passed thirty became plagued with frostbite at the end of January. Merlin tended to him and informed us that he would die soon. The snow never let up and all of us knew that our same problems would persist through February if things progressed as they were. We were all thinking the same thing, but nobody said it out loud.

I was lucky for *there* during those long weeks. I woke up in America and Miss Marion would make me breakfast and I could eat as much as I wanted. Still, I lost nine pounds even though I grew an inch that winter. All the other men lost much more weight and everyone grew irritable as they grew hungrier and hungrier, our only food being clothing, whatever was living in the dirt, and the ever so occasional, squirrel. I caught a possum at one point: Merlin made a broth with it, and the cavalrymen shared its destroyed carcass.

Sir Jameson died a week after his diagnosis.

The day after Sir Jameson's death, Lionel sat down with me and watched the fire. The fire was the only sure thing we had right now. By some saving grace, we were always able to find material to fuel our fire.

"We need to decide what to do about Jameson," Lionel said.

I looked at him weakly. He was not the impressive looking lion man he had been when he had first introduced himself to me. His skin was as pale as mine and seemed to hang off of him with malnourishment. His once full, curly, golden beard and mane now were stringy and sad looking.

"You have more compassion than me," I told him. It was true. Next to Lionel I looked like a mindless killing machine. "You know I would."

"I think I have my answer," Lionel said solemnly. "The men will starve if not."

I nodded, "I will tell Merlin for you."

"Thank you, Arthur," Lionel bowed his head to me. "You are my king."

"Not yet." I studied the ground. "If we can make it through this."

"Arthur, it pleases me to think of you being king."
He set his hand on my shoulder. "You are going to do brilliantly."

I smiled and stood, having nothing to say. I walked to Sir Jameson's tent where Merlin still was. My stride was a walk of melancholy.

Merlin had become the cook and the medic in the camp. He was not so good at fighting, but he did his job well and nobody questioned him anymore.

I delivered the message to him quickly and quietly and he simply nodded and shut the tent flap tight, making sure that nobody would come in and see what he was doing.

On February 7, the British tasted human flesh.

Not one word was said the entire day. Hardly any sound was made aside from Elaine crying and leaning against Ellion sadly. Lancelot crouched down next to her and whispered something in her ear that made her smile. Ellion did not suspect a thing.

I sat with Lionel and quietly drank the stew that Merlin had made. I told no one this, but I enjoyed it. I enjoyed it too much. I contributed it to my lack of nourishment or to my Pictish blood.

Sir Jameson had been a friend of my father's. I hoped that the king would find out his fate after death and maybe at least feel a twinge of sadness. I knew he would not though; he did not care about anyone but himself.

*****

Colorado Springs, America, 2011

Valentine's Day.
The most utterly pointless American holiday of them all. Or maybe I only think that because of what happened to me on my third year in America.

278

If I Could Tell It

It was a tradition at Harrison for all of the science teachers to give the biggest test of the year on Valentine's Day for some reason. My honors biology teacher, Mrs. Arnold, was no exception. She had scheduled our entire genetics unit test for that day. We had been covering the topic since October, and there were forty-seven pages of notes in our notebooks devoted to it. It would have been nearly impossible to remember everything unless one was willing to sacrifice days to study for it, which most of us were not. That happened to be a problem, however, because most of our grade depended on it. At that point, I had a B+ in the class, which was dragging my entire GPA down, and the only way to raise it would be to ace that Valentine's Day test.

"I'm telling you guys, it's a bad idea," I said as I sat on Helix's bed eating popcorn while I watched Ty and Helix play a video game the week before the big test. I was honestly just trying to put the things that happened *there* the previous night out of my mind.

"Why?" Ty asked. "You're the one that's obsessed with grades after all."

"Helix's mom alphabetically organized all of his assignments for him," I sneered.

"So Helix is a mama's boy," Ty laughed. "That doesn't make you any less of a geek. I've seen your room buddy, you math draw."

"Shut up." I rolled my eyes. "It's still a bad idea."

"Look, Matt will just take pictures of the test tomorrow when he takes it and then send them to us for fifty bucks," Ty relayed. "It's not even technically cheating because we would have to remember the answers."

"And what if we get caught?" I asked. "We'll fail the class or worse."

"So, we won't get caught," Helix said. "Pass me that bowl."

I handed it to him. "It's just not right. It's like in a duel, agreeing to fight one way, and then breaking the rules. Like hitting below the belt."

Suddenly Ty paused the game, he and Helix both turned around and looked at me. "What the hell are you talking about?"

"Forget it," I said and shook my head. "I'm just saying this is wrong."

"And I'm saying this is the only way you're going to get a good grade in the class," Ty said. "Not even you are going to be able to memorize all that crap."

"Okay, fine," I sighed. I felt a wave of guilt wash over me and I ignored it.

"How much do we owe him?"

"Fifty bucks," Helix said and urgently shook his video game remote like a maniac.

"That's like twenty-three bucks per person...?" Ty asked.

"You have got to be kidding me," I said and aimed an exasperated glare at the back of Ty's curly head. "Fifty divided by three is sixteen and two thirds; that's about sixteen dollars and sixty-six cents per person."

"And you say you're not a geek," Ty muttered.

"Shut up."

"I don't want it," I said firmly as Matt tried to hand me an envelope in the locker room before winter football weight training. He was leaving the next day to go to Hawaii with his family for a week and a half, which was why he had taken the test early in the first place.

"Well, I'm not giving you your money back," Matt said and shoved the envelope at me.

I took it and stared at it for a moment. In reality, it was just a piece of paper with some multiple-choice questions on it, but to me, in that moment, it represented all cheating of any sort and my conforming to do it. I sat down on the bench and cringed as it squeaked under my weight. Matt left the locker room and about two minutes later I heard Coach's voice echo through the chamber, "Ector! Get the heck out here! Do you want to be on this team or not?"

"Coming, Coach Knox!" I yelled back. I ripped the envelope and its contents in quarters and threw it in the trash.

Chapter XXII

Colorado Springs, America, 2011

Three weeks before my birthday, March 3, just as our test scores were about to be released, I was called into the vice principal's office.

I waited outside the office and stared at the gold-plated name plaque next to the door. 'Clarence Washington' was spelled out in clear Times New Roman font.

The door clicked open a few moments later and Mr. Washington stood at the threshold.

He wore a pristine white collared shirt, gray slacks, and a red patterned tie. His dark hair was combed carefully to the left and not a hair grew on his smooth milky brown cheeks. He was a handsome man, probably around thirty-two, and he spoke with an accent somewhere between African-American and Hispanic. It had an odd effect as one might imagine.

"Arthur," he smiled at me and pulled out a red cushioned chair for me to sit across from him. I complied and looked across his desk as if it were a wooden sea that separated the two of us. "Do you know why you're here?"

"No, sir," I said and scooted my chair into the desk and tried to sit with the best posture as possible in order to seem more confident.

"We have heard from an anonymous source that there may have been some cheating in your class on the infamous Valentine's Day science test," Mr. Washington said, looking down at a paper on his desk. "Do you know anything about that?"

I froze in my chair.

"It's okay, Arthur," he said. "We know you didn't cheat. A custodian found an envelope addressed to you with the material in it in pieces in the trash."

I still said nothing. Anything I did say would betray my friends and likely everybody on the football team who was in honors biology.

"Nobody will tell anyone it was you who helped us find out who cheated," he said. "In fact, Mrs. Arnold has agreed to raise your grade to an A for your honesty."

Apparently, the school system was not above bribery.

I blew my hair out of my face and bit the inside of my cheek.

"I don't know," I said. I felt like my entire body was vibrating with adrenaline at this decision. It was almost how I felt in the heat of battle.

"Arthur, come on," Mr. Washington said, "I know you know. You are just choosing not to tell us. Who got the questions to the test and who used them?"

I bit the inside of my cheek harder. "I don't know, sir."

"I know they're your friends," he told me, "but you should think about what you're throwing away for a second. Do you know what you got on that test?"

"No, sir," I said in monotone.

"A C+," he said looking me straight in the eyes. "If you tell us what happened on the test, that grade won't count and you'll have an A."

"I can't say what I don't know for a good grade, sir," I told him through the stiffness in my jaw.

Mr. Washington shook his head. "You're a good kid, Arthur, and I can tell you're very smart. You're just a little too loyal to see what's best for you."

I went back to biting the inside of my cheek.

"Well, if you really aren't going to tell me anything, I suppose you can go back to class." He sighed, "If you change your mind, you know where to find me."

"Thank you, sir."

"I heard that you saved our hides," Helix said to me that day in the locker room.

"Yeah," I said and gritted my teeth, thinking about how my grades were suffering because of it.

Nobody even said thank you, or anything about it, aside from that one comment Helix made to me.

I should have told Mr. Washington.

*****

Central British Battle Camp, Britain, 648

Nine months.

The snow melted at the beginning of March and we were finally able to hunt effectively again. It was a miracle that only one of our men had died.

Bedivere and Kay walked into the village and bought flour and dried fruits and vegetables. They also bought four new horses to replace the ones we had eaten. But the best thing of all that they brought was honey. Two big pots of the sweet and sticky liquid. I still remember the moment I stuck my fingers into one of the pots and contentedly proceeded to lick the golden stuff off, savoring every bit.

The battles started up again mid-March and we seemed to slog through them as if we were walking through a deep and dark marsh full of thick mud. Only one archer and one footman died in March.

On my fifteenth birthday, there was drinking and a bit of a celebration held by all of the men at camp. I did not receive much, unlike my other birthdays at which it had seemed the entire country would get me presents; only a small pot of honey was presented to me by Lancelot. He and Ellion had been saving up their shares of it all month for me when they saw how much I liked it.

It was almost the best present I had ever received. Almost.

The steel knotwork ring from my mother still hung between the two sides of my chest, and it was cold against my skin. I could almost feel my heart beating next to it.

I pulled it up out of my shirt and stared at it in my palm.

I thought about what my mother had said when she had given it to me two years ago today, *When you look at this, I want you to remember me, and my people, and that they are a part of you as well.*

I was not fighting the war for my father.

I was fighting it for her.

*****

Colorado Springs, America, 2011

Two months after I turned fifteen, in May, I started a Drivers Ed course at Harrison after school.

Personally, I had no desire to drive because the entire concept still felt foreign to me, but Miss Marion insisted it was an essential skill for me to be able to drive myself. So, as soon as I was registered in the Drivers Ed course we went to the Department of Licensing and waited a full two hours for them to take an unattractive picture of me and write down my information. About a week and a half later, an envelope arrived addressed to me with my drivers permit inside. Promptly, the moment after I opened the paper, Mr. Ector dragged me out to the car and sat me down in the front seat commanding me to drive out into the street. Promptly, the moment after I tried that, we discovered that I had little to no coordination when operating a car.

None of my friends were in the Drivers Ed course that quarter, so on my first day I lamely walked to the back of the classroom, sat at a desk and started drawing little lines and circles on the first page of my notebook. No sooner had I done that had Jeanette, Ty's ex-girlfriend, came flitting into the class in a skirt that was too short for her. I unsuccessfully tried to hide behind my notebook, hair, and glasses from her. Sadly, she noticed me and sat right in front of me.

She had broken up with Ty about two weeks before, claiming that she "just wanted to be friends" after they had started dating at homecoming. Ty, however, did not see it that way. He was completely heartbroken. I had never seen him that way either; he had always seemed so nonchalant and unattached to anything, but when Jeanette broke up with him, he was a mess. And, being one of his best friends, most of his mess, fell into my mess. I was not Jeanette's biggest fan at the moment.

She tossed her light brown curls behind her shoulders and turned around in her seat to face me. Her mean, hazel eyes were inches away from mine, and, suddenly, I felt uncomfortable. Like I was being caught by a wild cat.

"Hi, Arthur," she said and moved her eyes down to the straight lines in my notebook and then back up to my messy hair.

"Hi, Jeanette," I said awkwardly, grimacing at her.

"Do you mind if I sit here?" she asked and grinned at me.

I shook my head through my grimace and looked back down at my notebook.

About two minutes later, another girl came and sat next to Jeanette: Claire Woods from middle school, the meanest, prettiest girl in America.

In all, there were about twelve kids in the class, none of whom I knew the names of aside from Claire and Jeanette. The teacher, a fat, middle-aged woman, came in a few minutes late and introduced herself.

"My name is Ms. Mazepa," she said in a smoker's voice that seemed to match her looks exactly. "Why don't you go ahead and introduce yourselves to your neighbors while I get ready."

My plan to avoid contact with Claire and Jeanette quickly evaporated as soon as Claire turned around toward me with a big fake smile and stuck her manicured hand out to me. "Hi, my name's Claire. What's yours?"

"Arthur," I said. I had no doubt that my face showed a cynical sneer. *I sat behind you for an entire year and you do not even remember me? You must have been too busy being an awful person to notice. You must get bonus points for being mean AND stupid.* "I went to Carmel."

"Oh!" she squealed. "That's funny, me too!"

It took every ounce of willpower I possessed not to come back with a sarcastic remark. Instead, I nodded and looked dutifully back down at my notebook.

Ms. Mazepa started the class a moment later and began talking about how important it was to drive and how important our safety was when driving. I felt my eyes glaze over for most of the lecture and then I was suddenly snapped back into perspective when I heard her say,

"You will be taking your drives with a partner. Please choose those partners now."

Jeanette and Claire quickly chose to become partners and hugged each other. I noticed American girls did that quite frequently, hugged each other. Personally, I thought it was a little strange, but maybe that was just because of my own aversion to touching other people.

Because I knew nobody in the class, I decided to hang back and wait for somebody to come to me. That was a poor decision because the boy who came up to me was incredibly overweight and smelled very bad.

"My name's Dustin. You wanna be partners?" I looked at him for a second, wishing with all my soul to reject him, but, seeing as I had no other options, could not.

"Yeah, sure. I'm Arthur," I said and looked back down at my notebook.

"You're that really smart kid who got a hundred on the circle geometry test right?" he asked. Apparently, I did know him; he was in my class.

"Uh, yeah, I guess," I said and looked at him again.

"How are you so good at geometry?" he asked and came closer to me. *Please go away gross kid.*

I wanted to come up with some half intelligent, half sarcastic remark that would leave him pondering why he came up to me, but instead all I said was, "I like circles."

He raised his eyebrows for a second and then sat at the desk next to me.

His smell did not go away with time.

*****

Central British Battle Camp, Britain, 648

One year.

It had been one year since I had come to that camp to fight in the war. And I had. I had fought, and I had killed. It had been one year, but I had aged a decade; all my scars were painful reminders of everything that had happened.

*****

Colorado Springs, America, 2011

Surprisingly enough, I was quite a terrible driver.

When maneuvering a car, I never seemed to judge distances quite right, or speeds for that matter. I could never quite be aware of every single thing around me and backing up...was a little too backwards for me. It was odd because I had been riding horses since I was barely four years old, and I was therefore fine at navigation, but when it came to the mechanical aspects of the car, I was simply unadept.

I think this may have been because I did not grow up riding in cars and therefore had not had the opportunity to observe people driving. After I came to this realization, I spent every moment I was riding with Miss Marion in the car observing her movements and what she did instead of looking outside at my surroundings as I had grown accustomed.

The worst part of all of it was that Dustin, my driving partner, was unmistakably good at driving. Every maneuver the instructor told him to do, he did perfectly, and this infuriated me beyond measure. Worse still, Jeanette and Claire were also excelling quite well at the driving program, both of them whom I thought to be stupid, ignorant girls. I could not believe that they were doing better than me. I was always the best at things, and when I was not, it was simply unbelievable.

*****

Central British Battle Camp, Britain, 648

Thirteen months.

I was homesick. I was truly longing to go back to Camelot, to Avalon. To fight in tournaments where everything was just a game and to play capture the flag. To go on trivial adventures that really did not matter. A quest to kill a dragon that may or may not exist or find hidden treasure in the forest. Things that were all too much a fantasy right now.

*****

Colorado Springs, America, 2011

In July, after the Drivers Ed course was finished, my driving began to improve, and regular school football practices started up again. It was fine, I suppose, and life in America continued on as normal. Or, as normal as it could be when I went to medieval Britain in my sleep.

*****

Central British Battle Camp, Britain, 648

Fourteen months.

If war has made me see anything clearly, it was that people are the greatest danger we can ever face.

I have fought and killed both a dragon and a phoenix, both creatures that were fearsome and worthy of fright. However, in my opinion, they paled in comparison to what I had seen men do and what I had done to survive. Being afraid of nonhuman things seems silly after seeing the things I have seen.

*****

Colorado Springs, America, 2011

Sophomore year began with all the excitement of the disappointment of summer ending. Students and teachers slipped back into the dull and laborious routine of school. Going to class, going to football practice, going home, going to sleep (which I dreaded most of all), and then the whole process repeating itself. However, it was at the beginning of sophomore year that someone began to suspect there was something different about me.

It happened the fifth day of school when the second-year Latin teacher, Mr. Tribiani took us out in the hall for our oral pre-tests. The objective of the oral pre-test was to see where our class was at in our progress in order for Mr. Tribiani to determine where our material should be. We were quietly filling out word searches in Latin while he called students out to test them.

"Arthur Ector," he called stepping into the classroom for a moment. I set my pencil down and followed him out into the hall.

"Please sit," he told me, and we sat across from each other at a desk while he prepared a piece of paper and a pen to write my progress on. I complied.

"*Salve*," he said. (Hello.)

"*Salve*."

"*Quid agis?*" (How are you?)

"*Bonum, et vobis?*" I replied. (Good, And you?)

"*Bonum. Quid enim tuum est ventus genus?*" he asked. (Good. What is your favorite class?)

"*Meus ventus genus est mathematica*," I replied. (My favorite class is mathematics.)

"*Quod mathematica sint in genere?*" (What mathematics class are you in?)

"*Algebra duo*," I answered. (Algebra two.)

"*Quid censes schola anno tantum?*" he asked next. (What do you think of the school year so far?)

"*Suus 'bonum. Velim mihi scribas, et classes. Sed nervous quia ego football sed simul excitatur*," I said. (It is good. I like my classes and my teachers. However, I am nervous for football but at the same time excited.)

Mr. Tribiani put down his pen and looked at me. "Do you speak Italian at home?"

"No, sir," I replied.

"Romanian?" he tried. "You must be exposed to one of those languages in order to speak the language so fluently…and with such an old-fashioned accent."

I swallowed. "No, sir…"

"Is there something you aren't saying? Am I missing something?"

Yes, the fact that I am completely fluent in Latin after fourteen years of private tutoring and abuse by a Roman Priest in the year 647!

"Ah, no, sir," I said again. "I just really understand the language."

Mr. Tribiani and I exchanged a few moments of intense stares.

He gave up first.

"I suppose you can go back to class then, Arthur," he sighed.

I nodded to him, pushed my glasses back up on my nose and returned to the classroom.

*****

Central British Battle Camp, Britain, 648

Seventeen months.

November arrived with an icy chill and a shiny frost coating.

I dreaded winter as if I were a dead man walking to the executioner's block. I thought that winter was worthy of it too, looking back on what had happened last year.

It was late morning and all of the men were sitting around the bonfire when the crow came. And I do mean a crow. A vicious looking black bird swooped down so close I thought it would take a bit of my hair with it. With that swoop, it dropped a tiny scroll in my lap.

It was a little roll of yellowed parchment tied with a thin rope of braided grass. I picked it up with two fingers and stared at it carefully like it was a bomb that might go off at any second. All the men were watching me.

"Well, read it already!" Bedivere said excitedly.

With shaking hands, I untied the grass rope and the tiny slip of parchment unrolled in my hands. It was about two inches wide and six inches long. The corners were ripped and frayed, not right angles like paper was in America.

The message written in black ink was in Latin and I read it aloud.

Frater,

Tollerent unam parted et ad merydiem hodie in campo certaminis eo.

I noticed that *meridiem* was spelled wrong; Morgain was never much good at Latin. I translated for my listeners.

Brother,

Bring one man and go to the battlefield at midday today.

Lionel held out his hand and I put the scroll in it so he could make sure that I had translated right. He looked it over and then nodded to me. "Who are you going to take with you?"

"Should I even go?" I asked.

"This means results, Arthur," Lionel said. "You must go."

I nodded and looked around the circle of men. I knew who I was going to choose before my gaze even met theirs.

"Lancelot," I said with my stare angled directly at his dark eyes. "Will you go with me?"

"Of course."

"You had best get going," Lionel said and pointed to the sun. "It will be midday soon."

We got up and left silently. There was nothing left to say, only a silent prayer abounded around the men. They needed us to stop this war.

It was about a half hour walk from our camp to the battlefield. Probably about two miles. It felt like much longer when we were marching with a hundred pounds of armor and weapons.

"Lancelot," I said when we were about halfway to the valley. "I know about Elaine and you."

He looked at me, stopped walking for a moment, and then started again. "What do you know?"

"I know that for the past year, you have been sneaking off into the forest with Elaine and doing…" I trailed off for a moment, looking for the right word, "…questionable things."

"We have not lain together," he stated, "if that is what you think."

I shook my head. The thought had not crossed my mind that someone as nice and refined as Lancelot would have sex before marriage. "No, but I still do not think Ellion would approve of what you have been doing."

Lancelot shrugged. "Elaine's actions are not his to dictate."

"I suppose," I agreed. It alarmed me how American Lancelot sounded, as if he would let his morals slip through his fingers for simple pleasures. That was one of the most bothersome things about American people, they had no respect for traditions or even for their own honor. Many peoples' philosophies seemed to be "if it feels good, do it, no matter the consequences." I suppose that it was good to take risks, but on the other hand, it did not seem good to sacrifice one's code for it. "Just be careful, my friend."

He nodded and looked down at the ground and our worn boots. His right boot had a tear beginning near the toe and his stocking was bloodstained from blisters underneath.

"Do you remember when we used to sneak out and walk to Avalon and collect those white stones when we were young?" Lancelot asked me after a veil of silence—we would arrive at the place of battle soon. "We thought we were so brave."

I smiled at him and moved a strand of hair out of my line of sight. It bothered me that I could only have my glasses in America, I could never see so well here. "And then there is now."

He chuckled. For the first time in ages, I really looked at Lancelot, at his face and the entire impression that he must exude.

Even though he was sixteen and I was only fifteen, I was still a good two inches taller than him, but we had both grown and Lancelot's cheeks, neck, and upper lip had become thickly covered in little black hairs in the beginnings of a beard. Dark, mysterious eyes peered at me from a chiseled face that was set in a serene, thoughtful expression under silky black hair. He was still slim and small-framed, as I guessed he would always be, but his shoulders had broadened. His voice had deepened, as mine had, but not as much and his words flowed sweetly and smoothly like honey. He could sing well because of this.

Lancelot had become a man. A good looking man.

I wondered how I looked in comparison, a tall, awkward, blonde boy with too pale skin and jagged hair. I shaved every day in America now so there was no hope of my growing a beard to look more manly, not that the minuscule amount of stubble I had managed to sprout from my face would make a difference. The only hair I had managed to grow was on my chest, legs, and under my arms and that was not that impressive. I probably looked exactly the same as I had two years ago, just taller and skinnier.

"We are here," I said solemnly. I did not let on to Lancelot that I was analyzing his appearance in comparison to my own.

Lancelot just nodded and bit his lip. We carefully made our way down the side of the valley, where corpses and bloodstains dotted the ground, and meandered to the center where two dark figures stood waiting for us, their dark cloaks blowing in the wind. As we came closer, I made them out to be Setanta and Morgana, Setanta dressed in his signature tight deer hide under his cloak.

Morgana smiled cryptically when we were close enough to see their faces clearly. "Brother."

"Morgain," I said. I regarded her coldly. I would not let her see the emotions that brewed and bubbled like acid beneath my skin.

"Morgana," she corrected. I refused to call her that, she would always be Morgain to me. "I see you have brought Lancelot."

Lancelot inclined his chin slightly and subtly stepped closer to me.

"Do you remember when we all used to play together as children?" she asked warmly as if we were reminiscing at a family reunion. "You two used to be the brave knights who rescued me from a tall tower in the palace that we pretended was guarded by the griffin. Remember?"

Lancelot spit on her black leather slippers. I wanted to fist bump him.

Setanta almost hit my friend, but Morgana coolly put her hand in front of his chest to stop him.

"What do you want?" I asked her. My voice imitated the cool roughness of a jagged rock.

"To propose a deal to you," she said. She looked up and moved her eyes as if searching the sky for something.

I crossed my arms as nonchalantly as I could and glared at her.

"It is silly for us to keep fighting when there will obviously be no result. All of the men will be dead within a matter of moons, and surely no one will make it through winter, considering how harsh last year's was," she explained as she looked Lancelot and me over. Her gaze lingered on Excalibur that was hanging at my left hip. I tried to stand a little higher, undeterred by the fact that I was already taller than all three of them. "My proposition is that we stop all of these silly battles. We will stay on our side of the border and the Britons shall stay on theirs…for now."

"For how long?" I pressed.

"One year," Morgana offered. "We will stay out of British territory for one year."

I wanted to inform Morgana that she was, in fact, British, but I only said, "Two years."

"Eighteen moons."

I considered tackling her and holding my sword to her neck in threatening negotiation. Morgana's gaze narrowed as if she could read my mind. "I am doing you a favor, Arthur Pendragon. I have men watching your camp at this very moment. If you dare to test me, I will have them all killed."

"Twenty moons," I said and laced my hands on my stomach. I could nearly feel Lancelot's nervous energy on my skin.

Morgana's face broke into an intelligent smile. "You always were good at negotiating. Twenty moons it is."

I nodded and held out my hand. She took it and we locked eyes for a moment. She let go before I could give it a firm shake.

"I would rather seal our agreement in blood." She wet her lips. "It is more certain that way."

I drew Excalibur from its scabbard and raised it to cut my hand for its blood flow.

"Oh, not like that dear brother," Morgana raised her hand to stop me. "*Þidercyme!*"

A giant winged figure descended from the sky to land right next to Morgana, who put her hand on the creature's large, eagle-like head. She ran her hand down its furry, golden back as if it were her housecat.

"This is a griffin, Arthur, like in our games," she said and looked at it lovingly for a moment. "Her name is *Ácennicge.*"

297

"What are you doing, Morgain?" I asked her as I looked over the terrifying creature. Its intelligent, amber eyes seemed to look straight through me as if I were transparent. I wielded my sword offensively, and Lancelot drew his long cavalry sword and did the same.

"If you can spill her blood, our agreement will be sealed," Morgana informed us. "Sealed with blood, the sacred blood of a griffin."

Lancelot and I looked at each other for a moment. His eyes had widened in fear. I gripped the hilt of Excalibur tighter and braced myself to fight.

Setanta spoke for the first time since we had arrived, "Do you accept these terms, Arthur?"

"Can I fight you instead?" I asked as innocently as I could muster. "Or are you too afraid to fight me yourself?"

Setanta smiled. "I am not so juvenile as to be tempted by your taunts. Answer my question."

Lancelot and I glanced at each other. He nodded slowly.

"First, I have a question," I said eyeing the griffin cautiously. "Do you love him?"

Morgana studied me carefully as if deciding what to tell me. She was calculating which answer would give her the upper hand. "Yes, Arthur, I do."

I gave her no acknowledgement that I had even heard her answer. Lancelot and I backed up a step into better positions to fight.

"*Aflygennes!*" she shouted. The griffin lunged forward at us. I stepped forward, and Lancelot jumped back to run around to its backside.

I waved my sword so the creature could get a good view of Excalibur. It simply reared up on its lion-like hindquarters and let out the most horrifying avian screech I had ever heard. Raptor talons with points sharper than arrows raked at me. I swiped Excalibur up to keep the griffin from shredding my face. The magic sword bit easily through two of the three claws as if it were a hot knife through butter. They fell onto the battlefield like any weapon a man would have possessed. I picked one up and held it threateningly like a knife.

I remembered Viviane's words when she had given me the sword, *This is the sword Excalibur. It is the most powerful sword in Britain. It has the power to kill anything.*

The griffin screeched again, more frustrated than anything. I saw the glint of Lancelot's sword above its head as it cut through one of its feathery ears. It did not even seem to notice that it was now missing an ear; its attention was completely and utterly focused on me. Its eyes were like fire. It stalked toward me in a limp from two of its talons being missing. Still, it strode with the absolute grace of a lion. I ran backwards to give myself the maximum amount of time possible to think.

"Cut its tail off!" I shouted at Lancelot while the griffin continued to advance.

I kept my gaze on its fierce eyes, not bothering to look where I was walking, which was very much a mistake. I tripped over a rotting cadaver and landed on my back, Excalibur flew out of my hand and landed a good six feet away. I swear I saw the griffin's beak form a rough smile when I fell.

It raised its still intact claw to rip my heart out.

Then I heard the sound of flesh being cut and the griffin shrieked and spun around to face my friend who was holding a limp lion's tail. He raised his sword to defend himself. I knew it would not do much to save him from the griffin, however. I got to my feet and snatched Excalibur up by the hilt.

"Switch swords!" I yelled at Lancelot.

I threw Excalibur in an impossible arc above the griffin's body. By some immeasurable amount of good fortune, he caught it and did not cut himself in the process. I was not so lucky. His sword flew in a spinning pinwheel of glinting steel and sharp blade. I had to sidestep and run after it when it landed a good ten yards away from where I was standing.

I picked it up and griffin blood ran onto my hands.

"Morgain!" I yelled and sprinted toward her. "Its blood has been spilled! Call it off!"

"What fun would that be?" she asked and smiled evilly.

I jumped fiercely and my hands found a collar to grip. I held Lancelot's sword to a beating heart as I knelt on ribs that were slowly being crushed by my weight.

"Stop it, Arthur!" Morgana screamed. "I have men poised to attack your camp!"

"Honor your agreement!" I yelled at her. I pressed the sword point into the deer hide. Setanta was struggling to breathe now, his lungs were collapsing under me.

We all heard the sickening sound of blade sliding through several layers of flesh.

The griffin gave one last terrible screech, and then it fell onto its side with a loathsome *thump*. Lancelot stood panting with my bloody sword drooping in his hands.

"Fine!" she shrieked. "I swear it on the Goddess! No more attacks for twenty moons! Let him go!"

"Morgain," I looked at her with complete and total hatred. "You took someone I loved away from me."

"Arthur, no." Tears streamed down her face. "I will kill all of your men."

"You are bluffing," I snarled, and the sword ripped through his clothing. I could feel his life in my hands. It was exhilarating.

I heard Lancelot's exhausted voice in the background, "Arthur, you are not this kind of man."

"Listen to him!" Morgana cried. "Please, Arthur, please. I will surrender! I will end the war!"

"Arthur!" Lancelot yelled. "Listen! Use your head!"

I stared at Setanta's face that was struggling for life. I remembered when I had been poised to kill Morgain on the executioner's block. *I had let up for less than one second. I had felt sorry for her.*

I would not make the same mistake twice.

"Some things are worth more than war," I breathed.

I plunged the sword deep into his chest, piercing his heart. I could feel it stop in the hilt of my sword. I twisted it all the way around and then got to my feet, staring at Setanta's body ruefully.

Morgana fell on him and kissed his bloody mouth. She stared at me with boundless terror strewn across her face.

I walked away.

I felt nothing.

Chapter XXIII

Central British Battle Camp Britain, 648

ave you ever felt victorious but so
entirely despicable at the same time?
I have.

I told myself that I did not feel one speck of guilt in my soul or mind for killing Setanta. I felt that it needed to be done and that was all. Morgain had taken who I loved from me, so I felt it was only fair that I take who she loved from her. She had also dishonored our agreement through her trickery by trying to kill Lancelot and me with her griffin; it was only fair that I punish her for it. It was only fair that Setanta died for all of the terrible things that he had done to my people. For all of my men that he had killed, my friends, my brothers. *It was only fair.*

Excalibur hung heavier on my belt than it had on our way to the place of battle. Lancelot and I did not say one word to each other the entire two mile walk back to the British war camp. I was thankful; I do not have a clue what I would have said. There was nothing to be said.

When we returned, I called for all the men to meet in the center of camp. They complied quickly, and I stood in the middle of the remaining thirty-five men and Elaine, our single woman. I noticed that she quickly rushed to Lancelot's side, a common occurrence recently.

"The war is finished—" I started but I was quickly cut off by the cheers of all the men.

I smiled cynically and held up my hand, calling for their silence.

I realized something in that instant.

It had become a natural instinct for me to raise my hand to the crowd to call for silence and respect. I did not use to do that. I used to stand like a scared little boy with wide eyes staring at the men in fear of having to speak as a leader. It had become instinctive to call for respect and ordinance. It had become instinctive to lead. Authority had grown into inclination.

As soon as the men had calmed down, I finished my announcement, "The war is finished for twenty months. We will be departing camp to return to Camelot tomorrow." I remembered that I was still under the jurisdiction of Lionel, who had become somewhat of a mentor to me, and I looked at him and paid my respects. "If Lionel agrees, of course."

He nodded and touched his curly blonde beard with his fingers.

"What happened?" I heard someone in the crowd of men whisper. I could not make out who it was.

I felt my authoritative stance crumble in that moment. I heard my sister's cries of anguish. I felt Setanta's heart on my sword. I felt the rush of life and death in my hands. And then I remembered the most appalling thing of all, Morgana's words just before I plunged Excalibur deep into the life of her love.

"Please, Arthur, please. I will surrender! *I will end the war!*"

She would have ended the war. I could be telling all these men that they were going back to their families. *For good.* I could have told my father that I did it, that I ended the war. I could have told the starving, helpless people of Britain, *my* people, that there would be peace. I could have told the mothers they would no longer have to send their ten-year-old sons off to war. I could have told the peasants in the fields they would no longer have to live in fear of Saxon invaders. I could have told them that all was not lost, and yet…and yet I chose to exact my petty vengeance and kill him. I chose to kill our chance at peace.

I swept my eyes over the men, their hopeful eyes staring innocently up at me. I felt like a shepherd who had just sold his flock to the butcher for a tiny fee.

Because, while I did not feel anything for killing Setanta, I did feel something for killing my own men.

*****

Colorado Springs, America, 2011

"Good morning, Arthur!" Mr. Ector said cheerfully as he entered the kitchen that morning.

I was quietly eating my cereal at the counter and doing one of the extra credit worksheets for algebra II. I definitely was not interested in Mr. Ector's abounding cheerfulness and forced conversation at the moment. I replied with a weak, "Good morning."

"How are you this morning?" he asked as he poured himself a cup of coffee.

"Good," I muttered and wrote 'x=7' at the bottom of the problem I had just completed.

"Just good?" he asked. "It's a great day! You have the districts game tonight!"

I do? I mentally asked. I looked at the calendar: Friday, November 4. It was the districts game tonight. I had completely forgot about it, last night's events having taken a toll. I suppose that made sense. Generally speaking, killing someone and potentially extending a war were slightly more important than some American game.

"Yes," I agreed with my adopted father.

"Are you excited?" he asked. At this point, I could tell he was only trying to make conversation for the mere nicety of it. I suspected he had lost interest in me just as I had no interest in him.

"Mhmm," I agreed and finished another problem.

"Do you want me to leave you alone?" he asked. I could tell he was not actually hurt by the sarcastic lilt in his voice. That pleased me. It meant that I did not have to make amends with him.

"Maybe," I said and brought my empty bowl over to the sink.

"Well, that's too bad," Mr. Ector said.

I looked at him in question and blew my hair out of my face.

"I'm driving you to school today; Marion's busy with some charity thing," he informed me.

I followed him out to the car and strapped myself into the passenger seat with my backpack between my legs. We had just gotten into the car when he realized he had forgotten his coffee and quickly darted back into the house.

I took a deep breath in Mr. Ector's absence. I put my face in my hands and closed my eyes.

You can do this Arthur. It's time to be normal now.

The cheering seemed to blast in my face as I ran onto the field with the team. Then gradually, it formed one dull sound in the back of my mind. I looked at my shoes They had been white at the beginning of the season, but now they had faded to a dirty eggshell. The band played a peppy tune behind me that I could not quite make out. It may have been the school fight song, it may have been a funeral hymn for all I knew. The grass blurred into an expanse of green before me.

Suddenly, I was no longer at the school football field.

I no longer saw the white lines that sectioned the grass, the bleachers full of students, or the row of houses that stood behind the football stadium. I no longer could hear the shrill voices of the cheerleaders, the booming sound of the drummers in the band, or the screaming student section from Harrison. Instead of the broad football pads strapped on my shoulders, I now felt the heavy steel plates of my armor weighing heavy on my back. Ahead, I saw Morgana. Her mouth was open in a silent scream and she held the limp body of Setanta. I looked down at my hands; they were wet, blood dripping from them, Setanta's blood…

"You good, buddy?" A senior clapped his hand on my back and suddenly my world was snapped back to where it should have been—the cheering fans, the stadium, the smell of popcorn wafting from the stands.

"Y-yeah I'm fine," I said quickly and picked up my pace, running closer to the front of the team who were now running laps around the track.

I looked down at my hands again. Only the scars from my battles marked them. There was no trace of blood on my pale and reddened palms.

A cry arose in Harrison's side of the stadium stands as the 0:08 counted down to 0:00 and the band blasted a loud and positive note. The cheerleaders formed some sort of pyramid and the whole team ran from the field and the benches to the front of the stands as the fight song played. I smiled with the happiness of our victory, but every time I closed my eyes I could still see my sister's face, twisted with anguish.

"Do you want a ride to dinner with me?" a junior named Luke asked me in the locker room as we changed out of our sweaty uniforms.

I shoved my helmet unceremoniously into the locker and turned to him. He was shirtless, and I stared with jealousy for a moment at his unmarked chest. I never took my clothes off in front of anyone in America for that reason. I could never explain the battle scars that covered my body.

"I'm okay," I told him solemnly. I took my glasses out of their case and put them on. "I think I'm just going to go home."

"You sure?" he asked suspiciously.

"Yeah," I said, "I'm not feeling great."

"Okay man," he said and clapped me on the shoulder. "Feel better before next week. We need that win to get to state."

I nodded and sat down on the bench as he left. The sound of the door connecting with it's frame echoed through the room. I was alone.

I stared at the black and gray lockers in front of me for a second. I thought about what I had seen when I ran out onto the field with the team. I knew exactly what it was too. It was what I had feared all along, every day since I had woken up in America, and then in Britain, and then in America again.

I truly was insane.

My head hit the palms of my hands and my elbows rested on my knees. My shoulder ached. I wanted nothing more than to die; to simply let my consciousness fade into blackness along with my worries. No more *here*. No more *there*. No more war and no more Morgain. I wished it had been Setanta driving Excalibur into my chest instead of the other way around.

"Hello?" said a male voice with a slight Italian accent.

I lifted my head from my hands and shook my head as if trying to shake off my problems.

"Yeah?"

Mr. Tribiani appeared from around the corner of the locker row. "Your father told me I would find you here."

"He's not my father," I said, shaking my head again, this time slowly, refusing to look at him.

I saw him nod out of my peripheral vision. "I wanted to talk to you."

"Then talk," I said harshly. At the moment, my tolerance level for anyone was below zero.

There was a long pause before he spoke again. "I got my undergraduate degree in medieval literature. I did my capstone project on the Arthurian legend."

"Good to know," I said, trying to keep a cavalier tone. I heard my voice crack a little on *know*.

"Did you know that in the Middle Ages every document was written in Latin?" he asked. "Anyone with a high rank would have to speak and write it almost fluently."

Of course I knew that.

"Huh," I said. I bit the side of my cheek nervously. I did not know exactly what was happening, but I had a feeling that Mr. Tribiani knew something more than he should have about me.

"You know what else is very interesting…" he trailed off for a moment and I felt his gaze on the side of my face. "Arthur was sent to be fostered by a man named Ector when he was a boy."

I turned to face him. "What are you trying to say?"

"I think you know."

We stared at each other for a very long moment. It seemed like a lifetime. At first, I was set on glaring harshly at him, trying to attain dominance, and then I began to study his face. He had the thinnest glasses I have ever seen, so thin they were almost invisible.

"Do you know about the Saxons yet?" he asked finally.

And then I lost it. I felt tears stream down my face and I looked at my scarred hands to avoid looking at him. I turned away and took off my glasses to wipe my eyes with my wrists. I had wanted the war to end, but I wanted this moment to end even more.

"Oh, Arthur, I'm so sorry," he said, suddenly sympathetic. He was expecting a confrontation, but instead he got a mess. The mess that was my life. "Please, you can tell me about it. I won't tell. I promise."

And for no reason in particular other than the fact that there was no other way to explain my breakdown, I told him. I told him everything. I told him about the first time I came to America and how I did not understand so many things. I told him about Caliburnus, and how my sister had killed my mother, and even about Viviane. I choked when I tried to tell him about the war and how I had killed Setanta and stopped Morgana from ending it. When I stopped speaking, I let my head drop back into my hands and I rocked softly, as if somehow that would make it all go away.

"You think I'm crazy, don't you?" I asked him at last, trying to swallow my emotions.

"No," he said thoughtfully. "I believe you."

I felt my whole body seize up with those words. The words I had been waiting to hear for the last two years.

"Y-you do?"

"Of course I do," he said. "It makes sense. King Arthur coming to America would be the missing piece of the legend. It would explain his return as well as where he got the ideas for his modern policies."

I felt like a science experiment. "But I'm not King Arthur. I couldn't even save my own mother or stop myself from killing someone for no reason! I can't even have a real conversation with you I'm so messed up!"

He put his hand on my shoulder and I did not flinch away. "But you will be. And that's what matters."

I looked up at him. "Mr. Tribiani, sir, I'm just a boy whose life has gotten so messed up that I can't even tell what's real and what's fake. I-I'm just a boy that's had an awful lot of bad luck and gotten put into places that I shouldn't be."

He looked at me for a long moment as if summoning wisdom for me.

"Everything happens for a reason," he said solemnly. "It's not about who you are now; it's about who you will become."

I closed my eyes and saw darkness. I opened them and saw the bright white American lights of the locker room.

"They write legends about you, you know."

Epilogue
Camelot, Britain, 648

There is nothing quite like a hero's welcome at Camelot.

I felt guilty the entire ride back from the battle camp, but as soon as I crossed the threshold into the village at the base of the palace I felt my feelings shift.

I rode in front with all the men in flank behind me— all the men from all the battle camps.

I had been under the impression that there were not many men fighting in the war in view of the fact that there were only thirty-five men left in my camp. What I had not realized was that there were over fifty battle camps all along the borders of Britain, from the kingdoms as far north as Orkney and as far south as Cornwall. That meant that there were almost two thousand men now behind me.

It was rather exhilarating to have all of these people following me. I remember when I first went to the war camp a year and a half ago I was so afraid to be a leader. I never felt confident addressing people from an administrative position and my voice deserted me when I spoke to the men in the camp. Now, I sat on my horse proudly, without any doubt in my aura. I smiled authoritatively and looked over the crowd with an air of certainty.

The people of the village threw flowers at me and I smiled and waved a few times. I tried to be as congenial as possible, contrary to my normal stoic state where I tried to avoid all human interaction. We reached the castle portcullis and two bugle players sounded a cheerful fanfare as we entered the palace square.

311

I saw my father on the palace steps. He was dressed in old battle armor from his earlier days. A scarlet cape with the Pendragon crest hung from his shoulders and blew softly in the wind. It made him appear even more powerful and commanding. He looked like a centurion from the old days of Rome. A hero. I hated that he looked that way. It was so far from true.

I stopped my horse and dismounted about ten yards from the base of the steps. I handed the reigns of my stallion to a stable boy and then knelt at my father's feet.

"Rise," the king said to me. I noticed that he did not acknowledge me formally as his son.

I stood and looked into the face of my father. I was still a good six inches shorter than he was, even though I was already six feet tall at fifteen. The world seemed to freeze at that moment, my father's harsh, disapproving glare the only thing of which I was aware. His distaste of me hung in the air like an icy fog.

"Father," I said finally without respectfully inclining my chin.

His glare did not waver.

"How long is the peace for?" he asked. His voice was crisp and solid. He had not been drinking for once.

"Twenty moons," I said. My glare did not waver either.

He nodded, then took a step back from me to make an announcement to the whole of the troops that had come to Camelot. "All of you will be lodging here for the next week so that I may congratulate your victory over the Saxons. You will be celebrated and many of you will be considered for knighthood by the various leaders of the camps, however, the main decisions will be made by me and my son."

I looked up at him. I doubt I suppressed the ecstasy in my gaze. A glimmering streak of pride came over me and I smiled. As much as I hated my father, I could not help but bask on every bit of praise he gave me, no matter how insignificant.

"All of you will join me in the banquet hall for supper tonight," he said and nodded. "I trust the palace staff to help you to your quarters. My captains will attend me in the great hall."

I began to leave to go with Lancelot and the rest of my camp, but my father grabbed my wrist. I turned back to him.

"Where are you going, boy?" he asked. I felt as if his eyes were boring into my soul.

"W-with my troops, sire," I said. My hand shook slightly and I grabbed the hilt of Excalibur to keep it still

"Come with us, Arthur." he sighed and dragged me by my wrist into the entry hall with his captains. Suddenly I felt like a little boy again, with my father controlling me in front of all the war captains. After what seemed like an eternity, he let go of me and I walked behind him next to a man who was obviously Roman. He had dark, brooding features with a clean-shaven face and cropped black hair. He reminded me of someone, but I could not quite place who it was.

"Sir?" I asked him. "Have we met before?"

"Yes, son," he answered with a chuckle. "But you must have been all of six years old. I would have visited Camelot sooner, but what with the war going on and my son going missing things have been stressful in Orkney."

"King Lot!" I said in sudden realization. "Sir, I mean. You are Gawain's father!"

"Yes," he said solemnly. "So you have heard about his leaving?" He looked sad. I suppose I would be sad as well if my child had run away from home without a word. I wonder what my father would feel if he never heard from me again. Probably nothing.

"Sir, I know where your son is," I told him. We entered the great hall, and I took a seat at the table on my father's left to the right of King Lot. I noticed that Lionel was at my father's right hand as he was second highest rank, and I was in my mother's place.

"You do?" he asked, his interest sparked. However, at that moment my father began the meeting by clearing his throat.

"As I mentioned previously," he began, "the purpose of this meeting is to nominate men for knighthood and awards of valor. Of course, the same rules for knighthood still apply. Each of you may pick up to ten men."

The men around the meeting table nodded in accordance with his stipulation.

"Lionel, please start," the King said in a rather cordial voice.

"If I may, I request that Arthur nominate the men from our camp," Lionel said. I felt my eyes widen unintentionally. "I have grown to trust wholly in him and I am sure he already has men in mind for knighthood."

"Arthur, then," my father sighed. "Who do you wish to nominate?"

"Kay, son of the late Sir Halpin, and Bedivere, his foster brother," I began. The scribe that stood behind my father nodded and wrote the names down. "Lancelot, my mother's ward, Perceval, Sir Lionel's adopted cousin."

I paused for a moment so the scribe could get it all. My father looked unimpressed with who I had chosen. He was about to be shocked.

"Ellion, who has fought valiantly at my side for many months," I said confidently. "The boy who became our camp medic, Merlin. He has healed me as well as many of our men."

"And where are those two from?" my father asked. Lionel bit his lip.

"Ellion is from one of the northern villages," I told him. I noticed my voice shake slightly. "And—"

He cut me off before I could finish, "Are you stupid, boy? A knight must be of noble descent."

"But, Father," I said, "Ellion has done more for Britain than almost anyone else I know. He deserves knighthood more than anyone else I know."

"The rules are there for a reason," the king said gruffly. "Those of proper bloodline are trustworthy. I do not want a traitor among my most decorated and regaled men."

"The rules are useless," I snapped.

The room fell silent. I felt all the men's eyes on me. Standing up to Uther Pendragon was simply not something that was done. And I was his son. Still, I did not break my fierce stare with my father.

He looked away first. "Because I know that you are rather simple, I will ignore your words. Finish your list now, Arthur."

"Just one more," I said. I tried to keep the heat of embarrassment from turning my cheeks bright red. It was worse that my father acted so civilly about my comment, as if I truly was stupid and should be ignored. Instead of submitting and bowing my head in respect, I stared my father straight in the eyes. "Prince Gawain of Orkney."

There were a few gasps around the table. Even the scribe paused a moment before writing Gawain's name down.

"Thank you, Arthur," my father said, quickly trying to fill the silence and change the subject. "King Lot, please."

I felt Gawain's father's gaze on me as he recited the names of the men he wanted to nominate for knighthood. I ignored it and took to staring at my hands and the little scars that covered them.

The rest of the meeting seemed to blur together, a mix of names I did not know and the different voices and accents of my father's captains. I felt rising tension between my father and me. By the end of the meeting, I was nearly shaking with anticipation of what he would do to me.

"I suggest you tell the men you have nominated so they can be prepared for their knighting ceremony." Even though his voice was directed toward the entire company, he stared directly at me. "You are dismissed."

The men all bowed to him and left. I noticed Lionel look back wearily at me as he left last through the tall doors. At least he cared for me.

"Arthur." My father regarded me.

"Are you going to hit me?" I asked him weakly.

"Do you deserve to be hit?" he growled.

I said nothing. No, I did not deserve to be hit. However, my father did not punish people according to what they deserved.

"You do," he said. There was a long and uncomfortable pause. "However, I will let your disrespect go this once. You are obviously still not thinking straight because of the war."

"Thank you, father," I said quietly.

He just looked at me. "I want to know."

"Know what, sir?" I asked him.

"How you got that Saxon bastard to give you a peace treaty."

I looked down at the table. "I killed him."

"You killed Setanta?" he asked curiously.

I nodded and bit my lip.

A smile spread across his scarred face. "Well done, my son. I am proud of you."

I beamed. At that moment I did not regret my decision to kill Setanta. It did not matter that the war was not over; I had at least made peace for a while. My father was proud of me.

"You best get to your men," he said. "Go and tell those who are to be knighted to come to me. The ceremony for your men will be tonight."

"Yes, Father," I stood and bowed, then left, still grinning.

As soon as the doors shut behind me, I felt a heavy hand on my shoulder. I whipped around to its owner.

"Nephew, please take me to Gawain," King Lot asked.

"Of course," I said and bowed my head to him. I lead him to the wing that I knew the men in my battle camp were staying for the victory week. I knocked on the first door where I guessed Lionel was placed.

"Come in," Lionel answered and I pushed open the ornate oak door. He was sitting at the table writing something on a scroll.

"Where is Gawain staying?" I asked him. I noticed that King Lot had stayed outside in the hall.

"Third room down with Perceval," Lionel answered and dipped his quill in the inkwell. "How was your father?"

"Surprisingly well," I told him.

"Good." Lionel nodded. "If I may take leave to write this?"

"Of course," I said and left.

"This way," I said to the king and he followed me down the corridor to Gawain's room.

I tried to open the door, but it was locked. I frowned and knocked.

"What?" a voice yelled. It sounded like Perceval.

"Let me in!" I yelled back.

"No!" Perceval yelled. I was not in the mood for his immaturity.

"Perceval!" I growled. "This is Arthur! Let me in!"

"Fine," I heard him huff. The door unlocked with a sharp click and swung open. An air wafted to me that was permeated with the sharp scent of raspberry liquor. Perceval, Gawain, Kay, and Bedivere were all sitting at the table drinking the potent stuff from silver cups and laughing like idiots.

"Compose yourselves!" I barked at them and took the pitcher. It was almost empty. I set it on the other end of the table. "You are in the presence of a king!"

I think they assumed I meant my father, so they all immediately dropped to the floor on one knee. When King Lot entered the room, their expressions were quite surprised.

Gawain rose immediately. "F-father."

"My son," King Lot embraced him in a bear hug and Gawain stood limp in his arms, his silky black hair encasing his face. I saw his father's eyes begin to shine. "I am so glad you are alive."

"Yo-You are not mad at me?" Gawain asked once his father had released him.

"I was…" he trailed off, "but now…now that I see you, my son, all grown and to be knighted! How can I be anything but proud?"

"Knighted…?" I saw Gawain mouth.

"That is right!" I said. "All of you are to be knighted tonight!"

"All of us?" Kay asked excitedly. I walked over to their table while Gawain and his father continued to talk by the door.

"Yes!" I told them excitedly. "And Lancelot too!"

"What about Ellion?" Perceval asked quietly.

I looked at my boots and shook my head. "I tried. My father called me simple."

"Oh…" he trailed off. "I am sorry."

I shrugged. "I need to go talk to them anyway. I hope you will wish me luck."

"We will," Kay answered solemnly.

"Greetings," I said as I entered the room.

The scene in Lancelot, Ellion, and Merlin's chambers was quite different from the one in the other room. Lancelot and Ellion were at the table playing chess on a wooden board and Merlin lounged on the bed reading a papyrus scroll marked with the seal of Avalon.

"How did it go?" Lancelot asked me, looking up from the game. Ellion stared up at me hopefully.

I sighed and sat down next to my friends. "That is what I have come to discuss."

Ellion dutifully slid the board to the other end of the table in order to give me his full attention.

"I asked my father to knight both of you, Merlin too," I said quietly. "But he just called me simple and gave me the speech about a knight having to be of noble blood. He said he would only knight Lancelot. I really am sorry."

"About what?" Merlin snapped from the bed. "I for one definitely do not want to be a knight. Having one's arse so high cannot be good for blood flow. I am a bard of the Druids and proud of it!"

I did not dignify Merlin's comment with a response. "Ellion I want you to know that if it was up to me, you would be joining the cavalry tonight."

Ellion bit his lip and nodded. I could tell he was upset, but doing his best to hide it. "I knew it was never going to happen and so did you. We really should not have ever fantasized that way. I never—"

I cut him off, "Ellion, I promise that someday you will become a knight. I may have to knight you myself, but I will do it."

"Arthur, please—" he started.

"No, Ellion. I will," I said firmly, suddenly sure of myself. "I will."

He bowed his head.

"As for tonight," I said. "congratulations, Lancelot. Servants will be along to dress you shortly."

I stood up to leave.

"Too proud to stay with us low ranks, my liege?" mocked Merlin.

"Oh, I could never be too proud for you, Merlin." I felt a smile spread across my face. "You seem to think you are much higher than I after all."

"Because it is true, you dirty blooded one," Merlin said gruffly. "Now come help me with this. I do not know this word in Latin."

I grinned and jumped onto the mattress next to him, scanning the scroll he had in his hands.

"Now, the most central camp, captained by Sir Lionel and my son, Arthur," my father announced, sitting back in his throne for a moment.

I drummed my hands quietly on my knee in anticipation of watching my friends be knighted. I looked at Ellion. He was doing a good job of being stoic. Lionel laid his hand on my shoulder for a moment.

"Kay, son of Sir Halpin and his foster brother, Bedivere," the king read off a scroll in his hands. "Please come up."

They got up from beside me and walked to the front of the great hall, their footsteps echoing on the stone floor. I could tell they were trying to keep from grinning.

They knelt before my father and bowed their heads accordingly. He stood in front of Kay first.

"Do you promise to be loyal to the Pendragon bloodline for as long as you live, any form of treason punishable by death and nothing less?" he asked.

It was at that moment that I realized just how lacking the knight's code and oath was. It was not really a code at all, rather a glorified promise to do whatever the king might tell you to do. That would have to change.

"I do," Kay said and bowed his head even further.

My father laid his sword on both of Kay's shoulders and his head then said, "By the power vested in me by the sacred blood and people of this land, I dub thee Sir Kay of Camelot and Brittany. You may rise."

The newly knighted Kay stood up, his face shining. Two squires came forward. One hung the red cape with the gold Pendragon crest about his shoulders and another handed him a ceremonial sword which had been engraved with the same symbol. He bowed again to my father and came to sit next to me in the front row of pews.

I patted his leg as he sat down and he showed me his sword proudly. I nodded and looked back up to the front of the room where Bedivere had just taken his oath. He was cloaked and given a sword in the same way that Kay had been.

"Prince Gawain of Orkney, Kingdom of Uriens and Perceval, fosterling to Sir and Captain Lionel of Camelot," he read aloud. He waited a few moments for the two of them to make their way to the front of the room.

They knelt; both of them swore their oaths and were knighted, then cloaked and given their swords. They sat back down. I glanced at Ellion. He was gazing around the room at the various banners and tapestries hanging on the cracked and weathered stone walls.

My father took a moment to compose himself before asking the next set of men up. Personally, I found it rather stupid to have so many men knighted at the same time. Not only did it make for a long and laborious ceremony for us to sit through, it also made the knighting ceremony less special. When I became king, along with changing much of the knight's code and oath, I would try not to knight more than five or so men on the same day.

"Lancelot, my former wife's ward. I also call on Arthur, crown prince to the high throne of Britain and my only son."

I looked wearily across the aisle at Lancelot and we both knelt at my father's feet, still glancing at each other from our knees.

"Do you, Lancelot of the Lake of Avalon—" I noticed my friend prickle at the mention of his true heritage. "—promise to be loyal to the Pendragon bloodline for as long as you live, any form of treason punishable by death and nothing less?"

"I do," Lancelot said solemnly, still looking at me under his mane of dark hair.

My father lay his sword on Lancelot. "By the power vested in me, I dub thee Sir Lancelot of Camelot, Avalon, and Brittany. Rise."

Lancelot completed the ceremony still regarding me with his gaze.

"Arthur," my father said to me once Lancelot had been seated, "rise."

I stood and followed his gaze to stand at his side.

"I am afraid that many of you are not aware of the reason for the current peace in the land," my father said. It sounded as if his voice echoed throughout the castle. "That reason is my son. The boy standing next to me today. He has killed a prominent leader of the Saxons, Setanta, and given us this period of peace. I am happy to tell you that one day, this boy will continue the Pendragon dynasty and become your king. It would do all of you well to acquaint yourselves with him and show him respect."

I smiled. It was the greatest praise I had ever received. The greatest praise I could ever have hoped for. It was also the first time I had ever truly thought of myself as the man I would become. Someday, I *would* be king and I *would* rule over Britain. And the best part? That was what I wanted. I wanted my kingship like I wanted to breathe. I knew I could do so much for my people, so much for the people to come. I could become the man that everyone wanted me to be. The man they *needed*. I had grown up from the Arthur who felt only circles made sense.

I would make things make sense because I was going to be king.

I was going to be *King Arthur*.

And I'm going to do it with America.